RIVER WALKER

Visit us at www.boldstrokesbooks.com

Praise for Cate Culpepper

"*The Clinic* sets the tone for what promises to be a terrific series. Culpepper's writing style is spare and evocative, her plotting precise. You can't help but feel strongly for the Amazon warrior women and their plight, and this book is a must-read for all those who enjoy light fantasy coupled with a powerful story of survival and adventure. Highly recommended."—*Midwest Book Review*

In *Fireside*, "Culpepper's writing is crisp and refreshing, even in the midst of the difficult subject matter she has chosen for this story. Her turns of phrases are unique and resonate like harp strings plucked to create a beautiful tune."—*Just About Write*

The Clinic "is engaging and thought-provoking, and we are left pondering its lessons long after we read the last pages… Culpepper is an exceptional storyteller who has taken on a very difficult subject, the subjugation of one people by another, and turned it into a spellbinding novel. As an author, she understands well that fiction can teach us our own history without the force and harshness of nonfiction. Yet *The Clinic* is just as powerful in its telling."—*L-Word.com*

By the Author

Tristaine: The Clinic

Battle for Tristaine

Tristaine Rises

Queens of Tristaine

Fireside

River Walker

RIVER WALKER

Cate Culpepper
12 / 14 / 10

by
Cate Culpepper

2010

RIVER WALKER

ISBN 10: 1-60282-189-5
ISBN 13: 978-1-60282-189-7

This Trade Paperback Original Is Published By
Bold Strokes Books, Inc.
P.O. Box 249
Valley Falls, NY 12185

First Edition: November 2010

CREDITS
EDITORS: CINDY CRESAP AND STACIA SEAMAN
PRODUCTION DESIGN: STACIA SEAMAN
COVER DESIGN BY SHERI (GRAPHICARTIST2020@HOTMAIL.COM)

Acknowledgments

My thanks to my excellent editors Cindy Cresap and Stacia Seaman for their skillful nurturing of this ghost story, and to Radclyffe and Bold Strokes Books for publishing it. My beloved beta readers Connie Ward, Gill McKnight, and Jenny Harmon supplied many months of helpful critique. Kudos also to talented BSB artist Sheri for her evocative cover design.

The translation services of my fine YouthCare colleague, Jose Luis Bonilla, saved Elena's beautiful language from my atrocious Spanglish.

My longtime friend Katherine Unity Porter provided both warm encouragement and invaluable practical support. Thank you, KUP.

I'm also grateful to my sister, Connie Warren, for prowling through the Mesilla cemetery and roaming the Organ Mountains with me, and for her general kind spoilage of her little sister whenever I visit our home state.

Dedication

For my mother, Joyce Culpepper,
enjoying her well-earned rest at the Heart of the Mountain,
and for my sister, Connie Warren,
the classiest straight woman I know.

Chapter One

The dark river rolled silently beneath the desert's full moon, shadowed and implacable as Grady Wrenn's heart.

Her boots rasped through the dry grass lining the riverbank. She lifted one hand to keep her balance on the uneven ground, the night air soft and warm against her palm. It was cresting midnight, and her eyes felt as hot and arid as the plains that lay west of this storied river.

Grady had heard the desert was an acquired taste. She hadn't acquired it fully yet, but perhaps it was growing on her. The Mesilla Valley held a crystalline beauty that still seemed alien after the easier, gentler allure of the Pacific Northwest. The blue velvet sky was spangled with stars, and she was half dazzled by them. The clouded heavens of Oregon never offered much sky. New Mexico's skies were an embarrassment of riches, especially on nights like these.

She settled cross-legged onto the sandy bank, the faint popping of her knees the only sound besides the lonely chirping of river crickets. Grady had always thought the ocean was grief's most natural habitat, but she found solace here, too, watching the slow currents of the Rio Grande. There was subtle comfort in the ceaseless movement of the river. Just as the ageless waters sluiced away the embedded grit of the riverbed, she was starting to hope this gentle flow could do the work of her unshed tears and ease the pain of her loss. Her nightly wanderings often drew her to the Grande and usually brought her enough peace to find a few hours' sleep.

Only one small, smooth rock in the center of the river's narrow span interrupted its patient flow. Grady scraped a handful of fine pebbles from the bank and tossed one after another at the rock. Her throws were short and her aim hopeless, but the whole point was to hear the soft plunk as the stones hit the water.

She was plunking pebbles into history itself. She relished the moment, breathing in the distinctive rain-like smell of the creosote brush dotting the bank. Billy the Kid drank from this river. Pancho Villa led his rebels across its waters. If rivers could talk, this one had centuries of gossip to dish, and Grady only wished she spoke its language. As a cultural anthropologist, her greatest pleasure was to unravel the mysteries of—

It began as a low, snarling cry, so mindless Grady thought a wild beast had to be near, and she spun on her butt in alarm. It seemed to come from everywhere. The keening moan rose from a growl to a harrowing shriek, an all but unbearable cacophony of rage—a wail of very human fury, and unmistakable grief.

Adrenaline streaked through Grady in a painful burst, and she scrabbled in the dry grass of the riverbank, her only conscious thought to get *away* from that sound. She groped for the bank's edge and it crumbled beneath her hand. She slid down the shallow side and her churning boots plunged into the cold water. She flailed on her back like a turtle, helpless as a child and terrified as one caught in a nightmare. She sat up and looked around wildly, her heart punching hard in her chest.

"What the *fuck.*" Breath whistled in and out of Grady's lungs in sharp bursts. She had walked between a mother grizzly bear and her cub once during a study of a mountain Klickitat tribe. Even that towering beast's roar hadn't frozen the blood in her veins like this.

The wailing rolled on, impossibly prolonged, a disembodied

wave of enraged suffering. There was something inescapably feminine in that discordant melody that chilled Grady to the bone.

Then, as abruptly as it began, the sound faded. The night was silent again, and the river continued its peaceful, serpentine trek through the desert valley undisturbed.

Undisturbed except for the rock in the center of the stream, which was rising slowly to its feet.

"Jesus!" Grady yelled. She kicked her way back up the bank, clawing for purchase. She gaped at the lush form that rose gracefully from the water.

It was a woman, the moonlight revealed that much. A naked woman. A young naked woman, her dark hair a smooth, wet sheen around her bare shoulders. She stood in the center of the shallow river, the water lapping against her thighs.

"Cálmate," the woman called. *"Usted no tiene nada que temer."*

"What *are* you?" Grady croaked. Perhaps a person with a doctorate should be capable of a more articulate greeting, but she forgave herself that lapse for now.

The woman seemed to study her for a moment, apparently at ease with her nudity. Grady was finally able to accept that this strange creature was mortal and not the source of that nerve-shredding wail, when she took a quick side-step to steady herself in the sluggish current.

"You have nothing to fear." Her words carried clearly across the water to Grady. "Maria has no interest in you, or in any woman."

"Good," Grady called back. She was glad to hear this. Her pulse was only now slowing its frenzied pace. "Who's Maria?"

The young woman turned carefully in the river and began making her way toward the opposite bank.

"Hold on!" Grady scrambled to her feet and tried to inject some authority into her voice. "Who is Maria? Who are *you*? What was—"

"Go home to your nice bed, gringa." The woman paused and glanced back over her shoulder. There was no mockery in her voice; she just sounded tired. "Any night Maria walks the river is a night to stay indoors."

Grady folded her arms, shivering. She watched the woman step nimbly up the bank, water streaming from the rounded swells of her hips. The moon's illumination was too faint to pick up much detail, but Grady placed her in her mid twenties. Her body didn't carry the sculpted sleekness of the gym, but her curves held a softer and more natural appeal that reached Grady even through her daze. Her wet hair looked dark against her pale shoulders.

Grady had felt no desire to touch a woman in well over a year, and she didn't feel it now. But she recognized a sweet sensuality in the girl's movements, in the obvious comfort she felt with her body. A slight breeze caressed Grady's face, and she imagined it reaching across the river to touch the girl's cheeks. She wished she could see her expression.

The distant figure lifted a folded pair of pants from the ground and pulled them on. She shook out a loose shirt and snaked her arms through it, then stepped into a pair of sandals. She walked to a spindly tree and the small horse—yes, a *horse*—tethered to it. Grady had been so enamored of the river, and then scared shitless by some banshee's cry, and then fascinated by this naked naiad, she had missed an entire horse, not fifty feet away. The woman mounted the unsaddled beast with one agile leap, then lifted the rope reins from its neck. She looked back toward Grady, and the moonlight flashed briefly across her smile. "Sleep well," she called. "I'm sorry you were frightened."

Grady lifted one hand in feeble acknowledgment. The adrenaline rush left her mildly nauseous. She watched the small horse canter gamely off, headed east toward the town of Old Mesilla. The woman's shining curtain of hair lifted and fell with her mount's gait.

"Good night," Grady whispered. She was chilled in spite of the warm air, and she snuck her hands into her armpits. Her pickup was parked on a frontage road about a half-mile away, and she shuffled toward it, looking over her shoulder to keep the horse and rider in sight. They dwindled into the shadows in moments.

The clock of Grady's boots on the stony path echoed hollowly in her ears. If she had hackles, they were still prickling high on her neck, and she pulled the collar of her cotton shirt around her throat. She listened so hard her scalp twitched. If she heard even the faint beginnings of that growling cry again...

Grady reached her lonely truck unmolested. She ducked into its cab and keyed the ignition, the wet cuffs of her jeans chafing her ankles. In the dim glow of the dome light, she caught a glimpse of herself in the rearview mirror; the dark circles beneath her eyes aged her a decade beyond her thirty-four years. She drifted her fingers through her hair, noting the strands of gray that had been there even before the banshee—Maria?—scared her stinking witless tonight.

Grady gazed at her image in the small mirror. Through the dust on her skin, she traced the track of a tear. She remembered the terrible grief that had saturated that shrieking voice, a sorrow even greater than its rage. Her own mourning had found resonance there, an answering sadness. The river and the cry that haunted it had released the first tear Grady had shed in months.

She glanced out the side window at the flowing Rio Grande and shivered again. The primeval river could keep her mysteries, if they included demons like that.

Grady turned her truck east, back toward the glittering lights of the city of Las Cruces. It rumbled over the wide dirt road, its headlights gleaming weakly through the dust. The Grande's mysteries also involved a shapely young woman who sat naked in rivers at midnight, and the wonder of that almost overrode Grady's initial fear.

Almost.

Grady was tired and shaky and lonely and she needed a bathroom in the worst way. She needed long hours of decent sleep, too, but the night's events all but guaranteed those would elude her. Again.

Her truck rumbled over a small rise, leaving the muddy Rio Grande behind to keep its silent course throughout the night.

CHAPTER TWO

*G*ood *evening, sweet Goddess, mi Diosa.*
Ha ha ha. You hear me laughing down here. You must
be very pleased with Yourself. Like my mother when she covers
my pillow with packages of condoms. I bet You and my mother
cackle just the same. You are a very funny Goddess.

My Catholic neighbors, who do they get for a god? They get
to worship this wise old man who cuts tablets out of mountains
and parts seas. I get a stand-up comic.

How long have I been asking You for help, Diosa? How old
am I, that is the answer. All my life. All my life I have prayed that
You would send my family an ally, someone to help us. This is too
hard to do on my own. You know my mother cannot help. I have
told You all this every night for years and years.

So what do You do? Who do You send to help me? A skinny
gringa so brave she falls on her ass and tumbles into the river!
She is not what I had in mind, Diosa. She was even scared of me,
and all I did was stand up.

But this Anglo woman did hear Maria's cry. I have never
met a female who is able to hear Maria. How have You afflicted
this woman? What sadness does she bear, that she can hear the
wailing of the River Walker?

Questions for another day. Mamá is asleep at last and
there is peace in our home, so I suppose there is something I

can sincerely thank You for. Comfort all Your errant daughters, Diosa. Guide me all my days.

Smile down on Your loving Elena.

Chapter Three

S orry, sorry, sorry." Burdened with an armload of books
and maps and balancing a box of doughnuts, Grady
fished her keys from her back pocket and stepped through the
small cluster of students waiting outside her office. "I'm usually
a lot better about being on time."

"That's okay. I've forgiven you already." A plump Hispanic
girl grinned broadly and lifted the toppling box of doughnuts.
"I'm Sylvia."

"Hey, Sylvia." Grady nodded at the other two and kneed
open the door. She genuinely enjoyed her students for the most
part, but she always had a devil's time remembering their names
at the beginning of a term. She had committed these three to
memory before she peeled out that morning, and luckily she had
a name for each face: Sylvia Lucero, Cesar Padilla, and Janice
Hamilton, the full roster of her summer seminar.

She let the others introduce themselves as she navigated
behind the oak desk that dominated her small space. Her office
was in Breland Hall, not one of the new and shinier complexes
dotting the New Mexico State University campus, but it suited
Grady well. Built in the 1950s, Breland struck her more as an
old-time public school house than a center for higher learning,
and she liked its informality. The old building housed both the
anthropology and sociology departments, and as new faculty she
was lucky to merit even this wedge of a private office.

"Is this yours, Dr. Wrenn?" Sylvia gestured at the cedar-framed tapestry hanging on the west wall, where the morning light could reach it. "It's beautiful. I've never seen these designs."

"That's one of my favorites. It's a ceremonial mantle from the Klickitat River area, a tribe on the northwest coast." Grady poured water into the coffeemaker. She hoped these kids could stand some high-octane caffeine this morning; decaf was not an option.

She turned and rested her butt against the desk as the others settled into the folding chairs forming a small circle in front of it. She felt a little like Saint Francis addressing the lambs in this crowded space, with those young faces tilted up at her.

Grady was already learning what she'd need to know about each of her students to inject useful knowledge into their heads. Sylvia gazed with open pleasure at the sand paintings and small carved animal totems that adorned the office, her eyes alight with curiosity. Cesar sat beside her, fumbling with his notes, trying to find a working pen, his brow creased and his broad shoulders hunched. Grady noted his affectionate hold on Sylvia's hand. Janice was a bit of a cipher, so far—she returned Grady's regard seriously, motionless, her gangly legs crossed at the knee.

"So, let me start by coming clean with you guys about my near-neophyte status, here," Grady said. "You all saw my bona fides on the syllabus, so you know I'm pretty well-versed in the Native American cultures of the Pacific Northwest. I'm handy with a half dozen other Native and Hispanic community models up and down the West Coast. But I can't claim any great expertise in the social mores of southern New Mexico. I only moved here six months ago, so I'll be on a learning curve myself this summer."

"But this is just an undergraduate seminar." Cesar blinked up at Grady through his wire-rimmed glasses. "You know all the basic stuff to teach us, right?"

Grady smiled. *I have a PhD and eight years in the field, laddybuck. Eat a doughnut.* She extended the box to him pleasantly. "Sure, I know the basics, and I've done a lot of research on the area the past few months. I'm excited about our project. I just want you all to know I'll welcome your input in its direction."

"It's a full three credits for this paper we're going to write together." Janice spoke so softly Grady had to crane to hear her. "And it has to be on the folklore of the Mesilla Valley? That's all I know so far."

Grady nodded as she filled her tanker-sized mug. "We'll want to narrow it down a bit, and that's where we can start today. Did any of you grow up around here?"

"Cesar and I did." Sylvia bumped Cesar gently with her shoulder. "We were born in Cruces, two weeks apart, not four blocks from each other. And we're getting married in six weeks."

Cesar looked down at Sylvia with unabashed adoration, and Grady locked her eyes to keep them from rolling. She really needed this coffee; she wasn't ordinarily cynical in the face of young love. "Great, congratulations. You two give us the hometown advantage. What about you, Janice?"

"I grew up in Albuquerque." Janice accepted the doughnut Sylvia offered her with a timid smile.

"So toss out some ideas." Grady blew on her steaming mug. "The Fountain Theater in Mesilla has an interesting history. Lots of great characters in and out of those doors."

"The San Albino Church in the plaza probably has some kicking folklore attached to it, too." Cesar perked up a bit. "Have you heard, Dr. Wrenn? The Vatican named San Albino a basilica. A minor one."

"Yes, I read about that," Grady lied.

"Ooh, I think we should write about the witch!" Sylvia sat up and bounced lightly in her seat. "That's like, vintage Mesilla folklore. It's perfect."

Janice brushed her lank blond hair out of her eyes. "What witch?"

"The witch all our mothers warned us about when we were little, to keep us in line. *La Llorona*..." Sylvia put her lips close to Cesar's ear and emitted a low, menacing murmur. "Any night Llorona walks the river, is a night to stay indoors...bwah-ha-ha!"

Grady's ears pricked up. She noted Cesar didn't return Sylvia's smile this time. He cast his eyes down.

"*La Llorona*, that's this witch's name?" Janice looked intrigued. "Spelled with a *Y*?"

"With a double *L*, which sounds like a Y in Spanish," Sylvia said. "Yo-rone-ah. In English, it means 'the woman who weeps.'" She seemed to register Cesar's discomfort, and she patted his arm. "I'm sorry, baby. I know you don't think she's a joke."

"She's just a legend," Cesar mumbled.

"La Llorona?" Some faint memory was tickling the back of Grady's sleepy skull. She edged around her desk and consulted the bookshelves behind it. She flicked her finger across several titles, searching. "Llorona. Why does that sound familiar?"

"They also call her the River Walker. It's just a local story." Sylvia sounded more subdued now as she watched Cesar. "I shouldn't laugh about her. They found another body this morning."

"A body?" Janice looked from Cesar to Sylvia. "Whose body?"

"Some rich farmer, I don't remember his name. They pulled him out of the river last night. We heard it on the news."

"Wait," Janice said. "What's the dead farmer got to do with this River Walker witch?"

"It's not just one dead farmer." Cesar cleared his throat. "This is the fourth one. Four guys from Mesilla have killed themselves since last April."

Grady turned from the shelves and stared at him. "Four suicides in a few months? In a town the size of Mesilla?"

"Yeah, and they were all healthy, and they came from good families." Sylvia shrugged. "Well, the first three were. I don't know about this guy today. But I think they were all pretty old men, in their fifties."

Janice sat back. "I'm sorry, I still don't see the connection between this witch and four guys who killed themselves."

"Some people believe Llorona drives men to suicide." Cesar brushed his palms soberly over his knees. "The legend says she lived a long time ago. She murdered her two babies to get back at her husband, who was sleeping around on her. Now she walks up and down the Rio Grande looking for her sons, and if she sees any living kids, she pulls them into the river and drowns them. And any man who hears her scream kills himself, the noise is so horrible."

A screaming, weeping ghost-woman who haunted rivers. Grady settled carefully into her chair, an unbidden and unwelcome echo of last night's wailing sounding in her head.

"She didn't live all that long ago," Sylvia said. "She's buried in the old churchyard in Mesilla, and those graves only go back about a hundred and fifty years."

"This witch is buried in a churchyard?" Grady wondered if Sylvia picked up her skepticism, but apparently not; she was nodding earnestly.

"Everyone knows where the witch's grave is. It's almost a rite of passage to go there in the middle of the night." Sylvia squeezed Cesar's arm. "We first saw it when we were in middle school, right, *querido*?"

"The witch is buried in San Albino Cemetery." Cesar seemed certain of this. "The town fathers painted her portrait on her headstone, to keep her spirit trapped underground." He smiled wanly at Grady, a handsome kid in spite of the acne scars marking his cheeks. "You should go there, Dr. Wrenn. You won't have any trouble finding her grave, with that face painted on the stone. It's pretty wicked."

"Call me Grady, please." Grady swiveled in her chair and gazed out the small window to the left of her desk. "Dr. Wrenn sounds like a character in a children's book." It was back, and

Grady hadn't been sure she would ever feel it again—that light flickering up and down her spine that went off whenever she heard a really intriguing legend. Her love of the past ran deep, and she cherished the folktales born of a community's historic triumphs and tragedies. A culture's legends revealed far more about its people than any dry book of dates and laws, and the story of this murderous witch was mesmerizing.

She had built her career—her avocation—on listening to long-silent voices whispering their stories. Her loss had robbed her of that pleasure for two long years. Perhaps some of the enchantment of that privilege was still within her reach.

"Does this sound like a go?" Janice reached into her backpack and pulled out a small notebook. "This La Llorona legend? It would be very cool to spend the summer researching a juicy ghost story like this."

"It has possibilities." Grady remembered the ghastly scream she heard last night, and a shiver went through her that had nothing to do with an appreciation of folklore. Her throat went dry, and suddenly her office seemed too confining. She slapped her knees and stood up. "Come on, it's beautiful out there. Grab the doughnuts and let's find a patch of grass on the quad to talk this out."

Grady reached for her coffee mug and saw her fingers tremble slightly before they closed around it.

Chapter Four

G rady had never had problems sleeping in the past, even through the rigors of graduate school and other periods of high stress. Sharing a bed with her wife had offered long nights of sweetly peaceful rest. Since the tragedy that ended her marriage to Leigh, she often wrestled with stretches of wretched wakefulness. This one was a killer. Grady hadn't caught more than brief, troubled naps in the week since her last visit to the river.

If it were just a matter of being awake all the time, Grady could live with that. But true insomniacs were never fully awake, or asleep. She passed entire days in a torpid haze of exhaustion, a twilight existence that drained all her energies. Grady had finally kicked off her sheets just after dawn, and pulled on her boots.

Hours later, fortified by killer coffee, Grady stood at the edge of the Mesilla Plaza. Southern New Mexico was less conducive to insomnia than cloudy Oregon. The relentless cheer of the sun in that incredible blue bowl overhead defied any craving for sleep. Grady slipped on her extra-strength sunglasses and sighed in relief.

She stepped off the high, cracked sidewalk into the plaza just as the stately church bells tolled the end of Sunday morning Mass. San Albino kept queen-like watch over the north end of the pretty square, a dignified sentinel of the faithful.

If Grady had to meander by a Catholic edifice, San Albino was more welcoming than most, with its cream-colored statue of Mary beckoning all toward the arched doors. The young mother's uplifted gaze seemed both hopeful and weary, as if she still saw good in the world, but she wasn't getting enough sleep.

The plaza was coming alive around Grady as the church emptied in a colorful babble of mixed English and Spanish. She noted a fair share of tourists, drawn to the art galleries, jewelry shops, and restaurants lining the red-brick courtyard. She sidestepped a scrambling toddler, his mother in hot pursuit, and turned down a quieter side street.

She lifted her sunglasses, wincing, and checked the street sign and then the small map she'd sketched on a napkin that morning. The church cemetery would be found at the end of Calle de Guadalupe, an elegant name for such a humble little path. Grady followed it as the clamor from the plaza faded behind her, and she walked out of the new twenty-first century and back several decades.

No cars passed her on the narrow road, and only the shrill buzzing of cicadas in the high grass disturbed the morning's stillness. Grady loved that about this desert valley—turn any given remote corner, and all vestiges of modern life seemed to disappear. Even the simple wrought-iron gates of the cemetery ahead recalled another time, appearing without fanfare at the end of the street.

Like any anthropologist worth her salt, Grady considered cemeteries among the most culturally rich acreage on earth. Exploring them had always been her pleasure, even the green-saturated, manicured hills of more modern yards. But a quaint burial ground like this, dating back a century and a half—she should have been in heaven.

But Grady couldn't see death impersonally anymore, and she avoided the tree-shaded collection of small white crosses that likely marked the graves of young children. She made her way respectfully through a proliferation of lots marked by small plaster representations of Catholic saints, protecting the slumber of their devout.

The cemetery was almost empty of visitors, which struck Grady as odd for a mild Sunday morning. She saw only one family clustered by a wide headstone flanked with fresh flowers, and an older woman in a light shawl standing near a larger block monument.

The newer graves were closer to the entrance and fairly well kept. But as Grady walked on, the San Albino churchyard assumed a kind of genteel shabbiness that seemed more poignant than indifferent. The loved ones who buried these people so long ago probably rested beside them now, and there was no one left to pull the weeds or patch the cracked stones above their graves.

The monuments here were more ostentatiously pious than in the newer section. Many of the epitaphs were in Spanish, and Grady had only a rudimentary grasp of that language's basic vocabulary. *Descanse en paz* was easy enough to·translate, and *Sueña con los ángelitos* had something to do with dreaming with angels.

She wended through the graves, keeping carefully to the narrow dirt paths between them. There was nothing even faintly witchy about any of these headstones. Instinct drove her toward the elderly woman by the taller monument. The shawl that covered her head and her long skirt marked her as a local senior, and she might have a wealth of knowledge about an old graveyard.

"Hello? Excuse me." Grady didn't want to startle this grandmother into an early grave by yelling at her right in front of one, so she approached her carefully. The shawl shifted as the woman glanced her way, but Grady couldn't see her face. "My name's Grady Wrenn. May I ask you something?"

"I was surprised you could hear her, Grady Wrenn."

Grady stopped. "I'm sorry?"

"I'm almost finished." Her head dipped briefly before the

grave in apparent prayer. Then she crossed herself and slid the shawl back from her abundant dark curls.

Grady's mouth fell open. This woman was several decades too young to be anyone's grandmother, and the musical Hispanic lilt of her voice was familiar. She wasn't naked and she wasn't dripping wet, but she carried herself with the same grace Grady had admired the night she stepped out of the moonlit Rio Grande.

"Grady…" It was all Grady could think of to say, and she extended her hand to shake although they were still a good ten feet apart. Her hand hovered lamely in the air as her mind galloped to catch up. "I thought you were…your clothes…"

The young woman sighed and turned back to the grave. Grady had assumed she was elderly because of her calico skirt and antique shawl, and the way her shoulders had seemed to hunch toward the double-block gravestone. Now it appeared she was hunched because she had been scrubbing the upper stone with a stiff wooden brush. She started doing so again now.

"Do you have a name?" Grady didn't want to make any more assumptions.

"Elena Montalvo." She swept her forearm across her damp brow and kept scrubbing.

"Elena Montalvo," Grady repeated. She stepped cautiously closer. "Is this a bad time?"

"This is a disgrace." Elena spat out the words, and now Grady was near enough to see the anger in her dark eyes. The bristles of her brush rasped over one corner of the granite block that stood upon a larger square foundation.

Grady edged around so she could see the front of the grave, and her knees locked in place.

It wasn't a terrible face. It was a terrible portrait, but it wasn't frightening in any visceral sense, except for its jarring oddity among the surrounding icons of serene saints. The flat stone surface bore the painted image of a woman's head, with wild black hair and blunt features. Her dull eyes stared directly at Grady, with no more expression or humanity than the granite itself. The only splash of color lay in the woman's heavy lips. They might have been scarlet when the paint was first applied, but years under this sun had aged them to a dingy brick red.

Grady watched Elena saw her brush across the graffiti marring the upper corner of the stone, just above the face's Medusa-like hair. Elena bent and rinsed the brush in a small bucket of water that stood beside the grave, then scrubbed some more, the muscles in her forearm dancing. Grady waited until the last of the profanity was washed away.

"Is this Maria?" Grady asked quietly.

"What?" Elena glared at Grady over her shoulder. "Of course this isn't *Maria*."

"I was told they painted her face on her grave to trap her spirit." Grady gazed at the crude image in fascination. "But I've never heard of that custom, among Catholics or any other—"

"Because such a custom doesn't exist." Elena dropped the brush into the bucket. She lifted her hair as if to cool the back of her neck and watched Grady silently. When she spoke again, the sharpness had left her tone. "This portrait has nothing to do with trapping evil spirits. It was painted by a girl of fourteen whose heart was broken by her mother's death. She was a loving daughter, but not a very good artist. She meant this picture as a tribute to her mother."

In a calmer state, Elena's voice was musical, even soothing. She gestured at the lower block, and the words etched faintly into the stone.

ROSA ANGELINA DE LA FUENTES
1917–1951

"She wasn't evil," Elena said. "And she wasn't a witch. She was my great-grandmother."

"Your great-grandmother rests here, Elena?" Grady stepped closer and crouched by the stone. She traced the letters with respectful fingers. "Why is this known as a witch's grave, then? Just because of the face?"

"Because kids around here are fed cruel lies." Some of the bitterness had returned to Elena's voice. "They get some kind of sick thrill out of defacing the headstone of a woman who never harmed a soul."

"And it was your grandmother, then, who painted this portrait when she was a girl, to honor her mother? Do you think she would be willing to tell me about her?"

"You can ask her. She's buried over there."

"Oh." Grady got to her feet. She wiped the palms of her hands on her jeans, looking at Elena uncertainly.

"Would you take those off?" Elena flicked a finger toward Grady's sunglasses. "If we're going to talk about such things, I need to see your eyes."

"Oh. Uh, sure." Grady dreaded the bombardment of sunlight, but she did as she was asked. Light drilled into her burning eyes, and she had to blink rapidly for several moments before she could see Elena clearly again.

The younger woman's expressive face underwent subtle changes. She studied Grady closely, with keen interest, and then her features softened into contrition. "Thank you. It's very bright out here. Please, put them back on."

Grady did, and blew out a breath. "So you look after this grave now because this woman was family?"

"Because I am of Rosa Angelina's line." Elena nodded. "But also because my ancestor was a good person, and she doesn't deserve to be mocked by children."

"How often do you come here?"

"Often. Almost every day, the last few months."

"Since the suicides started?"

Elena's dark eyes glittered, and she folded her arms.

"My students tell me some people in Mesilla blame a witch for these deaths." Grady paused. "They blame La Llorona."

"You've asked lots of questions since the first time we met."

"I guess I have."

Elena picked up the small bucket. "Yes, the vandalism has gotten much worse since the suicides began. Mesilla wants to blame a *bruja*, a witch, for these deaths, but they punish an innocent woman here. Come with me."

She set out toward the back of the burial ground, lifting her skirt as she stepped around a brick-lined plot.

"Are we going for a walk?" Grady called.

Elena turned back to her. "I thought you wanted to see the grave of a witch."

That intrigued flicker skated up and down Grady's spine again. She followed Elena through the loose rows of graves, which only grew shabbier as they reached the northern border of the cemetery. It was fenced by a sagging, waist-high wall of rusted chain link. Elena opened a screeching gate and waited for Grady to pass through.

Elena closed it behind them. "My turn for a question. How many lashes did Christ suffer before he was crucified?"

"Oh, no. A Bible quiz." Grady smiled, but Elena merely waited. "I'm afraid I don't know."

"Then you don't know how many paces you must walk from consecrated ground before you can bury a witch."

Elena started walking, and Grady started counting paces.

The deserted area north of the churchyard was no one's idea of pastoral. The ground was featureless, the earth dry and cracked underfoot. Trash was snarled among the weeds. They walked past the corrugated tin cylinder of a drainage ditch and a sparse stand of mesquite brush as the sun pounded on the back of Grady's neck. She had counted about forty steps when Elena stopped, and they both stared down at the flat rock embedded in the parched earth. The writing on it—a single name, no dates—was even fainter than the epitaphs of the oldest graves in the cemetery.

HIDALGO

Grady tried for some levity. She would probably regret it, but Elena's still presence beside her made her oddly nervous. "Please tell me this isn't your grandmother's grave."

"No." Elena lowered the bucket to the ground and knelt before the stone. "The woman who rests here is my grandmother's grandmother's mother."

Grady regretted her levity. She lifted her sunglasses and rubbed her eyes hard. She watched Elena brush dirt and small pebbles off the flat stone with her hand. She took the wooden brush out of the bucket and began scrubbing a white splash of bird droppings off the craggy surface. Grady crouched beside her and began plucking snarls of dead weeds away from the marker.

"Juana Hidalgo was a witch, and everyone in the village knew it." Elena's tone held the same soft sadness as when she'd spoken of her great-grandmother. "Mesilla was just a small village a hundred years ago. Men suddenly started to kill themselves back then, too. And Juana was blamed—they thought she was in league with Llorona, that she drove those men to their deaths. But it wasn't true. Juana was good to her neighbors. She always tried to help them."

Grady hesitated. "A witch who helped her neighbors?"

"There are many kinds of witches, Grady."

Grady leaned back on her hands and looked at the lonely grave. "What happened to her? Do you know?"

"The people's hatred finally broke Juana's heart, and her mind. She went to the river one night and opened her wrists with a knife."

Grady watched Elena's profile, the coffee smoothness of her skin. The sun coaxed red highlights from her dark curls. "Juana

Hidalgo killed herself, then? Was that another reason she was buried outside the churchyard?"

Elena made a contemptuous sound. "Do you think the *men* who took their own lives were forbidden burial in holy ground? You'll find them all back there." She jerked her chin toward the cemetery.

"I'm sorry, Elena." Grady wasn't sure exactly what she was sorry for, but Elena's expression compelled some offer of comfort.

Elena's long fingers brushed the little stone. "I'm sorry, too." She looked up at Grady, and a smile passed over her lips. "Don't look so sad, Grady Wrenn. I know you didn't set church doctrine way back then. You can't even pass a simple Bible quiz."

Grady smiled back.

Elena sighed and returned the wooden brush to its bucket. "Have you seen enough here?"

"Yeah. Thank you for showing me this."

Elena nodded and got gracefully to her feet. She lifted the shawl from her shoulders and covered her head. Grady waited until she finished her prayer and crossed herself, and then she rose, too, and brushed the dust from her hands.

"Do you have to go now?" Grady heard the plaintive note in her own voice, and Elena looked up at her questioningly. "I mean…I've enjoyed our talk."

Elena seemed to think about this. "I've enjoyed it, too."

"May I walk you home?"

Again, Elena didn't answer at once. Her gaze drifted east, toward the purple crests of the Organ Mountains that girdled that side of the desert valley. "Yes, you may. I'd like that."

Grady picked up the bucket and emptied the water in a patch of weeds, then followed Elena back toward the cemetery. She looked over her shoulder once at the small gray stone receding behind them, alone again under the cloudless blue sky.

❖

Grady's somber mood improved as they strolled together toward the plaza. Perhaps because she sensed a similar lightness in Elena, a new ease in her step as they left a witch's sad history behind.

"You're a teacher?" Elena asked. "You mentioned you have students."

"I'm an anthropologist. I do teach, yes, at NMSU."

"I don't know very much about what anthropologists do."

"Well, my kind studies the ways different cultures work. How people try to make sense of the world, through their customs and traditions."

"That must be a wonderful job." Elena's nose crinkled with her warm smile. "Do you study the religions of these cultures?"

"Sure, spiritual systems are always a big piece of the puzzle."

"But you have no faith yourself?"

It was a question, not a statement, and respectfully phrased, but it took Grady aback nonetheless. "What makes you ask that?"

"Ah. I'm sorry." Elena clasped her hands behind her as they walked around a curve in the narrow road. "Faith is a very personal matter."

"I don't believe in God," Grady found herself saying. "I never have. But I do respect the beliefs of others, Elena. Your own Catholic faith seems to mean a lot to you."

"Catholic?" Elena actually giggled. "I'm not Catholic, Grady. Oh, my. How much more not-Catholic can I possibly be?"

"You're not?" Grady frowned. "Then what's with the…" She mimed pulling a shawl over her head. "And the…" She crossed herself clumsily.

Elena laughed outright, an alluring sound. "I just pray the way my mother taught me to pray, the same way her mother taught her." She nudged Grady playfully. "I'd think an anthropologist wouldn't jump to such quick conclusions, Professor Gringa."

Grady wanted to know more. She wanted to sit down with

Elena over a plate of green chile enchiladas and listen to her talk about her faith, and her mother, and why she sat in rivers, and anything else under the fierce desert sun. Mostly, she wanted to soak up the friendly interest in Elena's eyes all day long. But she needed answers to other questions.

"You said it surprised you that I could hear her," Grady said.

Elena looked puzzled for a moment, then she glanced back toward the cemetery and nodded. "Yes, that's what I said. I was surprised you could hear Maria's cry, that night at the river."

"Why were you surprised? Didn't you hear her? She was hard to miss."

"No, I didn't hear Maria. Very few women can. Only particular women."

"What kind of women?" Grady tried to sound casual, but her throat felt dry.

Elena didn't answer. She wrapped her shawl more tightly around her shoulders in spite of the growing heat of the day. They were nearing the plaza now, and Elena nodded down a pleasant shaded street dotted with small adobe buildings. "I live down this way."

"This Maria." Grady cradled the bucket in her arms as she walked, half glad she hadn't received a reply. "Was she a witch?"

"Yes, she was a witch."

"And Maria is the one they call Llorona?"

"That's right. They're one and the same."

"Elena. Please help me understand this." Grady kicked a pebble out of their path and sorted her thoughts. "I've looked into this legend. La Llorona, The Woman Who Weeps, is featured in the folklore of three different continents, over the past five hundred years. The same story, about a woman who drowned her children and now haunts a river, is known in Mexico, El Salvador, Venezuela…this folktale isn't specific to this area, or to New Mexico. Or even North America."

"That's true." Elena seemed unperturbed by Grady's revelation. A dreamy cast had come over her features. "Maria is the River Walker. She searches for her lost sons in many rivers. She's been seen and heard in many Spanish-speaking countries. But her life began here, in the Mesilla Valley, and it ended here, when she drowned in the Rio Grande."

"You're saying Mesilla is the seat of this legend? Maria lived in this valley, five hundred years ago?"

Elena nodded. "She still wanders far and wide, searching streams and rivers, but she and her babies were born here, and they died here. And every hundred years or so, Maria comes home. And men begin to die."

Two cracking pops sounded farther down the street, and Elena gasped.

Grady stopped abruptly. "Was that a gun?"

Elena snatched the hem of her skirt and took off, her sturdy legs taking her from zero to full speed in a heartbeat, so what could Grady do? She ran after her.

"Mamá!" Elena streaked straight toward a two-story adobe shop and the group of people milling around it. She cut through the gawkers like a linebacker and threw open the door.

Grady was right behind her, and she was stunned by the hostility she saw in more than one sullen watcher's face. She jumped onto the wooden walkway that fronted the shop and saw that the large, arched window by the door was half shattered. Her boots grated on chunks of stained glass as she entered the store, and she heard feet pounding up a staircase. "Elena?"

After a moment, Elena's voice sounded above her. "It's all right, Grady."

"Should I call the cops?"

"No! Just stay down there."

Grady put a hand to her heart, panting. At least she wasn't sleepy anymore.

She peered out the broken window. The people outside were

clumping into small groups, murmuring quietly. They weren't turning into an angry mob; that was some comfort. Grady slid off her sunglasses and took in the shadowy interior of the shop.

There was a light, pleasant scent in the air, not of incense but of recently kindled sage. The interior adobe walls were lined with antique wooden shelves bearing labeled packets of herbs, small jars of oil, and bundles of dried leaves and grasses. Artwork proliferated. There were representations of a dozen different religions on the adobe walls, from traditional crucifixes to candles associated with the practice of Santería, as well as small statues of various pagan gods.

"I'm in a spiritual Wal-Mart," Grady murmured.

She heard drumming footsteps again, then Elena shot past her and out the front door, the small bell over it clanging wildly. Grady followed quickly.

"What do you want here?" A high flush on her cheeks, Elena set her hands on her hips and barked at the stragglers still hovering in front of the shop. "Why do you stay? You're not going to tell me which of your brave sons shot out my window and terrified my mother. Go on, you righteous citizens. Go to your afternoon Mass!"

Grady stood near Elena and studied the crowd uneasily. There were still some angry glares, watching Elena in what seemed like defiance. But several people simply dropped their eyes and turned away.

Grady noticed an older couple whispering heatedly near the wooden walk. Finally, the woman pinched the bearded man's vest in her bony fingers and forced him to walk with her. They approached Elena, and the man crossed himself surreptitiously.

The old woman regarded Grady narrowly for a moment, then spoke to Elena in English. "We're sorry this happened, Elena. Your mother, is she all right?"

"Yes. She's fine, Mrs. Valdez." Elena's fierce stance softened a little. "I don't suppose you saw what happened?"

"We only heard the shots." The woman glanced up at her husband, who nodded, his eyes on the ground. "We have been afraid for your safety, *hija*. Ever since the first man was taken from the river in April, we have been worried that the town would take its fear out on you. You heard that a fourth man was drowned a week ago, *sí*?"

Elena glanced at Grady. "Yes, ma'am. Enrique Acuña. I was sorry to hear of his family's loss."

"And he died in the same way *she* always kills men, with that terrible look in his eyes. *Madre mía*, I have heard his poor wife fainted when she saw his face." Mrs. Valdez's husband cleared his throat, and she sighed and laid a wrinkled hand on Elena's arm. "Shooting out windows. This isn't Mesilla's way, Elenita, all this vile meanness. We want you to know we're praying for you."

Elena covered her hand with her own. "Thank you, *abuela*, for your prayers." As the couple shuffled away, Grady heard Elena add under her breath, "If nothing else."

They went back into the store, and Grady blinked in relief to be out of the sun's glare. Elena clicked a switch on the wall, and the lamps suspended over the center of the room shed a pleasant gold glow.

"I don't see much damage, except for this window," Grady said.

Elena walked to a far wall, searching. Finally, she reached up and lifted down a crucifix the size of her hand—or half a crucifix. The wall behind it bore a neat round hole. "It must have taken a lot of courage, to attack such a dangerous window."

"Do you know who did this, Elena?"

"I know a half dozen men who might have." Elena kissed the broken cross, then opened a small drawer and laid the pieces inside. She slid the drawer shut, then lifted a broom from behind a counter. "Careful, Grady, there's glass everywhere. Don't cut yourself."

Grady realized she was still carrying the bucket. She went back to Elena and knelt in front of her, tipping the pail on its side so she could sweep the glass into it. "Why would anyone want to scare you and your mother?"

"They don't care about my mother. They haven't seen her for years."

Grady glanced toward the shadowed stairway that led to the second floor, which must serve as the family's home. "Is she ill?"

"She just never comes downstairs."

Grady pondered that while Elena finished sweeping up, and then set the full pail of shattered glass by the wastebasket.

"Sit down, Grady." Elena disappeared through an arched doorway curtained by strings of beads. Grady settled at the oak table in one corner of the store, a comfortable nook apparently set aside for conversation. Elena returned, carrying tall glasses of iced tea, and joined her at the table. Grady sipped the sweet tea tentatively, and then pulled hard at it, relishing its cold splash down her parched throat.

Elena emptied half her glass too, at first swig. Then she sighed and slipped off her shawl. She wore a white cotton peasant blouse beneath it that left her shoulders bare. Grady's gaze lingered on the small wine-colored birthmark that graced the swell of her left shoulder. Elena sat back and swept her fingers through her dark curls, her eyes sad and distant.

Grady waited patiently, finding the silence comfortable. Finally, Elena looked at her and they both smiled, acknowledging explanations were in order.

"All right." Elena flattened her hands on the table, the silver rings on her fingers clicking softly against the wood. "Remember your history lesson, Grady. A hundred years ago, men began killing themselves in Old Mesilla. They blamed Juana Hidalgo, the village witch. Today, men have started dying again. And Mesilla is still blaming the village witch."

"Really?" Grady blinked. "You?" She infused as much friendliness and acceptance into her voice as possible. She had met witches before, or men and women who claimed to be, in her field work. "Are you a witch, Elena?"

"No." Elena smiled faintly. "I'm a *curandera*. Does the gringa professor know the difference?"

"Sure." Grady rested her elbows on the table, intrigued. "A curandera is a folk healer. A spiritual healer, right?"

"That's right." Elena nodded at the surrounding shelves. "Mostly I'm an herbalist, and I have a nursing degree from our community college. But I try to help people through prayer and trances, too. I deal with the spirit world. So the more ignorant and superstitious bullies around here insist I'm a witch."

"And they're blaming you for these recent suicides? I thought they held La Llorona responsible. Maria. She's supposed to be able to force men to take their lives."

"Yes, but Maria was a witch, and all witches are believed to be her spiritual sisters." Elena blew a lock of hair off her forehead in disgust. "All witches are supposedly in league with her, they help Maria do her killing. But that's absurd, Grady."

Grady had been trying to redefine what she considered absurd for most of the past week. She kept her eyes on Elena's face and listened carefully.

"Juana Hidalgo was a witch, but she cherished human life, she would never have aligned with Maria. Juana was another innocent woman, wrongly accused. Just like my great-grandmother—she was a devout Catholic! But once you're labeled a witch in this town—" Elena broke off, and looked at Grady unhappily. "I'm sorry. I get real emotional about this, sometimes."

"No need to apologize." Grady studied the palms of her hands. "Let me try to sum up. La Llorona was once a real woman named Maria, and now she's a vengeful spirit. She haunts rivers and drives men to suicide. The people of Mesilla think you're a witch and you're helping Maria kill these men, so they're out to get you."

"No, that's not fair." Elena sipped from her glass. "Most of the people of Mesilla are good-hearted and sensible. There's only a very small faction of religious fanatics that cause me any trouble."

"I guess that's reassuring."

"Tell your new *gringa amiga* the rest of it, Elena." A rasping voice from the stairway startled Grady. She twisted but couldn't see the woman who stood in the shadows at the top of the stairs. "Tell her why Maria loves you best of all! Why crazy men are trying to kill us both, because you won't stop talking—"

"Hush, Mamá, *cálmate*." Elena's voice was firm, but she sounded more weary than angry. "Go back to your TV show. I'll be up soon."

Grady heard a muttering of Spanish curses recede upstairs.

"She's still pretty shaken up. I need to be with her." Elena looked at Grady closely. "Wait a moment."

Elena got up and went to one of the shelves behind the counter. She took down a small packet and came back to Grady. "This is a special tea blend. It has valerian and a few other herbs. It's not a heavy sedative, but it might bring you enough peace to get some real sleep."

Grady took the packet of ground leaves, surprised her insomnia was so obvious. She was surprised again when Elena stepped nearer and reached up to cup the side of Grady's face in her hand.

"It must be very lonely," Elena said quietly. "Not believing there's a loving deity out there who cares about your pain. Thinking you're alone."

A ready quip came to Grady's mind, but it died on her lips. Elena's palm was cool and soft against her cheek, and the kindness in her voice turned Grady into a young child. For a moment, she wanted badly to close her eyes and turn her face into Elena's hand, and something told her Elena would allow that. But she held still.

Elena tapped her cheek gently. "Go home and take a nap, nosy gringa. I need to babysit my crazy *madre*."

Grady got to her feet. "Thanks, for this." She slipped the packet of tea into her pocket.

"That will be six dollars. I take Visa and MasterCard." Elena smiled. "I'm teasing you."

"Take care of yourself, Elena."

"I always have." Elena showed her to the door and patted Grady's shoulder sweetly before she closed it behind her.

Grady snapped on her sunglasses as she stepped down off the wooden boardwalk. She headed vaguely north, unfamiliar with this particular warren of winding streets, but knowing the plaza, where she parked her truck, lay that way.

Three men stood behind another truck, a big battered blue one, a block up the street. They watched Grady as she walked past, muttering to each other.

"*Buenos días*," Grady called, deciding to acknowledge their obvious scrutiny. She checked the position of the sun. "Well, *buenas tardes*, anyway."

She received neither a returned greeting nor a single smile. The men, two middle-aged and one younger, all Hispanic, stared at Grady silently long after she passed them. She could feel their muddy gazes on her back.

Grady glanced back at Elena's shop, but made herself keep walking. Elena and her mother were grown women. And Grady had had a long day, considering it was just past noon, and she had much to think about. There was a six-pack of Corona calling her name, chilling in her fridge at the condo that passed as her home.

Grady touched the packet of tea in her pocket. Maybe she'd pass on the beer. The side of her face tingled pleasantly all the way to the plaza.

CHAPTER FIVE

*W*hat an interesting voice this strange gringa has. Have You heard her speak, mi Diosa? Of course You have, even though she never talks to You. Her voice sounds like she's talking through rich, dark cocoa all the time. I don't mean that she sputters. You know what I mean. Grady Wrenn has a nice, low voice.

They could have gotten in today, those men with their rifles. The lock on the front door is not very strong. They could have smashed it and destroyed everything in the shop. They could have run upstairs and shot my mother. How much time do I have, Diosa, before it gets that bad?

The deaths are coming faster now. They are only weeks apart. And after every body washes up on a riverbank, Mesilla's fear grows, and so does their rage against Mamá and me. I must stop these killings. How many more men will die if I don't? Sweet Mother, I feel their blood on my hands.

I begin to understand why You placed Grady Wrenn in my path. She is like my grandmother in one way; when she listens to me, it's like there is no one else in the world who is more important. She listens to me with her whole body. But of course, she doesn't believe anything I tell her. She doesn't believe in anything. You could have saved me a lot of time and trouble by sending me a person who came equipped with some small faith in an afterlife, mi Diosa. I'm not complaining, I'm just pointing out.

But I must admit, tonight, for the first time, I don't feel so alone. As the sun goes down I have the anger of the street mob in my mind, yes, but I also have Grady Wrenn's warm chocolate voice drawing me out, hearing my story.

I'm glad she took the tea. Glad that she was willing to let me help that much, at least. How old is the soul behind those green eyes? They seem to carry the wisdom of many long years, but Grady is still a young woman. She looks so tired, like she has never slept, not since the day You put her on this earth.

I pray she has found healing sleep tonight, and now I must seek my own. Sweet Goddess, send my abuela, my grandmother, to me in my dreams. I so need her comfort now, and her strength.

As always, with love from Your Elena.

Chapter Six

A week later, Grady again found herself standing beside the Rio Grande at midnight, but not solely because she thought Elena Montalvo might be sitting in it. She had purely professional reasons for being there, but she admitted other motivations occurred to her. She had scanned the water's rippling surface more than once for nubile Hispanic curanderas. No luck so far.

And no Llorona. The night was peaceful and still.

"Shrouded she comes, gliding silent on the water," Janice intoned, reading from a worn, hardback text. "La Llorona seizes the unwary child. She snarls his shirt in her taloned hands and drags her small screaming victim into the river. Blood flows from the boy's nose. He howls and retches with terror. The merciless wraith—"

"*Man*, Janice, is this some slasher novel?" Sylvia tossed a twig playfully at Janice's sneaker.

Seated cross-legged on the ground beside Sylvia, Cesar smiled, too, but a bit stiffly. "It sounds like a horror movie."

"It's from the Cordova text, that compilation of Southwest ghost stories." Janice showed them the cover of the book, illuminated by the fire that crackled between them. "Listen, this is great stuff. We can excerpt this in our paper. 'The merciless wraith drags the thrashing child beneath the chill waters of the river…'"

Janice's voice faded behind Grady as she left them and wandered farther down the riverbank. Her students had managed an hour of silence awaiting Llorona as the stars filled the sky, but then their scholarly focus had faded. These guys had far to go if they wanted to build the discipline to do real field work, but Grady hadn't the heart or inclination to rein them in.

The moon was all but invisible tonight, and she missed its friendly light. It had been in its full glory two weeks ago, when she first saw Elena. Funny, in Grady's mind that had become the night she first saw Elena, not the night she heard the shriek of a centuries-dead witch. Talk about losing scholarly focus.

She'd actually tried to talk her students out of this nocturnal jaunt, but they were adamant. They wanted to preface their paper with a descriptive passage about Llorona's natural habitat, the Rio Grande by moonlight. Janice was especially keen on the idea. And these weren't high school kids, Grady couldn't forbid them a legal activity. But she felt antsy and protective, uneasy at the thought of exposing these callow bairns to a ghost that inspired five hundred years of terror.

And her worry was crazy. Grady didn't believe in ghosts. She didn't believe in God or in an afterlife, so there were no ghosts. Sylvia, Cesar, and Janice were in no danger from a folktale.

She bent and swept up a handful of pebbles and tossed them one by one into the river. Perhaps the mere casting of pebbles would again summon Elena, cause her to rise up from the dark waters to comfort lonely anthropologists. But the Grande seemed empty of such promise tonight.

"Grady?"

"Shit *fire!*" Grady whirled, knocking the hand from her shoulder, scattering the remaining pebbles.

Janice yelped and jumped back two feet.

Grady slapped a hand to her chest, high-fiving her own heart. "Are you trying to kill me?"

"God, I'm sorry!" Janice was wide-eyed. "I thought you

heard me coming. I tried to scuff my feet." She smiled, tentatively. "Did you think I was La Llorona?"

"I thought you were back there." Grady knew she sounded sullen. She was growing fond of Sylvia and Cesar, even given the sappiness of their young love, but she still felt no real connection to Janice Hamilton. The girl had an unfortunate tendency to fade into the woodwork. Or the adobe, as it were. "Are we about ready to pack it in for the night?"

"Oh, no. Do we have to?" Disappointment flitted across Janice's sallow features. "I've never been out to the river at night. It's really kind of cool out here. Beautiful, but spooky. I can almost hear the witch out there in the dark. Can't you?"

"Clear as a bell." Grady folded her arms, then nodded toward the distant campfire. "Did you guys get tired of bloody ghost stories?"

"Yeah, I guess. Well, mostly I thought those two might want some time alone." Janice glanced back too, her expression wistful. "They're really into being together. Very nice people. I like them both. But they're *really* together, you know?"

"I've noticed."

Janice seemed to pick up on Grady's lack of enthusiasm for this conversation. "Well, I'm going to take a little walk. I want to check out some more spooky riverbank."

Grady relented to a twinge of guilt. She had always known she was a good teacher, and her bond with her students meant something to her. It wasn't Janice's fault that she wasn't particularly keen on bonding with anyone with a pulse right now. And she didn't want any of her charges out of her sight tonight. "What did you learn about Llorona, in the Cordova?"

Janice turned back and her face lit up. "That is one gruesome text. I loved it. If getting a degree in anthropology means reading stuff like that all my career, I'm set for life." She walked back to Grady quickly. "Okay. So everyone can see Llorona, men and women both, right? And the descriptions of her are crazy consistent—a young woman in a shroud, walking slowly along, hunched over, always seen somewhere near a river, especially this river."

Grady stared at Janice, astonished. She had a notion she was meeting her for the first time. The shy, empty expression was gone. It was like switching on a lamp. The girl's face looked like Grady felt when that small shiver of academic pleasure ran up her spine. Janice was going to love this work.

"But only *men* can hear Llorona weep. What's up with that?" Janice looked at Grady intently. "Is there some kind of symbolism going on there? Like, Llorona's husband hurt her so much with his infidelity, now only men can hear her sadness, something like that?"

"Yes, that was Cordova's take on the legend." An uneasy quiver went through Grady's stomach. "Though I've heard recently that some women are able to hear Llorona, as well. Particular women."

"Really?" Janice's eyes sparkled with a new idea. "And when Cordova calls Llorona a witch, what does he mean, exactly? I don't know whether to picture an evil woman casting spells, or some Mexican version of a Wiccan."

"Wicca is neopagan. It's a nature-based religion. Those who practice it spend a lot of time dispelling the whole cackling crone image." Grady's shoulders relaxed as she warmed to her topic. She was rather enjoying Janice's rapt focus on her every word. "The stories Cordova collected sprang from a more primitive concept of witchery. Spells and hexes and the dark arts were involved." She looked out over the river. "But then, I've also heard recently that there are many kinds of witches."

"Well, I have to admit I find the primitive concept of witchery much cooler. Um, is it okay if I smoke?"

"Sure, if you stay downwind." Grady watched Janice pull out a crumpled pack and flick a lighter, the small flame illuminating her chewed fingernails.

Leigh had been a smoker in her twenties. She quit the habit, for sensible health reasons of her own, shortly after she met Grady. She took it up again during the last year of their marriage. Her cough had jarred Grady awake more than once during the few nights she truly slept that terrible year. She realized Janice was still talking and made herself focus on her voice.

"I'm glad your seminar was offered this summer. I'm really enjoying it." Janice's smile was tentative again. "I still don't know many people in Cruces. I'm wondering if you know of any places lesbians might hang out in town?"

Grady pondered this. She wasn't surprised or dismayed that Janice knew she was gay. Students often Googled their professors, and Grady had sponsored a gay/straight alliance group at Evergreen College that would have come up with her name. She had always been able to be fairly open about her life throughout her career, even here. New Mexico might not smack of the same progressive spirit as parts of Oregon, but Grady's current boss was solidly supportive. Still, she noticed that Janice's interest in her personal life was accompanied by that shy smile, so she decided to answer her literally.

"Actually, Cruces is a more open town than you might think, Janice. NMSU has a GLBTQ Student Resource Center, and this July is Gender Identity Education Month. They'll have panels on—"

It began as a low, snarling cry.

Grady's hands clenched at her sides and her spine grew rigid, stiff as a hickory staff. The sparse flatland bordering the river was empty. Llorona was invisible again tonight, but her rising wail went through Grady like a bullet through a stained-glass window.

"Grady?"

"Hush." Grady closed her eyes, shivered hard, and kept telling herself it would pass.

The ghostly shriek, in full power, carried both the insane

trilling of a young woman and the hoarse fury of an old one, bitter and lost. Somehow, if Grady could just block out the grief in that terrible howling, if she could hear only the rage, it would be bearable; she could endure this. But the stark suffering in Maria's unnatural song shredded her heart. It resounded there because Grady recognized this grief. She shared it.

After a full, excruciating minute, the roar dwindled to a keening and faded. Her ears still rang with it, but Grady couldn't miss the terrified bellows coming from the direction of the campfire.

"Come on!" She snatched Janice's wrist and tugged her into a run.

The distant spark of the campfire jittered in Grady's vision as she raced toward it over the uneven ground. When she got closer she could see Cesar on his knees beside the fire, his arms outstretched. Sylvia knelt beside him, clutching Cesar around the chest.

Grady forced herself to slow and step calmly into the glowing circle, already trying to ease the horror she saw in Cesar's face. His glasses hung askew from one ear, and his eyes were wide and staring. His mouth hung open in a fixed rictus of fear.

"Grady, he just started screaming." Sylvia looked frightened, too, but her attention was entirely on Cesar. Her arms around his chest were trembling. "He won't look at me."

Grady knelt slowly in front of Cesar, and moved into his range of vision. She called his name gently, twice. He didn't move, and his eyes didn't focus.

"He fell into the fire." Sylvia seemed to be making a determined effort to quell her panic. She reached across Cesar and clutched his sleeve. "He burned himself."

"Buddy, I'm going to touch you. I want to look at your arm." Grady kept her voice low but firm. Cesar didn't react as she took his wrist and lowered his arm. She heard Sylvia hiss as the firelight exposed the charred tear in his sleeve. Grady moved the cloth aside and saw a series of small burns and scratches across his elbow.

"That's not good." Janice stood beside them, her hands on her knees.

It wasn't, but Grady was more concerned about Cesar's fixed stare and the bellows-pumping of his chest as he drew in air. His shirt was soaked in sweat in the cool night, and a drop slid down the side of his face. She thought quickly and fished in her back pocket for her keys.

"Janice, here, go get my truck. I don't think we should try to walk him back to our cars." Her eyes still on Cesar, she handed Janice her keys. "Sylvia, bring us your backpacks over there. Cesar? We're going to lay you down for a minute—"

"I've got my cell," Janice said. "Shouldn't we just call nine-one-one?"

Grady shook her head. "Cesar doesn't need a medical doctor. Go on, Janice, get the truck."

"But—"

"Now."

There was a pause, and then Janice's swift footfalls sounded behind Grady.

"Are you going to let us lay you down, Cesar, or will we have to hit you with a body tackle?" To her great relief, Cesar slumped to the ground in jerky stages, guided by her hands and Sylvia's. She checked out Sylvia again, content that she was physically unhurt, at least.

"Baby, you're going to be fine," Sylvia's voice shook, but her hand stroked Cesar's damp forehead gently. "*Te adoro, querido.* Just lie still."

Grady lifted Cesar's heavy sneakered feet and rested them on the backpacks, hoping elevating his legs would do something to stave off shock. Cesar seemed to be calming slowly under his girlfriend's tender touch. "Tell me what happened, Sylvia."

"Grady, I swear I don't know." Sylvia looked up at her

through her tousled hair. "We were fine, and then Cesar just started screaming like a madman. He clawed at his ears and tried to get up, but then he fell into the f-fire."

Grady looked at Cesar's face, ashen now, his eyes still staring sightlessly into the sky. Every brain cell she had told her Janice was right; they should have called for medics. But every other cell in her being knew Cesar needed Elena. Her certainty was immediate and complete.

Grady shifted on her knees to Cesar's side, and took her folded bandana from her pocket. "Cesar, I'm going to wrap up your arm real lightly to keep it clean. We'll have those burns looked at right away." He still made no response, so she looked at Sylvia. "I want to take him to a spiritual healer, Sylvia. A curandera in Mesilla. What do you think?"

"A curandera?" Sylvia rubbed Cesar's chest in soft circles. She looked at him silently for a moment. "I know curanderas can heal. If it was me that was hurt…I'd say the hospital. But Cesar's family, they're very traditional. He believes in a lot of the older ways." She drew in a breath, then nodded. "Yes, okay. We'll take him to this healer."

Grady caught the flare of headlights as her truck roared toward them over the rough ground. "Come on, Cesar. We're going to help you stand up. And Sylvia's telling the truth, you're going to be fine."

❖

The tendons in Grady's jaw creaked, and she unclenched her teeth. Losing a filling wouldn't get Cesar to Elena any faster.

The big kid was conscious and sitting upright beside her, that was the good news. He was crammed between her and Sylvia in the small cab of her truck. Janice followed them in her own car, closely enough that her headlights glared in Grady's eyes in the rearview mirror.

"Can't you talk to me, baby?" Sylvia tried to pull Cesar's

head down onto her shoulder, but his body stiffened and resisted. "Please, Cesar, you don't have to look so scared. Nobody's going to hurt you."

Grady chanced a quick glance at Cesar's face. His mouth was still slack, and his eyes retained that vacant cast that resembled a drugged stupor, but fear still seemed to radiate from his pores. He shivered with cold now, and Grady was seriously worried about shock.

She braked hard, gritting her teeth again in hopes that Janice would slow down, too, and cranked the wheel to the left. The winding streets in Elena's neighborhood were even more disorienting by night, and she had circled this block twice already. With a rush of relief, Grady spotted the white boardwalk that fronted Elena's shop, and she pulled up in front of it, spinning gravel.

"Cesar, you and Sylvia sit tight for a moment. I'm going to go find our healer."

Grady saw a light go on inside over the stairway even before she raised her hand to knock on the glass-paned door. She randomly noted the neat plywood square fitted over the frame of the broken front window, then saw Elena's silhouette moving swiftly down the stairs.

Elena shook her hair out from under her long shawl, apparently tossed on hurriedly over the shorts and T-shirt she slept in. She unlocked the door, surprise and concern in her eyes when she saw Grady.

"Elena, I'm sorry to bother you and your mother so late."

"Are you all right?"

"It's not me. One of my students needs your help."

"Of course." Elena craned past Grady and saw her truck. "Can you bring them inside?"

"Yes, he can walk."

"Please, bring him in."

Elena vanished into the recesses of the store, and Grady loped to her truck to help Sylvia with Cesar. He was disturbingly pliant as he climbed out of the cab, and he shuffled between them like a shivering zombie. Janice followed them into the shop, looking around curiously.

Elena came out of a back room, drying her hands in a silk cloth. Her eyes went directly to Cesar, taking in every nuance of his stance and expression. She smiled briefly at Sylvia and Janice. "I'm Elena Montalvo. Tell me about our friend, here."

Grady started to speak, but then nodded at Sylvia. She might be young, but she was every inch Cesar's partner, and she was proving herself worthy of his devotion tonight.

"We were at the river just now," Sylvia said. "Cesar went from perfectly normal to terrified in about five seconds. He kept grabbing his ears and screaming. He fell in a fire and burned his arm."

"The burns aren't too serious," Grady added quietly.

Elena murmured and stepped closer to Cesar, and took his face in her hands. "Has Cesar used any drugs tonight?"

"No, he never does." Sylvia shook her head. "Except pills for his allergies."

"Any major health conditions I should know of?"

"No." Sylvia rested her head briefly on Cesar's slumped shoulder. "He's very healthy."

Elena measured Cesar's pulse at the throat, then stood on her toes to smell his breath. "Does he have a faith?"

"Cesar is Catholic."

Elena nodded and took Cesar's right arm from Grady. "Let's bring him back here."

Cesar moved when they urged him to, and he might have walked off a cliff as mindlessly as he stumbled between Elena and Sylvia toward the back of the shop. Grady started to follow, but Janice touched her arm.

"Grady, wait. I really respect any local customs in Mesilla around folk healing and everything. But does this woman have a license? Any kind of license? Is that how she takes a medical history? Why did she ask about Cesar's religion?"

"Elena is a curandera, Janice. She does both physical and spiritual healing."

"Spiritual healing?" Janice blinked. "As in exorcisms?"

"I guess, if necessary." Grady glanced over her shoulder, wanting to be with Cesar.

"Grady." Janice took a step back. "Do you really think Cesar was attacked by the ghost of a dead witch tonight?"

"What's important tonight is what Cesar believes. Come on, Janice."

Grady stepped through the curtain of beads that separated the back area of Elena's shop and saw a mild gold light glowing from a side room. Sylvia and Elena were there, helping Cesar stretch out on an elevated bed.

Grady let out a low whistle, her worry deflected by the uniqueness of this small chamber. She had never been in a space that doubled so well as a cozy place to rest and an area designed for healing. While Elena's outer shop featured artwork from dozens of religions, the walls of this small room carried every healing symbol Grady recognized, and several she wasn't sure of—the caduceus, the Eye of Horus, several Native American icons. The single raised bed Cesar rested on looked sturdy and comfortable.

Elena's fingers were probing the base of Cesar's jaw. She looked at Sylvia. "What is your name?"

"I'm sorry. I'm Sylvia." She smiled fleetingly, clasping Cesar's loose hand. "I'm Cesar's fiancée."

"I'm glad you're with him tonight." Elena glanced at Grady. "Sylvia, I have some hard questions to ask you. They might not make sense to you, but I need to know the answers. All right?"

"Sure, of course."

"You love Cesar, very much?"

"With all my heart."

"Has he ever raised his hand to you? Ever hit you in anger?"

"Cesar?" Sylvia's brow furrowed. "Oh, no, Elena. He would

never be violent with me. I've known him all my life, and he's never hurt anyone. He's a very loving person." Tears rose in Sylvia's eyes, but she held Elena's gaze steadily.

"That's what I needed to know." Elena patted Sylvia's hand and went to a maple chest of drawers in one corner. She slid open the second drawer and lifted out a small vial of clear fluid. From the top drawer, she took out a string of rosary beads. She went back to Cesar and wound the rosary around his right hand.

"Shouldn't we try calling him again?" Janice's voice was respectful.

"I'm afraid Cesar can't hear us right now." Elena dipped an eyedropper in the vial, then lifted one of Cesar's lids gently. "He's listening to someone else."

She applied the drops to both of Cesar's eyes, then laid the vial aside. "This is a highly distilled lavender oil, Sylvia. It'll help him see us again. You're also Catholic?"

"Yes, I am."

"Then keep hold of his hand and pray, in any way you see fit, while this remedy takes effect. I'll do the same." Elena laid her hand on Cesar's chest and spoke softly to him. "Cesar. *Usted no tiene nada temer de La Llorona, mi hermanito.*"

Sylvia looked at Grady in sudden alarm, and Grady nodded reassurance.

"What did she say about La Llorona?" Janice whispered.

Sylvia swallowed. "She told Cesar he had nothing to fear from the woman who weeps."

"Let's be still, please." Elena lifted her shawl over her head and crossed herself. She closed her eyes and her lips moved.

For the next few minutes, all Grady heard was the soft ticking of the clock in the other room, and the occasional creak of a floorboard overhead. Elena's mother couldn't have slept through all this drama, and she seemed to be pacing upstairs. Sylvia stood beside Cesar, holding his hand to her heart as she prayed.

His shivering began to ease first, and his big body relaxed by degrees against the white sheet. Cesar's staring eyes finally fluttered shut, and Grady sighed in relief. She felt an ominous tightness in the back of her neck and she rubbed it absently as Janice shifted from foot to foot beside her.

Elena traced a cross between her head and shoulders again and slipped her shawl off her hair. She touched Cesar's forehead as tenderly a mother caressing her child. Then she went back to the dresser and sprinkled a pinch of dried powder onto a small tin disk. She took out a box of wooden matches and struck one, sending a tendril of smoke to the low ceiling.

"Cesar's ready to come back to us now. This will wake him as gently as possible."

Elena held the disk beneath Cesar's chin and blew very softly, sending the light smoke from the flickering powder toward his face. Grady caught a mild scent of thyme, blended with faint traces of something like yucca flower. Elena set the tin aside and waited, her hand over Cesar's heart.

Grady watched Elena's calm profile. She could almost feel the curandera's hand on her own chest, the warmth of her palm against her shirt. Elena looked tired, as if the effort of this ritual had drained her, but she no longer looked worried. As if drawn by Grady's regard, she turned her head, and they smiled at each other.

Cesar awoke suddenly and with a titanic start, his entire body jerking hard on the bed. Sylvia cried out in surprise and Grady nearly bit her tongue, but Elena seemed prepared for this abrupt surfacing.

"Shh, Cesar, you're with friends. You're safe." Elena's tone was soothing as she helped him sit up against the headboard.

Cesar was gripping the sides of the bed and looking around wildly, but when he saw Sylvia, he sagged against her and closed his eyes. *"Madre de Dios,"* he gasped.

"Exactly." Sylvia stroked his hair and murmured endearments in two languages.

Elena measured Cesar's pulse at the wrist and waited until he lifted his head from Sylvia's breast. "My name is Elena, Cesar,

I'm a curandera. You're in my home, in Mesilla. Your friends brought you here for help."

"Was it her?" Cesar was starting to tremble again. He stared hard at Elena. "Was she really out there?"

"Tell me what happened to you, Cesar." Sylvia pried one of Cesar's hands off the bed frame and held it in her own. "Where did you go? You wouldn't look at me, you wouldn't talk to me. You scared the shit out of me."

"She became the sky," Cesar said, and Grady started. She couldn't imagine a more dead-on description of how Llorona's cry invaded the human heart. "Her screams, they poured all over me. It was like the whole world hated me. I just kept saying my beads." Cesar blinked at the rosary wrapped around his hand, then looked up at Elena. "It was her?"

"Yes, Cesar." Elena took his free hand in hers. "You heard the screams of the River Walker tonight."

Grady's head was starting to pound. She never should have caved and taken her students to the Rio Grande tonight. Cesar looked better. In spite of his trembling he was Cesar again, not that paralyzed zombie, but he should be home in his own bed. She was an idiot to expose any of them to this craziness.

"But I didn't hear anything." Janice shifted in the small room, apparently trying to catch Elena's eye. "I was right there, and there wasn't any cry. It's really true only men can hear her?"

"Only men." Elena didn't look at Grady. "And good men have nothing to fear from her."

"You believe the witch is real, Elena?" Sylvia's eyes were wide again. "That Cesar heard her ghost tonight?"

Elena nodded. "You can walk through the Mesilla Plaza and find a dozen men who have heard Llorona. Mostly, they hear her weep. But on some nights, she roars." Elena went to a bowl filled with water on a side table and bathed her hands in it. "But she hunts a specific kind of prey, Cesar. You were never in any danger. She wouldn't hurt you."

"I'm sorry, but what kind of prey?" Janice looked from

Elena to Grady and back again. "What kind of men is this ghost supposed to be hunting?"

"Men who hurt the women and children who love them." A stony note had entered Elena's tone, but she softened again when she looked at Sylvia. "Not men like Cesar. You love a good and decent person, *mi hermana.*"

"Yes, I do." Sylvia smiled tremulously.

Cesar lifted the rosary wrapped around his hand and kissed it. He leaned back against the pillows, looking spent.

"You're probably going to sleep for several hours, Cesar." Elena adjusted the pillow behind him. "Your system's had quite a shock. I'd like you to stay here, so I can keep an eye on you. Should we call your family?"

"No," Sylvia and Cesar chorused, and they smiled at each other sheepishly. That smile settled the last of the quivering uneasiness in Grady's gut, leaving only the thudding headache.

"Cesar's mama babies him too much already." Sylvia brushed a strand of grass from Cesar's shoulder. "I'll stay here tonight, too. I can sit right there." She nodded at an armchair in the corner, as if Elena might object.

"Then I'll sleep on the sofa in the shop," Elena said. "I'll be able to hear you if Cesar needs anything. I want to take a look at those burns, and then we'll let you get some rest."

Cesar's eyes were already drifting closed, but he lifted his elbow and peered at it. "What the hell?"

"Hush, Cesar." Sylvia tapped his head sternly. "Don't curse in here."

"It hurts, though," Cesar protested.

"We can help that." Elena went back to her dresser, then looked questioningly at Grady and Janice. "Will you two be staying as well? You're welcome, but I think things are pretty well settled for this evening."

"I'd like to stay, if it's all right." Grady hadn't spoken in so long her voice was slightly hoarse. She nodded her aching head toward the shop. "I can just crash in there somewhere. Janice, it would be nice if someone besides Cesar got a decent night's sleep. You should go on home."

"Yeah? Okay. I will, then, if we're sure Cesar's all right." Janice gave Cesar's foot a light tap. "Night, Sylvia."

Grady was relieved at Janice's lack of resistance. Her post-crisis edge was wearing off fast, and she was exhausted. She followed Janice into the shop to see her out.

"Grady." Janice opened the door and hesitated. "I know you were right to bring Cesar here for help. I'm still clueless about how Elena did it, but he looks like he's going to be fine. You're not going to be in trouble over this, right? We can all back you up with Dr. Lassiter, if she gives you any flack."

"Thanks, Janice, but I'm not worried. I'm seeing Dr. Lassiter first thing in the morning, I'll fill her in. Good ni—"

"Grady? You heard it, too, didn't you? That scream Cesar heard. You looked so—"

"I heard Cesar yelling, Janice. Go on, now. Try to get some sleep."

Janice stared at her. "Okay. Let Sylvia know she and Cesar can call me in the morning, if they need anything." Grady set the small chain on the door and watched through the thick glass pane until Janice made it safely to her car. She rested her elbow on the door frame and squeezed the back of her neck.

If Grady had grown up in Mesilla, maybe Elena's claims about Llorona would make more sense to her. But nothing in her academic training or her experience in the world prepared her to accept the possibility of life after death. The very notion was heartbreaking to her now. She still half hoped there was some kind of rabid cougar out there, bellowing its way up and down the river, some natural explanation for all this. But animals don't grieve. A cougar couldn't produce the terrible mourning in Maria's cry.

"I have some blankets in this chest."

Grady hadn't heard Elena come in. She was kneeling by an antique trunk in one shadowed corner of the shop.

"I think we can make you comfortable in here," Elena said. "On the floor, of course. I'm not giving up my sofa."

"I would never ask it."

"You can always go upstairs and bunk with my mother, if you wish." A dimple appeared in Elena's cheek.

"I think I've cost your poor mother enough sleep." Grady accepted an armful of thick folded blankets. "Thank you, Elena. I'm not sure what I'd have done if you hadn't been here tonight."

"This must have been very frightening for you, Grady." Elena got to her feet. "I'm grateful you thought to bring Cesar here. A medical doctor would just have sedated him. He needed help waking from his nightmare, not to be locked inside it." She studied Grady's face. "Are you in pain?"

"No. Well, yes, I have a headache. What do you think we should expect with Cesar tomorrow?"

"Sylvia will want to watch him carefully, not just tomorrow but for several days." Elena closed the chest and latched it. "He could have problems sleeping. He might relive what happened tonight. It might be hard for him to think of anything else for a while."

"All the symptoms of PTSD." Grady sighed. "Damn."

"A crisis counselor would tell you to watch for PTSD. I doubt if they'd encourage Cesar to go to Mass several times, but I'm recommending that, too." Elena slid her arm through Grady's. "Come and sit with me for a while. If you'd like something for your headache, I think I have some pure-grade heroin in one of these drawers."

Grady had to smile. She let Elena lead her down to the oak table, enjoying her warmth against her side. "I'll pass on the heroin. Just sitting for a bit will be nice, though."

They settled at the table, and it was nice, though neither of them spoke. Their silence was easy, in the ticking shadows of Elena's store. A streetlight glowed through a side window, but otherwise the large room was peaceful and dark.

Upstairs, a flare of mariachi music bled through the floor, then faded.

"Just in case there's any doubt we woke my mother?" Elena looked up. "That's her, saying yes, we did."

"I'll apologize, if she'll let me." Grady hesitated. "Can I ask why your mother stays upstairs, Elena?"

"Well. That's a little complicated." Elena pulled a small candleholder nearer, then struck a match to the wick.

"I'm sorry. Didn't mean to pry."

"You're not prying. It's just if we're going to talk about such things, I need to see your eyes." Elena slid the lit candle so it sat evenly between them, then sat back. "Mamá stopped coming downstairs about five years ago. It was around then that the people of Mesilla started to fear the return of La Llorona. As I told you, Maria returns to her home valley every hundred years or so. And everyone in Mesilla can count very well, from generation to generation."

"Wait. Why every hundred years?"

Elena shrugged. "We'll have to ask Maria. None of my— no one seems to understand her timing, but it's consistent." Her face looked sad in the flickering light of the candle. "I suppose Maria haunts the rivers of the rest of the world when she is not in Mesilla. She never rests."

"I hadn't heard about any of this." Grady rested her chin in her hand. "I've lived here for six months, and until my students spoke up in class, I never even knew Llorona was sighted here. And even Sylvia and Cesar, who grew up in this town, only know about half of this legend."

"You might be seeing the faint dividing line that separates Mesilla from Las Cruces, Grady. Sylvia and Cesar might know of Maria, but they didn't grow up with the same stories I did. Our village has a very different history than Cruces, and our memory is long indeed."

"So everyone here knew the time for the River Walker's return was coming around again." Grady didn't want to pull

Elena too far off track. "Did something happen five years ago, when your mother went to ground?"

"Went to ground is a good way of putting it. But nothing had to happen to Inez Montalvo to drive her into hiding. My mother's paranoia did most of the work. It did have help, however." Elena drifted her fingers through the waves of her hair. "About five years ago, some people stopped talking to Mamá and me on the street. Not many people, but a few. Then we found whenever we went to Mass, our usual seats were taken. Just small things like that, at first. Then one day, Mamá found a dead rattlesnake in our mailbox. A big one."

"Jesus."

"Yes. That was all it took. She's been house-bound ever since." Elena pushed back her chair. "Would you like some tea?"

"Sure. Thanks." Grady flexed her shoulders, trying to loosen her neck. She watched Elena cross the dark room to the small kitchenette against the far wall and fill two cups with water. "What's it been like for you, Elena, these last few years? Looking after your mother."

Elena didn't answer at once. She set the cups in a microwave, then went to a collection of delicate ivory figurines on a side table. She lifted one, an image of the draped Madonna, and turned it in her fingers. "It's hard, at times," she said at last. "Mamá can be impossible. Demanding. I can't travel, I can't be away from her for long. I can only pray this will not last forever, for either of us. Perhaps our lives will be easier after Maria moves on again."

"I'm still not clear on why the people of Mesilla connect you and your mother to Llorona." Grady spoke gently, aware she was still treading private waters. "You said the other day that all witches are believed to be in league with her, but you're not a witch."

"No, but I am a curandera, a calling too close to witchcraft for ignorant minds." Elena took the steaming cups from the microwave and brought them to the table. "And remember,

Mamá and I are the descendants of a witch. These men believe we sit in here, weaving spells that lead them to the river and Llorona. Just as Juana Hidalgo was blamed for Maria's rampage a hundred years ago, my mother and I are blamed for these suicides today."

They sat together in the silence of the dark shop. Grady sipped her tea, a mild floral blend that soothed her throat, and watched the candlelight play across Elena's features. She heard a muted, low whickering, and she looked at Elena, puzzled.

"That's not my stomach." Elena smiled. "That's our pack horse. He's fenced out back, a nice little stall."

"Ah, your horse." Grady remembered Elena riding that horse by moonlight, her dark hair lifting and falling on her shoulders. "Can you handle another personal question?"

"Of course." Elena snapped her fingers. "I am on a roll. Go ahead."

"Tell me why you like sitting in the rivers in the middle of the night."

"Well, part of it is just the river." Elena's eyes sparkled. "It's amazing, Grady. This time of year, when the Grande is this deep and warm, the current flows just below your eyes. You feel its gentle pull against your body. It's all you see, the centuries of water passing all around you, and you're part of it." The pleasure faded from her face. "But yes, I know what you're asking. I wait for Maria at the river, too. I want so badly to see her. I've never seen her. I don't understand why she won't come to me."

"But why would you want her to? Believe me, it's not a relaxing experience." Grady wanted to understand. "Why is it so important for you to see Maria?"

"So I can tell her she doesn't have to keep doing this. She doesn't have to kill." Elena looked at Grady pensively. "What does the legend say, the version you heard, about why Llorona drowned her sons?"

"She wanted revenge on her husband. He was unfaithful to her, and she went insane and killed her children to spite him."

"Right. That's the story that's been passed down for hundreds of years. The witch was jealous, and she went mad when her husband took another woman. She drowned his babies in the river, and then herself." Elena shook her head. "Grady, do you believe what I've told you about my ancestor, Juana Hidalgo? That she wasn't evil, she harmed no one in her lifetime? She was falsely accused?"

"Yes, I believe that."

"Then believe me when I tell you that Mesilla is wrong about Maria, too." Elena covered Grady's hand with her own. "I don't mean she's innocent, like Juana. Maria has drawn a hundred men to their deaths, and the sorrow she's caused might always keep her from the light, unless she atones. Maria is insane now, and deadly. But she wasn't an evil woman while she lived. She didn't drown her children, or herself, as Mesilla believes. Her husband did. He killed all three of them."

"Elena." Grady closed her eyes, willing herself to focus through the throbbing of her head. "How could you possibly know this?"

"I'm afraid you'll have to trust that I'm in a position to know." Elena got up and went behind Grady's chair. She rested her hands on her shoulders and began a careful massage. "If you won't accept my heroin, at least let me try another remedy for this headache. It hurts me just looking at you."

At first Grady couldn't relax beneath Elena's touch. Her physical closeness was too unexpected—too welcome—to invite easy surrender. But she couldn't deny how good her hands felt, kneading the tension out of her neck. "Okay. Tell me more."

"Maria's husband drank. He beat his wife and children without mercy." Elena's voice was a low murmur against Grady's back. "One night, in a drunken rage, he drowned both of his infant sons in the river. Maria tried to stop him, and he drowned her, too."

Grady shivered, and Elena's palms warmed the tops of her shoulders for a moment.

"The next morning, he started the rumors that grew into the lie most of Mesilla believes to this day." Elena's strong fingers resumed probing Grady's neck. "This man was a murderer, and he was never punished. He took Maria's children, her life, her reputation. Her hatred for him is powerful and deep."

"Powerful enough to kill a hundred innocent men."

"Maria drew all those men to their deaths, yes. But they weren't innocent, Grady. Not the men who died over the centuries, and not those who are dying now. The four men from Mesilla who killed themselves were all known for brutalizing their families."

Grady turned her head. "What?"

"They beat their wives. Their kids."

"Elena." Grady didn't want to believe it, so she had to ask. "Are you saying Maria is only righting old wrongs? You believe she's a victim, seeking some long overdue justice?"

"No." Elena's voice turned fierce, and she knelt at Grady's feet and looked up into her face. "Maria is a monster now, I know that. Grady, I swear to you, if it would save one human life, I would pull Maria's heart out of her chest myself, if I could. But if you want to help me stop these killings forever, you must know what Maria suffered before she died, before she became La Llorona."

"I'm listening." Grady wanted to fall into Elena's dark eyes.

"Maria doesn't kill to seek justice, or for vengeance. Maria believes she is still protecting her children from violent men." Elena let Grady sit with that for a moment. Then she got to her feet, and began rubbing her shoulders again.

"Wait." Grady rubbed her burning eyes. "Violent men. What about Cesar? He's never abused anyone, but Maria's scream sent him toppling into a fire tonight."

"Yes, her screams are said to be fearsome." Elena kept up the massage, her touch as gentle as Maria's cry was frightening. "Llorona screams only when she is hunting prey. Any man can hear her, as Cesar did, and they are often badly shaken. But only a man who has battered his wife, his children, responds to these screams by ending his own life."

Grady lowered her head, trying to muddle through this information. Elena's hands drew rivulets of warmth through her sore muscles, coaxing them soft. All that remained of her headache was a faint twinge behind her left ear, a discordant high note on a violin that just wouldn't fade. "I never should have let those kids go to the river tonight."

"*Ay.* Is that what this headache is about?"

Grady hadn't realized she had spoken aloud. "It was a stupid thing to do. Cesar half believes this legend. I should have realized he was susceptible. I should have talked them out of it."

"I see." Elena's fingers spiraled down Grady's upper back. "Are you that powerful, really? Can you stop Cesar from walking his own path? He isn't a child. You can't protect someone from their destiny, Grady."

"I'm not sure I can see it that way." Grady heard Elena whispering above her, and she frowned. "Elena. You know I don't believe—"

"Hush." Elena tapped her shoulder. "Just because you haven't found any gods to your liking doesn't mean She doesn't like you."

The whispering continued, and then stopped. With Elena's last word, the final lingering spark of Grady's headache winked out, and her body was suffused with peace.

"Huh," Grady murmured. "How about that."

She heard Elena chuckle, and her hands slid from Grady's shoulders. A moment later, she helped Grady out of her chair.

"Come on. I've laid out the blankets. You lie down for a moment. Has your sleep been no better?"

"Actually, that tea you gave me helped a lot, the last few nights." Grady could have asked for a dose now, but maybe she wouldn't need it. The two folded blankets on the hardwood floor could have been a plush queen-size in a five-star hotel.

Grady curled onto her side, tired unto death but her mind still reeling with questions. She waited for the inevitable frustration—her comfort would slowly fade, her body would tense, her mind would continue to churn. What seemed a certain, deep sleep would elude her.

"You rest, Grady. I'm going to check on Cesar."

Grady watched Elena's bare feet pad toward the back of her shop.

Then she awoke to the streaming light and birdsong of midmorning.

CHAPTER SEVEN

She sleeps like a child, mi Diosa, nestled on her side with her hands cupped beneath her chin. Here, beneath my roof, Grady feels Your benevolence, whether she recognizes it or not, and it brings her peace.

All my thanks to You, my Goddess, for helping me wake Cesar from the terrible dream that gripped him tonight by the river. What defense can such an honorable young man have against the immortal hatred of La Llorona? The only way he could escape the bloody fury of her cry was to flee into the dark recesses of his own mind.

Does Maria possess even a drop of human mercy, Diosa? When her cold, dead eyes alight on a man like Cesar, and she finds no cruelty in him, does Maria's grim heart soften for just an instant as she whispers, "Not you," and moves on? I pray that this most errant, most lost of Your daughters experiences such brief moments of grace. I pray that a spark of Maria's humanity remains, that her tormented spirit is not entirely chained in the prison forged by her murderer.

Grady stirs and calls out a name, twice. Now she lies still again.

Grady could not see what I saw tonight, the nimbus of beautiful light that surrounded both Cesar and his lady, Sylvia. That light sent out tendrils of luminous color, connecting the man and the woman, nourishing them both, the warmth of Sylvia's love coaxing Cesar awake again.

I saw just the smallest flash of that same light rise from Grady just now, when she spoke that name. A wisp of light left her chest and reached out, searching, and finding no answering radiance, it faded away into darkness. She is so alone, sweet Mother. Grady is another River Walker, as imprisoned in some ways as surely as Maria herself, and my heart aches for them both.

I will smudge my chamber with white sage in the morning, to cleanse the last traces of Cesar's misery from my walls. I wish I had thought to send some sage with the other girl who came with Grady tonight, the blond one. Janice? She had the look of one almost as lost and alone as Grady. I pray for her, too, tonight.

Thank You for allowing me to watch over Grady's sleep. And thank You for giving Mamá that little cold in her head, so she took some NyQuil and finally went back to bed. And while I am thanking You, mi Diosa, would it be all right if I reminded you how very old our little Ford car is? I hate to bring it up again. I keep wearing out the clutch because I can't stop riding it, and a new clutch costs about $400, even at Pepe's Auto, where I'll get a discount because I healed Pepe's little daughter. That's still a lot of money. I'm just pointing out.

Good night, my Goddess. Lead me home by Your path.

As always, with love from Your Elena.

CHAPTER EIGHT

Dr. Phyllis Lassiter, Dean of NMSU's School of Anthropology, stood barely five feet in the high heels she wore daily. Her pinched face held a perpetually stern frown. She was notorious for her mastery of delicate sarcasm and her ability to puncture an inflated ego with surgically precise disdain. Most of the faculty avoided her.

Grady adored her.

"I take it that it is now your mission in life to drag this department into one juicy lawsuit after another." Dr. Lassiter peered at Grady through her rimless glasses.

"No, ma'am."

"Is this my punishment, then, for inspiring you out here to the desert boondocks in the first place?"

"Yes, ma'am. I mean, no. Not really." Grady smiled. "Yes, you did inspire me out here. But no, I don't mean to make problems for you."

Dr. Lassiter—Grady figured her mother must have called her thus in the womb. She could not conceive of her as "Phyllis"— had taught Grady's first undergrad course in anthropology fifteen years earlier, at Evergreen State College in Washington. An opening on NMSU's faculty, in her mentor's department, had coincided with Grady's fervent need to leave the Pacific Northwest.

"So, Cesar Padilla, our sophomore." Dr. Lassiter swiveled in her chair and typed neatly at her keyboard. "Age twenty, a graduate of Las Cruces High. Mediocre grades—except in history, interesting. Father employed at White Sands Missile Range. I remember the boy, vaguely. Large, glasses, often with an anxious expression?"

Grady nodded, but she doubted her confirmation was needed. The dean remembered every student who had ever majored in her college.

"And is Mr. Padilla recovering well from his unpleasant night at the river?"

"He says he is. I spoke to him on the phone a couple of times over the weekend, and I've been in touch with his fiancée, Sylvia Lucero. I'll know more later this morning. My seminar meets at nine."

"Ms. Lucero is taking your seminar, too." Dr. Lassiter tapped more keys. "And the new junior, Janice Hamilton? I hope to see her in some of our advanced courses next fall."

"Janice might have a good knack for this field."

"I'm pleased to hear it. Her parents, in Albuquerque, are my old friends. I think they've sent Ms. Hamilton down to us for safekeeping."

"Uh-oh. She needs safekeeping?"

"Perhaps she just needs a good teacher." Dr. Lassiter glanced at Grady over her bifocals. "Her parents tell me the girl has been a loner much of her life. She's always had excellent grades, however. Consider taking her under your wing."

Grady sat back in her chair, unwilling to commit to be-winging anyone at this point. "Anyway, I doubt there's going to be much fallout from the other night. Unless we should worry about my not getting Cesar to a hospital?"

"No, I'm not concerned. You sought treatment for your student in the context of his ethnicity and religion. A viable decision. And this curandera you brought him to sounds fascinating, by the way. You win points for finding a new local resource." Dr.

Lassiter typed an entry, then closed the program. "Your trio has chosen an intriguing topic for their paper, Dr. Wrenn. Don't neglect Cordova's *Guide to Mexican Folklore*."

"It's on their reading list."

"Hmm. Care to explain that scowl?"

"Am I scowling?" Grady sighed. "Okay. You're right, ma'am. Llorona is fascinating. Everything I'm reading, everyone I talk to, hooks me more on this legend. But I think I…"

She what? Did she really want to tell the dean of the School of Anthropology that she'd been spooked by the wailing of a ghost? Spooked twice? Grady recognized the genuine interest and concern in Dr. Lassiter's eyes, but she couldn't ask her to go there. Not if she couldn't believe it herself. "I think I need to put a priority on keeping my students out of trouble."

"Ah. I recall thinking the same about you, during our field study of the Klickitat tribes."

"Oh. You mean the study where I asked the tribal chief about their oral marriage rituals?"

"The study where you voiced the phrase that effectively married you to the tribal chief, yes." Dr. Lassiter's gaze was still measuring. She knew Grady's recent history, at least its bleak outline. "You're looking a bit better rested these days. Are you managing to get some decent sleep?"

It occurred to Grady that she hadn't wandered the Mesilla Valley late at night in over a week. Elena's mild tea worked miracles. "I'll sleep like a baby once this summer project is over. I'm still holding out hope that after our river visit, my trio will opt for some other fascinating topic for their paper."

❖

"We want to go on with our paper," Janice said. "'The Mystery of La Llorona.'"

Grady raised her legs slowly and crossed her boots on her office desk. "Really."

Seated in front of her, Cesar and Sylvia were looking at Grady as if Janice had just spoken rationally.

"All three of us still want to write it, Grady." Sylvia cradled Cesar's big hand on her knee. "We believe what Elena told us. Cesar isn't in danger from the River Walker. We want to know more about her."

"Three nights ago," Grady said evenly, "Cesar about took a header into a campfire because of this witch. Today she's no longer a danger?"

"Oh, Cesar's not going back to the river." Sylvia spoke with a vehemence that defied dissent. "Neither of us are going anywhere near Llorona herself again, thank you. But maybe we can help find an answer to these suicides, Grady."

"And this could be a dynamite paper," Janice said. "It's got everything. Didn't you say there was a possibility we could get it published in a professional journal, if our research is good enough? That would be such a coup, for undergrads."

"I said that before I realized you decided to write about an undead murderess." Grady eyed Cesar. There were no physical aftereffects to his trauma that Grady could see. His coloring was good, his eyes clear. "You're really considering this, Cesar?"

"Yeah. I do want us to go ahead, Dr. Wr—Grady. We've decided to focus on the suicides. If we can learn more about the men who died, maybe we can help Elena stop them."

"Elena?" Grady unwound her legs and sat up. "Elena asked you to help her with this?"

"She didn't ask us." Sylvia sounded protective of Elena. "Cesar's been to see her a couple of times in the last few days, since it happened. You knew that, right?"

"Yes, it makes sense that Cesar would see Elena." Grady was struggling to tamp down a flare of anger.

"She told us her theory, that Llorona is innocent of killing her children," Cesar said. "And that all of the men who have died were violent men. She said she knows of a way to stop the killings. We both want to help her." He nodded at Janice. "All of us do."

"I see." Grady stood and stretched. She needed to get out of this office before she snatched up the phone and screamed at a certain curandera. "I need to think about all this. It's a pretty day out there. Why don't we take a stroll and chew this over?"

"Hey, that would be nice." Sylvia got up eagerly, apparently relieved that Grady was open to discussion. "A stroll to the doughnut store on Solano?"

❖

The doughnut store was not what Grady had in mind.

Over two hours and more than three miles later, she led her straggling students into the sunny Mesilla Plaza. Grady's nocturnal wanderings had accustomed her to lengthy hikes, but her three charges started flagging long before they stumbled up the steps of San Albino Church.

"There's a reason I majored in anthropology and not phys ed." Sylva propped a friendly elbow on Grady's shoulder, fanning herself and sweating profusely. "This is the reason! Death marches. Are you mad at us or what?"

"Nope, I'm not angry with you." Grady looked up at the dreaming marble face of the statue of the Virgin that stood in front of the church. "I just thought we should place this conversation in its proper context, as it were."

Grady opened her pack and lifted out a tall bottle of water. She took a swig, then passed the bottle to the others. She had needed the time afforded by this long hike to gather her thoughts. As they left the campus behind, Grady had forced herself to put Elena's role in encouraging this project out of her mind. She had to decide whether she could allow her students to face what might be real danger, supernatural or otherwise.

And Grady had to admit, in her heart, that she might be

overreacting to this danger. She did not have a good record for protecting the people who looked up to her, for keeping them safe. But then, no one here was four years old. "Let's go in."

She was banking on the church being open to the public this afternoon, and she was right. They followed her into the tall vestibule, shadowed and blessedly cool. Grady nodded at a smiling older man who held the door to the sanctuary open for them on his way out.

A church's interior tends to loom larger when there are no worshippers present. San Albino wasn't immense or particularly grand, but there was dignity in the cushioned hardwood pews in the nave and classic beauty in the arched apse over the high altar. Grady felt again that surreal slippage in time southern New Mexico seemed to inspire in her. She could imagine standing inside this very church a hundred years in the past and finding it much the same.

She let Sylvia, Janice, and Cesar precede her down the crimson-carpeted aisle, their steps all but silent in the echoing space. Cesar and Sylvia genuflected briefly before entering the pew—Sylvia bobbed, Cesar sank fully to one knee. When all three were settled, Grady rested her hips against the pew in front of them and folded her arms.

"It's a little different, isn't it? Discussing Llorona in my scholarly, multicultural office, and talking about her here."

They were feeling it, she could tell by their faces—the hushed solemnity of any house of worship, especially one as old as this. The grandeur of ritual infused this place—weddings, baptisms, funerals, the milestone moments of entire generations, beneath one roof.

"It does feel different, saying her name in here." Like Grady, Janice spoke softly. "Llorona feels more real here, just like at the river. It kind of reminds me what's at stake."

"But I still think we need to do this, Grady," Sylvia said. "People in Mesilla are dying, and we should help if we can."

"And Cesar." Grady studied him. "You agree? You want to finish this project because it's important to the people of Mesilla?"

Cesar nodded. "And because I don't want to let my fear control me. My parents taught me that part of being a man is learning to face your fears."

Grady frowned. She hadn't really expected this personal sentiment, expressed so openly by this quiet kid, and it moved her in spite of herself. She heard Elena's voice whisper in her mind, asking if she was powerful enough to protect anyone from their destiny.

"Look, it's important you three understand this." Grady made sure she had their attention. "A lot of heavy emotion is brewing around these suicides. Real bullets are being fired, from real guns. Are you aware of that?"

Sylvia nodded. "Yes, Elena told us some men in Mesilla were pestering her. She warned us to be careful."

Pestering her. Good of Elena.

"Maybe we can ask some questions in town that Elena can't, right now," Cesar said. "She wants to stop the killings, but some people in Mesilla won't talk to her. If we can give Elena more information about the suicides, it will help her plan."

"And what is her plan, exactly?"

Cesar shrugged. "She said she'd tell us when she was sure."

And you let her get away with that? Grady rubbed her eyes. She couldn't blame Cesar; she had allowed Elena Montalvo to get away with entire speeches filled with cryptic statements.

"All right. We're doing this paper." Grady blew out a slow breath. "And we're all going to be very careful. Being careful means none of you makes a move until you discuss it with me first. And none of you works alone—ever. If I give you a field assignment, all three of you go together. That's non-negotiable."

"How do we start, Grady?" Janice sat up, smiling.

Grady shook her head and repeated herself. "Clearing things with me, working together, are non-negotiable, folks. Do we have an understanding?"

"Sí, Mamá." The respect in Sylvia's warm smile took the sass out of her words. "Yes, Grady, we understand."

Grady waited until Cesar and Janice acknowledged her aloud. Then she tapped her thighs, thinking. "Cesar, you don't attend this church, right?"

"No. We go to Immaculate Heart, in Cruces."

"Do you know anyone who works here at San Albino?"

Cesar looked at Sylvia. "Doesn't your mother know the pastor here? They went to school together."

"Yes, that's right," Sylvia said.

"Good. This is where we start using that hometown advantage." Grady felt that stirring of the old excitement again, the thrill of the hunt for answers. "Here's your first assignment. Sylvia, ask your mom to call this pastor for us. See if you can arrange to meet with him. *All three of you.*" She paused, and they nodded staunchly. "Tell the pastor the truth about this project. Tell him we're trying to find connections between the four suicides, and answer any questions he has honestly. Ask him if he'll help you set up interviews with the widows."

"Excellent. I'll start writing out some questions." Janice slapped her pockets, apparently looking for a pen. "Wait, Grady. We can find the widows' names through back copies of the *Sun News*. Why don't we just call them ourselves? It'd be faster."

"No, Grady's way is better." Cesar waited for Sylvia's nudge of agreement before he went on. "We don't know any of the wives, but I bet they all know the pastor here. We'd be more likely to get interviews, and also, it's just more respectful this way."

"If the pastor declines, then that's a firm no." Grady ticked the points off on her fingers. "If any of the widows decline interviews, that's firm, too. You'll be talking to grieving families, and in any culture, that requires sensitivity and respect. Are we clear?"

They were clear.

"Then that's where we start." Grady pushed off the pew and stood. "Janice, get busy on those interview questions, which I will pore over with a fine-tooth comb. Sylvia, you and Cesar get back to me tomorrow about seeing this pastor. I'm sorry to leave you guys with a long walk home, but I've got an urgent medical appointment."

Grady started up the aisle, ignoring the aghast silence behind her. She heard a cell phone flip open.

"As if," she heard Sylvia whisper. "Don't worry. I'll call my cousin for a ride."

❖

Grady had a temper, but not a vicious one. She wasn't feeling especially vicious now, but the small bell over the front door of Elena's shop clanged rather loudly as she pushed it open.

Elena was behind her counter, wrapping a package in brown paper, laughing with a large young woman who must be a customer. They both turned in surprise at Grady's abrupt entrance.

"Drug deliveries in the back, gringa." Elena waved at her airily, and the woman giggled.

"Don't let me interrupt." Grady's voice was tight.

Elena looked at her, then reached across the counter to pat the woman's hand. "All right, Rita, *vámanos*. Tell your father I'll come by and see him tomorrow if his dreams are bad today."

"Thanks, Elena." Rita waved at Grady on her way out. "She's *muy linda, amiga*," she called over her shoulder.

"*Sí*, very cute and very *loca*." Elena smiled at Grady, but then her face sobered, and she came out from behind the counter. "Hey. Has something happened? You look grim."

"I had a meeting with my students this morning." Grady tried not to sound accusing, but she couldn't help it; she was ticked. "It sounds like you've been doing a little recruiting."

"Recruiting?"

"You've been talking to Cesar and Sylvia and Janice about these suicides."

"Of course I have." Elena's shoulders were gaining a little stiffness of their own. "They had many questions about Maria. I answered them honestly. Why are you so angry, Grady?"

"I need to know what you have in mind for my students, Elena. They seem to think they're going to help you stop these killings."

"And why wouldn't they want to help stop Maria?" Elena looked puzzled. "This tragedy is happening in their community. They care about—"

"Elena, people are shooting at your home. Men are dying. I've heard that damn wail twice now, and whatever it is, it's dangerous. You have no business drawing these kids into this mess."

"Why do you insist on thinking of your students as children?" Elena's dark eyes snapped. "Their grandparents were working and raising families at their age. What's happened to you, Grady, that makes it so hard for you to—"

"This is not about me." Grady controlled her voice. "This is about making sure my students are safe. I'm not going to allow them to do anything that might put them at risk, Elena."

"Yes, right, and I would feed them to the fire." Elena stalked away from her, then turned back and set her hands on her hips. "Do you seriously believe I would ask those young people to do anything that would endanger them, Grady? Do you think so little of me?"

Grady almost faltered, but went on. "I think you might be obsessed with Llorona, Elena. I haven't known you long enough to know how far you'll go to vindicate her."

Sorrow flickered across Elena's features. "Then let me be perfectly clear." She walked to Grady. "I did not ask Cesar or Sylvia or Janice to help me. They have reasons of their own for offering to do so. Their safety is as important to me as it is to you. And yes, what they learn about these killings might help stop them."

Grady clenched her teeth in frustration. "And what do you think my students can learn that could possibly help stop these suicides?"

"*Nada* that I don't already know!" Elena jabbed Grady's chest with one finger. "But perhaps *you* will believe what your students tell you about Llorona, Grady! You don't believe me, not yet. You're thinking here." She rapped Grady's forehead with her knuckles, rather hard. "And I need you here." Elena rested her hand against Grady's heart.

Grady felt her blood pound against Elena's palm.

Elena hesitated, and the fire in her eyes faded. Her touch grew lighter on Grady's breast. "I must face the fact that we live on two entirely different planets, Professor Gringa. You're older than me, and you come from good schools, and you've traveled to so many wonderful places. I've lived in Mesilla all my life. I believe in a loving Mother, and you believe in nothing but your textbooks. I don't know how to convince you I'm telling the truth, Grady. I'm hoping your students, who live on your planet, too, will be able to persuade you."

Grady's hand rose of its own accord and covered Elena's. "Why is it so important that I believe you about Maria, Elena?"

"Because I'm starting to care for you. And because you're the only woman I know who can help me stop her."

"Me? Personally?"

"Yes. If you believe me, Grady, you can talk to Maria for me."

Grady swallowed. "How do you figure that?"

"If you can hear La Llorona, then she can hear you."

"Elenita?" a voice called lightly from upstairs. "*Ven aquí, por favor.*"

"*Un momento, Mamá.*" Elena kept her hand in place after Grady lowered hers. "Listen, I can't ask you to face Maria with me unless you believe she is real, and she's innocent of those first crimes." She patted Grady's breast. "I just want you to start thinking *here* more. Can you do that?"

Grady searched Elena's face, and found no slyness there, no guile—only a wistful hope. "I can try, Elena."

"Aiiyeee, gringa, help me!" The cry from upstairs was a frightened shout, and Grady started. "My crazy daughter is insane! She holds me prisoner up here against my will! Come save me, gringa!"

"Madre de Dios." Elena sighed. She dropped her hand and stepped back, then looked at Grady apologetically. "You might as well go see her. She can keep this up all day."

Grady looked from Elena to the staircase.

"She has chained me to the *wall*," the distant voice sobbed. *"Ay, Dios mío*, save me, stupid gringa!"

"Go on, I'll lock up." Elena made a weary flapping motion with her hand. Grady went to the back of the store and climbed the stairs obediently.

As soon as she turned the corner, out of sight of the lower level, the portraits began. Dozens of framed drawings of women, all Hispanic, were tastefully arranged on either side of the hallway. Some were in pencil and some in ink, but each was in a homemade frame, and each featured a different solitary woman. Black-and-white photographs replaced the drawings at the end of the short hall. Grady did one of those leaning-backward walks, studying the portraits as she went. The faces of these women fascinated her.

"Rescue me, save me from my *loca* daughter before she cuts my throat in my sleep, *ay ay ay."* The frightened voice droned off into a bored monotone as Grady stepped into the bedroom.

The middle-aged woman lounged quite comfortably on top of the neatly made bed, her veined legs crossed, a cigarette dangling from her lips. She was applying pink polish to her ragged fingernails. The loose collar of her robe bared her shoulder, and Grady saw the same small, wine-colored birthmark there that graced the cap of Elena's shoulder. The woman studied Grady through hooded eyes, and Grady wondered if she was seeing Elena in twenty years.

No, she decided. There might be physical similarities, but Elena would never truly resemble her mother. Elena had a kindness and strength that shone through her features, and that light was absent in the older woman.

"I'm Grady Wrenn."

"Yes, you are." The woman blew on her nails. Her voice was deeper than Elena's, graveled by cigarette smoke, and her accent was more pronounced. "I am Inez Juana Montalvo."

Grady looked around the large, dark room, noting the continuing stream of portraits of women decorating the walls. The room was its own apartment, equipped with a small kitchenette, tidy and pleasantly decorated. A television sat on a dresser, neat stacks of movie magazines were on the bedside table. No evidence of chains. "It seems everything's okay up here."

Inez leaned back against the pillows and drew on her cigarette. She nodded at the wall. "Go ahead, Miss Grady, check out *la familia*."

Grady gave in and went to the framed photographs. Several of these were in color, from the early two-toned shades of the fifties to the full spectrum of more recent shots. Many of the newer photos had small shrines built around the frames, with shelves that contained offerings of dried flowers and polished stones.

"They all look like me, *sí*?" Inez sounded pleasant enough.

They all look like Elena. Grady's fingers hovered over what seemed the oldest of the photos, a tintype, a process deemed decrepit in the early 1900s. She studied the shawled woman's solemn face. Every woman captured in these portraits seemed to be in her mid twenties, but this one looked older, aged by tribulation, if not years.

"That's Juana Hidalgo," Inez said behind her. "I'm named for the poor bitch."

"Mamá, you said you'd leave the fan on when you smoke

in here." Elena sounded unruffled as she entered the room. She opened the curtains and drew up a window, and sunlight danced through beams of lingering smoke.

"My *estéril* daughter took you to visit Juana's grave, Miss Grady. You remember that?"

"Yes, ma'am." Grady figured Elena's mother was at least ten years her senior, so cautionary courtesy was called for. She couldn't stop staring at Juana Hidalgo's sorrowful face. "Elena told me Juana was buried outside the cemetery because she was a witch."

"Our famous ancestor, *verdad*, Elenita?" There was genuine fondness in Inez's voice as she spoke to her daughter, but then her tone hardened. "At least Juana didn't go out looking for trouble. She had the sense to keep her fat mouth shut."

"My mother doesn't like me telling our customers the truth about Maria, Grady." Elena pulled the chain of the ceiling fan, then settled into a comfortable chair next to the bed. "She thinks if I stay quiet, Maria will just go away on her own."

"And who cares if she doesn't?" Inez jabbed out her cigarette in an ashtray, spilling sparks. "The witch only kills worthless men who are too mean to live! It has nothing to do with us."

"It has everything to do with us, Mamá. All of us." Elena was watching Grady.

Inez snickered. "My daughter is wondering if you've figured out our family tree yet, college teacher."

Grady finally turned from Juana Hidalgo's tintype. "Sorry. Figured it out?"

"A smart college teacher like you should have figured us out by now. Or are you still thinking La Llorona had only two children?"

Grady lifted a hand. "Hang on." Calmly, she looked around the bedroom and saw a wooden chair in one corner. She went to it and carried it to the bed, then sat down. She folded her hands and reminded herself to listen with her heart. "All right, Inez. Did Llorona have more than two children?"

"She had three." Inez seemed to be enjoying herself. "She had a daughter. Her oldest child. Maria hid her from her father the night she and her babies were murdered. This girl saw everything that happened. She saw her father drown her baby brothers, and her mother, in the river."

"This child survived?" Grady spoke to Elena, but Inez continued.

"She did. She was raised by that *pinche* bastard of a father, who swore her to secrecy. And Maria's little girl told the true story of her mother's death to no one—except, years later, to her own daughter. And Maria's granddaughter told no one, except her own daughter." Inez gestured to the series of photographs on the wall. "In every generation since, Maria's descendants have all been girls—women, who have borne one daughter each. Never sons. Never more than one daughter."

Grady closed her eyes, needing darkness to do the math, but also because she didn't want to meet Elena's gaze right now. "You're talking at least twenty generations here."

"*Ay*, I knew Elena would choose a giant brain as an ally." Inez struck a wooden match and held it to another cigarette. Threads of gray wended through her dark hair, and like Juana Hidalgo, she looked much older than her years. "The story has passed down, mother to daughter, every detail exact, for hundreds of years. It's the legacy of Maria's daughters to carry the truth of her death."

"And the drawings in the hallway, the photographs in here—they're all portraits of Maria's descendants?"

"Ending with me and her." Inez jerked her chin at Elena.

"Elena." Grady made herself look at the silent curandera. "Your mother is saying the two of you are the last living descendants of La Llorona."

"*She* is the very last." Inez exhaled smoke in a harsh rasp. "This cursed line stops with her. I think my Elenita has not told you everything, brainy gringa. *Ella es una lesbiana y estéril.*"

"Mamá." Elena flattened her hand on the bedspread, but her

voice was patient. "She's saying I'm a lesbian and I'm sterile, Grady. To my mother, they are one and the same." The corner of Elena's mouth lifted briefly. "I can't bear children. I contracted a pelvic infection when I was in high school. Do you understand what I'm telling you?"

Not even remotely. The revelations were coming too fast, Grady was having trouble absorbing them, and Elena must have seen it in her face. She got off the bed, went to Grady's chair, and knelt beside it.

"Maria kills to defend her children, and I am her last child. There will be no more little daughters for Llorona to protect from violent men. There is no need for any more killing." She touched Grady's hand. "You must help me tell her, Grady. I've waited for Maria at the river, night after night. She never comes to me, and I've never understood why. You're the only one who can tell her she can stop."

"And has Elenita told her brave hero why she is the only woman in Mesilla who can hear Llorona?"

"Mamá! You shut your mouth." Elena's tone turned ice cold, and she rose to her feet. Mother and daughter engaged in a rapid-fire exchange in Spanish as Elena stalked to the bed. Grady registered none of it, but apparently Elena scored some telling points. Inez frowned for a long moment and then sank back against the pillows, looking honestly contrite. She looked at Grady fully for the first time.

"I apologize to you, Grady Wrenn. I haven't left this *pinche* room for years, and my Elena is right, my fear has made me mean. I wasn't mean, always. It was cruel of me to mention your personal sadness."

Having no better use for her head at the moment, Grady just nodded. Elena was looking at her with a compassion that chilled her. She jumped when she heard a tapping sound from the lower level. Someone was knocking politely on the entrance to the shop.

"*Ay*, it's Mrs. Ramirez, my two o'clock." Elena sighed, and rubbed her forehead. "She really needs the *ambra grisea* for her heart. Grady, I'll be right back." She went to the door, then looked back at her mother. "Are you going to be good?"

"Yes, I am. Bring me some more Pepsi from downstairs."

Elena smiled. "*Te amo*, Mamá."

"*Te amo*, Elenita."

Elena looked at Grady, smiled again, and left the room. Her step had barely faded down the stairs when her mother snapped her fingers at Grady.

"Okay. Are you listening to me?" There was no apology in Inez's eyes now, and no malice, just urgency. Grady fought off her confusion and made herself focus.

"I don't care what happens to Maria, Grady Wrenn. I don't care what happens to a bunch of men who beat their wives. But Elena is calling disaster down on both of us, and you have to stop her."

"What is she—"

"Elena waits on a customer, she has to talk about Maria. She heals a child, she has to talk about Maria. Elena walks through the plaza, all she talks about is that damn dead witch!" Inez folded her arms, and Grady could see the shiver that went through her. "Everyone in Mesilla knows she goes to the river, looking for Maria. They're going to try to hurt her, Grady. They think she's a witch."

"Do you know who—"

"Just them, them!" Inez flapped her hand at the window impatiently. "The same little mob of cowards that drove Juana Hidalgo to cut her wrists a hundred years ago! Their sons are still around today. But now it's my daughter they hate."

"I'm sure Elena wouldn't do anything foolish, though, ma'am. Surely nothing that would endanger you."

"Don't ma'am me. My home is not a bordello." Inez settled back against the pillows. "And if you think Elena would not risk my life, you don't know my ungrateful daughter as well as you think, Dr. Grady. The stupid girl believes it's some big holy mission, stopping Maria. It's all those bullshit stories her *abuela* put in her head. My mother."

"Stories?"

"About our grandmothers." Inez still sounded contemptuous, but Grady thought she glimpsed a sheen of tears. "Mamá made heroes out of those women to Elena, in these stories. How one or another of Llorona's descendants tried to haul her sick soul off the riverbank, to bring her salvation. Mamá convinced Elena that stopping the ghost must be our life's work. That the blood of every rotten man our ancestor kills is on our heads until we do this. She made Elena *loca*! She thinks stopping the suicides is worth getting us both lynched."

"But you don't." Grady let herself point out the obvious. "None of this matters to you, Inez? The family legacy, the suicides."

"Look, not every woman in my line is crazy, *Professor.* Some of us just want to live in Mesilla, pay our bills, and raise our measly one daughter in peace." Vulnerability crept into Inez's coarse features. "What matters to me tonight is the safety of my little girl. Grady, please. Look out for her. Elena is all I have." She shivered again.

Grady lifted the edge of the comforter at the foot of the bed and drew it up over Inez's legs. "What scares you most about all this? What are you afraid might happen?"

"I'm scared a bunch of bloodthirsty men will kill my daughter. I'm scared they'll kill me, too. I've been afraid this would happen for a long time. The last time Maria came was during Juana's lifetime. We've been expecting her, Elena and me. And I knew it would happen, all this—craziness. It's Juana's witch hunt, all over again."

"And staying inside the house will protect you? Do you think you and Elena are safe here?"

"Safe, hell, of course we're not safe here! But this building has been in my mother's family forever. I'm not leaving it. They'll have to burn it down around my ears." The bravado faded from Inez's tone. "The worst thing that scares me about all this, though. Thinking in twenty years, maybe it will be my Elena in this room. Too afraid of the world to see it again. No daughter to care for her. Turning bitter and mean, like me."

"Inez." Grady waited until she looked at her. "You really see all that happening to Elena? Are we talking about the same Elena?"

Inez studied her through lowered brows, and then a glint of humor entered her eyes. "All right. Maybe not. Elena's a lot smarter than me. But being smart won't help her if someone puts a bullet through her head."

A nasty chill went up Grady's back. "I'll do everything I can for Elena, Inez. I care about her, too."

"I believe you do." Inez stared at Grady and then nodded. She lifted a remote control from the bed and clicked the TV on. "Okay. Go away. I got a hot date with Jerry Springer in a few minutes."

For a moment, Grady was tempted to settle back into the chair and wait for Jerry, too. Instead, she pulled her wallet from her pocket and took out a business card. She wrote her personal phone number on the back and left the card beside Inez's bed. Then she walked out of the room, past the portraits of dead daughters, and down the stairs.

Elena was seeing an older woman out of the shop, her hand on her shoulder. Grady heard her murmuring instructions to the woman about using the remedy she carried. She didn't hear any mention of falsely accused witches.

Elena closed the door behind the woman and turned to Grady. They walked toward each other and didn't stop until they were standing fairly close. Grady looked down into Elena's mild eyes, and words seemed superfluous for the moment. Where would she start?

Elena's face grew somber. "Do you have a question for me, Grady?"

Yes. Grady had a hundred questions for Elena. But she knew

the one Elena had in mind, and she had every intention of getting an answer this time. Grady opened her mouth to ask why she was able to hear the cry of Llorona.

"How old are you, exactly?" Grady asked.

Elena blinked. "How old am I? I'm twenty-five."

"Twenty-five." Grady considered. "All right, so I'm older than you. But is thirty-four all that much older than twenty-five?"

Elena looked at her, puzzled, and then her expression softened. "Not too much older, no."

"Why didn't you tell me about your family's connection to Llorona, Elena?"

"I didn't tell you because I was afraid you would write me off as *obsessed*." Elena made quote signs in the air as she used Grady's term. "But I'm not sorry Mamá told you today, Grady. I believe the Goddess reveals the secrets of our world only when we are ready to learn from them." She went up on her toes, and kissed Grady's cheek. "Be well, Professor Gringa. You have some thinking to do." She patted Grady's chest. "From here."

Elena showed her out of the shop.

Grady walked all the way home—over two hours and more than three miles—thinking, and touching her cheek.

CHAPTER NINE

So tonight, Mother Goddess, I have two questions for You. Please pull up a throne and sit down, this may take some time.

Question number one. Why did You make me a lesbian? (I know I first asked this many years ago, but You have never seen fit to give me a satisfactory answer.)

Number two. If You had to make me a lesbian, why must I have a crush on an older gringa atheist professor? (All right, she is not too much older.)

You know how I have struggled with my loneliness, Diosa. When I lost the ability to bear children, I thought You were telling me I would never have an ordinary family life. I accepted this fate, because it meant I could channel all my energies into learning the healing arts. Other women might have the joys of motherhood, but I would have the rewards of my work. Other women might find loving husbands, but I... Well, as You know, not finding a husband never struck me as a particular hardship.

As the years passed, I felt more and more certain that You intended me to focus purely on caring for the people of Mesilla. You never expected me to find a partner. For one thing, You planted me down here in one of the most socially conservative plots of land in the entire desert Southwest. This little town is not a real hotbed of sexual freedom or progressive thinking, Diosa, I'm just pointing out. My poor Mamá took to her bed for two weeks when I started calling myself a feminist in the ninth grade.

Plus, when I was younger, being alone just felt like my natural state. Most of the girls I went to school with talked about getting married all the time, but no boy ever caught my eye or my heart. I figured You just designed me to live a solitary life.

But then there was Bella, in high school. I never told her how I felt, of course. I never told Toni or Melissa about my feelings for them, either. My other amigas knew that I cared for them, but always with the simple affections of friendship, the same platonic fondness they had for me. I've never told a woman that I love her—that kind of love. I've never heard those words from a woman, or felt her intimate touch.

And after all of this time, mi Diosa, I assumed I never would. I have become Your chaste priestess, a curandera made stronger by my chastity, and so forth. And now, out of some contrariness on Your part or Your typically warped sense of humor, You send me this maddening, fascinating, wounded, sexy, sexy Grady Wrenn. What are You thinking? I should be focusing all of my mind, all of my skills, on finding vindication for the desolate spirit they call the River Walker. Why now, of all possible seasons, do You delight in throwing this perplexing gringa into my life?

Someday, Grady's role in the fate of La Llorona will be over. She will go back to her students, her classes, her educated friends, and I will not see her again. Like Bella, like Toni and Melissa, she will fade from my life.

Please give me peace in this, Mother. Give me the wisdom to enjoy the innocent pleasures of Grady's friendship, and the grace to return to my solitude without bitterness after she has moved on.

I guess that is all I wanted to say.

My Goddess, how would I cope if I couldn't rest my weary head in Your lap every night, for these few minutes of reflection and solace? How does Grady manage, with No One to inspire or comfort her? Send an angel to her tonight, to lay a gentle hand on her hair and grant her restful sleep. Let Grady accept from Your emissary the sweet nurturing I can never offer her myself.

Good night, mi Diosa, I hope You sleep well. With love from Your Elena.

Chapter Ten

Grady kicked through another long, laborious step, her knees aching fiercely. For some reason she was wearing her damn boots, and they sank deep into the slimy mire of the riverbed every time she tried to lunge forward. The ice-cold water of the Grande came up to her breasts, and her body was locked in a vise of spasmodic shivering.

She had enough information now to know she was dreaming. This knowledge did nothing to ease her raging fear. This was little-kid panic, the dry-mouthed terror she hadn't experienced since the nightmares of early childhood. And here again was the most common theme of those nightmares—trying to run away from an unimaginable horror.

Grady pushed mightily against the heavy flow of the river, the water itself somehow denser and more viscous than any water should be. On either side, the riverbanks were thickly snarled with brambles, and the moon overhead was a red gash in a starless sky.

She would not look back again. Knowing how close it was getting would only paralyze her, and she had to devote all her exhausted energies to getting away. In the vicious logic of dreams, no sooner had she resolved not to look back than she cast a frightened glance over her shoulder.

Llorona was a serpent—a sinuous, fluid creature as big

around as a tree trunk and endlessly long, gliding effortlessly on top of the thick water. Her black metallic scales glittered balefully in the moonlight as she twisted and slithered closer to Grady, and her red mouth yawned open to reveal row upon row of dagger-like fangs. She was close enough now that Grady could make out the features of her human face, and the horror of it almost drove her under, choking.

It was the face painted on the grave in the Old Mesilla Cemetery brought to unholy life. No vision of a mother's features painted by a grieving daughter, this visage was starkly evil and deeply greedy, the forked tongue darting over heavy lips as she slithered closer. Llorona's hair was a wild streaming blackness behind her, and her wide, dead eyes were pinned on Grady. The hissing that issued from the immense snake was the witch's wail made reptilian, a sibilant, wet sound that filled Grady with sick despair.

She threw herself against the heavy current of the river, fighting for another few inches of purchase, and then she heard the running horse. She didn't see it—the red moon revealed nothing but the wild, overgrown riverbank and the churning snake behind her—but the clapping sound of cantering hooves reached her clearly. The horse seemed to be running alongside her, and Grady forced her head up. She half expected to see Elena flying along the bank on her pack horse, though that elderly animal could never produce the charging tympani that still thundered around her. For just a moment, in the middle of the black sky, Grady did see eyes—Elena's eyes, kind and sure and unafraid, looking down on her fondly. Then she was gone, and a small island appeared in the middle of the dark river, a bonfire blazing in its center. Grady staggered desperately toward it and managed to clamber up its warm, sandy bank, freeing herself from the sucking waters with great effort.

The witch-snake was closer and still coming, moving impossibly fast but somehow not reaching her, its hissing human face frozen in a snarling rictus of hatred and rage.

Grady crawled toward the bonfire and she was instantly warm and dry, embraced by the gold light of the flames. She saw a small bowl resting by the fire, its smooth wood surface etched with intricate carved designs. The bowl was filled to the brim with a steaming, amber liquid.

The serpent's hiss rose to an unbearable shriek as Grady snatched up the bowl, and its sinuous length whip-sawed over the river toward the island. Following her instincts and still shaking with terror, Grady drank the tea down in three large swallows. That's all the bowl held, nothing more powerful or magical than Elena's mild herbal tea, but it filled Grady with a soothing warmth and a calm assurance that stilled her shivering.

She looked back over the black river just as the enormous snake began to dwindle in the current, shrinking in on itself, its human features growing diffuse, then melting away into the water. Its last cheated scream echoed into silence.

The Rio Grande of her dreamscape changed, too, the water lapping gently and naturally against the island, the riverbanks losing their tangled brambles to frame again the familiar, sedate stream wending its way through the Mesilla Valley.

She stretched out on the warm sand and rested her head on her folded arms. In the long, gradual transition from the small island to the comfort of the cotton sheets on her bed, Grady thought of Elena. The heart-pounding fear inspired by the witch-snake had faded and gone, and what lingered in her mind was that brief glimpse of Elena's smiling, loving eyes.

CHAPTER ELEVEN

Three days later, Grady's small truck trundled down a wide dirt road, one of dozens that branched off the main arterial out of Mesilla. Grady let down her window and enjoyed the sunshine warming her elbow, and the pleasant company of the woman beside her.

Elena was humming tunelessly as she gazed out the dusty windshield, a smile playing over her full lips.

They were both smiling, which was odd, as this wasn't a particularly light occasion. They were on their way to interview a grieving widow. Only two of the wives contacted by San Albino's pastor had been willing to meet with Grady's students. Cesar, Sylvia, and Janice were taking one of those interviews. Grady had asked Elena to join her to conduct the other. Her spirits had lifted the moment Elena stepped into her cab.

"What made you ask me to come along today?" Elena asked finally. "I'm grateful, but I'm curious."

"Well." Grady peered up the road through her sunglasses, looking for the turn-off. "You recognized the name of this family I want to talk to, and you're in their good graces. So that gave you cool points. And I doubt I could find the damn place without you. We're on the right road?"

"Yes, straight ahead. It's several miles." Elena leaned her shoulder against the backrest and faced Grady. "This woman we're seeing knew my grandmother pretty well. I remember her visiting our shop when I was young."

"Your grandmother had lots of friends."

"She did. She was a very warm person." Sadness touched Elena's voice. "I still miss her."

"And your dad, Elena?" The question was out before Grady considered the consequences, and she braced herself.

"Ah, a nice guy." Elena smiled. "He's remarried and lives in El Paso now. He left my mother when I was about ten. He's a plumber. Still sends me money pretty regularly. The two of us have dinner a few times a year."

"Oh."

Elena's eyebrow rose. "What? Can't I have one normal family member? Are you disappointed?"

"I was terrified. I thought you were going to tell me he was a witchdoctor or a king vampire. Something like that."

"A king vampire?" Elena looked stern, but her body shook with suppressed laughter. "Grady, I think you are just too fanciful for me. You need to go to church more."

Grady grinned at her. The sun slanted through the truck's side window and illuminated Elena's face, the curve of her throat. "I hope you understand, Elena. Every time I learn about one of your relatives, I have to suspend about twenty years of disbelief. You can't blame me for being a little anxious when your family tree comes up."

"No, I don't blame you at all." Elena patted Grady's knee. "I can't imagine what I'd do if someone I'd known for three weeks asked me to upend my entire belief system." Her hand lingered on Grady's knee. "May I ask you about something, Grady? It might be very personal."

"Okay." Grady pretended fascination with the dirt road.

"The other night, when you slept on my floor. You called a name in your sleep—Leigh."

"Oh." Grady was a little surprised. To her knowledge, she never talked in her sleep.

"You said that name so quietly, a couple of times. Like you were asking for someone."

"Leigh was my partner." Grady glanced at her ringless finger on the steering wheel. "We were together a few years. We broke up about six months ago, just before I moved down here."

"Ah. And this breakup is still very painful for you?"

"It was a long time coming. And probably overdue." She and Leigh had tried hard to keep what they had, but they'd been thrown a blowtorch few couples survived. "I've accepted it's best for both of us."

"Are you still in touch with him?"

"Leigh's a woman. And no, we're not in touch." Grady smiled at Elena to break the moment. "I'd think your secret curandera superpowers would include some gaydar, Elena."

She laughed. "My gaydar is just fine. But with some secrets, it's best to wait for people to tell you. Remember, I grew up in Mesilla. You don't see a lot of rainbow flags in my neighborhood."

"No, I guess you don't. You're out to your mother, though?"

"Imagine what a pleasant conversation that was." Elena sighed, but with more affection than bitterness. "My mother knows. A few of my friends. Well, my very few friends."

"Not much time for a social life?"

"No. Between healing sessions, gathering herbs, paying the bills, scrubbing gravestones, and saving Mesilla from the murderous rampage of this dead witch I may have mentioned…"

"You don't have much time," Grady finished.

"Not even for a hot quickie."

Grady stared at Elena, at the sophisticated tilt of her head, and laughter burst from her. "Oh, Elena. I'm sorry. You just can't pull that off."

"I *know.*" Elena laughed and pressed her hands to her cheeks, which were filling with color. "I can never do sexual humor without sounding like a prostitute! And also, I just let you drive past our turn-off."

"Whoops." Grady braked smoothly, grateful for the deserted expanse of dirt road. She cranked the truck around. "No gaydar," she griped. "Gets me lost, can't pull off sexual humor…"

"Stop bitching, gringa. I give excellent neck rubs."

"Damn, yes, you do." Grady turned right onto a smaller road and followed its twisting curves through thickening rows of pecan trees. The path terminated in front of a pueblo-style adobe house, solid and round-edged, all soft lines and earth tones. A lot this size would cost a small fortune anywhere near Portland.

Grady stepped out of the truck and followed Elena up the small gravel walk to the entrance, a tiled patio with red chile ristras strung on either side of the door. Elena knocked lightly.

"So, this is Antonia Herrera." Grady dug a small notebook out of her back pocket to check Janice's questions and other pertinent notes. "She has two adult daughters, both married, who live in town. And one grandson, who lives with her."

"Yes, Manny should be in high school by now. I remember him. He's a nice kid." The door swung open, and Elena looked up. "Oops. I mean, a nice young man. Hello, Manny."

The nice young man was taller than both of them, and he didn't bother to remove the iPod buds from his ears. He kept the door close to his shoulder and stared at them.

"It's good to see you again," Elena said. "This is my friend, Grady Wrenn. Your *abuela* is expecting us."

The kid said nothing. Something in his slouched posture registered with Grady, and with an unpleasant start, she recognized him. She had last seen Manny Herrera three weeks ago, standing with two other men outside Elena's shop, watching her with the same hostility she saw in his eyes now.

Manny bumped the door open with his shoulder, turned, and disappeared into the interior of the house. They heard him call his grandmother, a barking command.

"I do remember him as a nice kid." Elena lowered her voice.

"I hope he's not turning out to be more like his grandfather than his grandmother."

"Elena, I think Manny is one of the men I saw outside your shop, after your window was shot out."

"*Ay*, no. I'm sorry to hear this." Elena shook her head. "Maybe we should scratch the part about my being in this family's good graces."

"Yeah."

"*Bienvenida*, Elenita. Please, come in." The voice was soft and Grady couldn't see the speaker. She followed Elena into the shadowed entry and closed the door behind them.

They stepped down into the kind of living room that made Grady wish she wore a hat so she could take it off. High-ceilinged and white-walled with a simple decor, mostly religious icons, the large room was rigorously clean. A portrait of the Virgin, a rather good one, was mounted over the kiva fireplace. The furniture was as tidy and fragile as the lady of the house.

Antonia Herrera was a lady, in spite of her stooped shoulders and the tremor in her veined hands. Grady placed her somewhere in her seventies. Her sparse hair was pinned into a neat bun, and she wore a summer dress suitable for receiving company. Mrs. Herrera seated them around a low table and served coffee mellowed with cinnamon while she and Elena exchanged pleasantries. Then the older woman sat back in her armchair, and real warmth filtered through her polite tone.

"You look more like your grandmother every time I see you, Elenita. Consuelo would be very proud to see what a beautiful young lady you've become."

"Thank you, Mrs. Herrera." Elena's formality didn't disguise her genuine pleasure in the compliment. "I was just telling Grady that you knew my *abuela*."

"And your mother? How is Inez?"

Elena shrugged and sipped her coffee. "My mother is just as she has been for many years. Only more so, these days."

Grady nestled comfortably in her chair, content to let Elena ease their way into this dignified woman's house. She watched a quick shift of emotions pass over Elena's features when her mother was mentioned. She wasn't being flip.

"We should have visited you when your husband died," Elena said quietly. "I regret to this day that we didn't have the courage."

"Elena, coming here would have been a foolish risk." The woman spoke like a mother accustomed to gently chiding her daughters. "Rumors about the River Walker were already starting, even then. You had to protect your *madre*, I knew that." She smiled at Grady uncertainly. "Should I call you Dr. Wrenn?"

"Grady, please."

"Grady, then. Has Elena told you about my husband?"

Grady wasn't sure how to answer that. Elena had implied some pretty terrible things about this widow's husband. "Well, I know that he passed away four months ago. I'm very sorry for your loss, Mrs. Herrera."

"Thank you." She folded her hands in her lap and seemed to wait for questions.

"May I?" Grady gestured to the coffeepot, and her hostess nodded. She refilled all of their cups, her movements slow and careful. "Ma'am, it's important to both Elena and me that we be respectful of your privacy. So if we ask anything that's too painful or just too private, please say so. Okay?"

"Yes, sure." Mrs. Herrera nudged Elena's elbow. "She's very polite."

"Only at times," Elena said.

Grady felt the tips of her ears warm. "Pastor Rodriguez probably told you that my students are looking into the string of deaths that have happened in Mesilla since last April."

"Manuel was the first." Mrs. Herrera spoke her husband's name without reverence. "Everyone in Mesilla knew she was back when Manuel drowned. We knew more suicides were coming. Manuel died *la muerte clásica*."

"I'm sorry?" Grady looked at Elena.

"The classic death," Elena translated. "The one associated with Llorona. Always the same method, and always at night." She glanced at Mrs. Herrera apologetically. "Last April, Manuel Herrera drowned himself in the Rio Grande, just after midnight. The same way the other three men have killed themselves since."

"Yes, four gone. *Madre de Dios*." Mrs. Herrera crossed herself and kissed her thumb.

"The same way each of Llorona's victims died," Elena added quietly to Grady. "All of them drowned themselves in rivers late at night. Many more than four."

"And all died with the same look of *miedo*, this terrible fear, on their faces." Mrs. Herrera closed her eyes. "They would not let me look at Manuel after they took him from the river. Manny wanted to see him, he fought to see him, but I would not allow it. I knew he would not see the face of his beloved *abuelo*, but that of a man chased into death by a demon. I did not want that to be his last image of his grandfather."

Grady could imagine the expressions on the corpses of Llorona's victims. She had no doubt her own features reflected the same terror when she heard the witch's screams. Her gaze drifted over the religious paintings and small statues that adorned the living room. She thought of the deep stigma against suicide that still gripped the traditional Catholic Church. There was that unworldly shift again, the blending of time and cultures. Antonia Herrera, steeped in the holy icons of the Vatican, apparently accepted the reality of La Llorona with ease. "Was there any warning, Mrs. Herrera? Any sign at all that your husband planned to harm himself?"

"No, there was no plan." Mrs. Herrera waved a hand dismissively. "Not by Manuel. He was healthy. He was retired. The pecan crops have sold well. We have savings. He was king of his home, and a good Catholic. He had no reason to suddenly want to die. His only plan was to take Manny up to the Lincoln Forest to hunt elk the next weekend."

Yes, nice young Manny, who apparently has a hunting rifle. "Then your husband was very close to his grandson?"

"Yes, Manny is named for him. The two of them were good friends." For the first time, clear regret filled Antonia Herrera's faded features. "Manuel was never any good with females. With his wife or his daughters, or even his *madre*. But he loved his grandson. I will give him that. Manny still grieves very much for him."

Grady hesitated. Her interview subject had offered an appropriate entry to the questions Janice had detailed in her notebook, but she left it closed on the coffee table. Grady had a good memory, and this woman seemed willing to talk. "Can you tell us what living with Mr. Herrera was like?"

"He was a good provider," Mrs. Herrera said at once. "Never in trouble with the law, not since he was a teenager." She glanced at the painting of the Virgin over the hearth. "But he was free with his drink, and with his fists. This was no secret to anyone in Mesilla. I walked into Elena's grandmother's shop with black eyes more than once."

Grady considered the pain of that, the humiliation of knowing all her neighbors saw what happened in the sanctity of her home. She was beginning to understand the stoop in this woman's shoulders.

"I hope you won't judge my family for this, Grady." Mrs. Herrera's voice was still soft. "I honored my husband, and I obeyed him as I promised to. I would defend Manuel's memory today, to anyone who insulted his name. But mostly, I feared him. So did his daughters. And there is peace in this house now, for the first time in many years."

"I understand, Mrs. Herrera. Thank you for your honesty."

"Grady, may we ask about the others?" Elena's tone was tentative. "Mrs. Herrera knows everyone in Mesilla. She's lived here all her life."

"*Ay*, anyone who lives in Mesilla can tell you about the other men who have died," Mrs. Herrera said. "We saw most of them every week at Mass. The second to drown himself was Jaime Barela, then Celia Guzman's husband, Raul, in late May. Then, just three weeks ago, Enrique Acuña."

Grady consulted her mental Rolodex. Her students were interviewing Jaime Barela's widow today. Anything Antonia Herrera told her about the other deaths would be hearsay and gossip, but Elena's stillness held a kind of muted urgency. "Do you think the men who have died have anything in common, Mrs. Herrera?"

The older woman turned to Elena. "Do you still go to the cemetery to wash your great-grandmother's stone, Elenita?"

"Yes, I do."

"And you know the section with the children's graves. With the little white marker for Jimmy Guzman. He was two years old when his father, Raul, beat him to death." Mrs. Herrera reached for her coffee cup. The tremor in her hands had increased. Grady remembered the sad white patch of stones in the San Albino churchyard and blew out a bleak breath. "Raul Guzman is the only man who actually killed a member of his *familia*. But they were all husbands and fathers, those who Llorona frightened to death, and they were all violent men."

"Was Raul Guzman never prosecuted for the death of his son?" Grady asked.

"Yes. He served seven years at the penitentiary in Santa Fe." Mrs. Herrera shook her head. "Seven years. And then Celia let him come home. And his violence poisoned them all until the night he died."

Grady's eyes lingered on the portrait of the Virgin over the hearth, silenced by the simple weight of human misery bound up in these tales. Elena had been right about the link between the suicides. Now all Grady had to do was accept that these suicides were actually murders, brought about by a protective and/or vengeful ghost. She wished matrons in New Mexico served tequila instead of coffee at brunch. Elena threw her a look that was both sympathetic and searching.

"Sometimes I look at the Mother, and I see La Llorona." Mrs. Herrera had followed Grady's gaze to the portrait. "I would never say this to Pastor Rodriguez, Elena. But they were both mothers who lost their sons. I know Llorona is a murderess, but I pray to Mary to intercede for her forgiveness."

"So do I, *abuela*."

Antonia Herrera saw them out with the same courtesy she had shown throughout their visit. She pressed two slim boxes into Elena's hands. "Our chocolate pecans. Both sugar-free, since your grandmother had the diabetes. Has Inez gained much weight in the past years?"

"Not really. But she drinks too much Pepsi." Elena accepted the boxes with a grateful smile, and Grady saw a new softness in her face. Exposure to this woman's friendly maternity seemed to warm Elena, as if she were holding chilled hands before a fire. "Thank you for the candy, and for seeing us today."

Grady couldn't shake her pensive mood as her truck rumbled back toward the main dirt road. "Four men dead. I wonder how many more there might be. How many lives does Llorona take every hundred years, according to legend? Ten? Twenty?"

Elena seemed immersed in her own thoughts, and she pulled her gaze from the truck's side window with effort. "As terrible as these suicides are, there have never been many of them. All my grandmothers kept a careful tally over the years. Less than ten men die each time Llorona returns to the valley. I doubt there will be a greater number in this visitation. Considering how many men beat their wives around here, ten is a small number."

Elena winced as if in apology for this cold summary. "The men who died in the past four months all met certain criteria, Grady. They were all out on some business late at night, and always alone. Their business brought them somewhere near the river. They heard Maria's cry. Only men who have met all these criteria drowned themselves."

"How does it happen, do you think?" Grady had been trying to picture Llorona's attacks. "Mrs. Herrera said the men who died were frightened to death. So they're near the river, they hear Llorona's scream, and they're so terrified they just dash for the water and jump in?"

"That's how it's said to happen, yes. Everyone believes the men Maria kills die of terror as much as drowning."

"But were these intentional suicides, then?" Grady remembered a fervent desire to save her own butt while under the ghost's aural assault. "Or were they just trying to get away from Llorona, to escape her?"

"I've imagined it in my mind. Maria's cry is said to be hideous to hear, filled with a killing rage. But it's not like the roar of a wild animal. Men don't simply run away from it to seek safety." Elena stroked the top of her shoulder, and Grady recalled the small birthmark that rested there. "My own belief is that her voice fills these violent men with remorse, as well as fear. Something in that sound finally goads their conscience, and it's penitence, as much as terror, that leads them to the water. It's not a pleasant thing to imagine."

"There's as much grief there as rage." Grady stared at the narrow road disappearing beneath the wheels. "In Maria's voice. Her suffering is…immense."

"I've never heard this." Elena was watching her closely. "But of course, there would be great sadness. Maria is mourning her children. We only hear accounts of her cry from men who babble about her fury. A woman would hear her grief as well."

Grady felt a suspicious tightness in her throat and swallowed grimly. "I wonder if these men actually saw Maria before they died. I know she's been sighted many times, and almost everyone describes her the same way—this mild young woman in a shroud, floating along the riverbank. She seems so harmless. But in all those descriptions, Llorona is weeping. How does she appear when she screams?" She was picturing the kind of creature capable of such a sound—a floating wraith of gargantuan proportions, with hypodermic needle fangs and wild streaming snakes for hair. She remembered the huge black serpent of her nightmare.

"There's no way to know how Maria looks to these men when she is on the hunt, Grady." Elena nudged her. "But here's a new wrinkle of Llorona lore for you, Professor. Maria's wail is loudest when she is very far away. No one who hears it is close enough to see her. But if her cry is soft and faint, if it seems to come from a great distance, you know she is quite near. Look for her then."

"Yeesh. You look for her then. I'll wait here." Grady shifted on her creaking seat. "Are you sure you didn't get some of this stuff from Stephen King, Elena? That's genuinely creepy."

"I know." Elena chuckled, apparently unoffended. "Can you see why the mothers of Mesilla still use the threat of Llorona to keep their children home at night? She—"

A blue truck shot suddenly out of a side road and hit the left rear of the cab. A glancing blow, but sharp and powerful enough to punch them into a slide, and the back side window shattered in a spray of glass. Grady gasped, her right arm whipping out to brace Elena. Elena surged sideways against her, knocking her shoulder hard, but their lap belts kept them both in their seats. Grady's truck rocked to a stop, dust boiling around them.

"What the *fuck*!" Grady's vocabulary deserted her. "Elena, are you all right?"

Elena was breathing a series of Spanish curses of her own. She looked past Grady, and her eyes widened. "He's coming back!"

Grady didn't turn to verify Elena's warning. The engine was still running, and she floored it. The rear of her truck slewed in the dirt, but then the tires grabbed and she took off down the road. The broad grill of the blue behemoth behind them loomed in the rearview mirror.

Grady had faced some dicey situations in her field work before, a few of them fairly harrowing, and she kept her cool now. She drove fast and well, pressing the motor to its fullest speed, hyperalert for any oncoming traffic. The jittering road before them remained empty. Her senses were highly attuned to

Elena beside her, and she was aware of an unexpectedly strong and protective resolve to see her safely out of this.

"I recognize the truck." Elena was craning to see out the back window. The wind whistling in from the empty side frame and the jouncing of the cab almost drowned out her voice. "It belongs to Rudy Barela. His cousin was the second man to kill himself."

That garish blue color was unmistakable. Grady had seen Manny Herrera lounging with two men against that truck, near Elena's store. "Can you see how many are back there?"

"Just the driver. It's Hector Acuña. His brother was the third to die. I can't see anyone in the truck's bed, but—Grady!" Elena's hand clamped hard on her shoulder, and the next second Grady felt the fearsome thud against the back bumper. Her tires spun in the dirt and she lost control. The blue truck shot past on her left as she wrestled for traction. She caught a quick flash of a flushed face behind the wheel.

"Muerte a las brujas!" Death to the witches.

One raw shout and the man was gone, but Grady had lost interest in him by then: she was busy crashing. She kept one arm pinned across Elena's chest as they crested the lip of a shallow irrigation ditch. She braced to capsize, but the truck thudded down into the ditch hard on its front wheels. Grady's head caught a nasty crack against the side frame as the airbags deployed in an explosive rush, and things grayed out for a moment.

"Grady." Elena's eyes were inches from her own, and her fingers were cold on her face. "Are you back now?"

"I'm falling in love with you," Grady said. She moaned and touched her head, her thoughts scattered and then lost in confusion. "Are you okay?"

"I'm fine."

Grady opened her eyes. Elena sounded very odd. "Are you sure?"

"I'm fine. Grady, you blacked out. Where are you hurt?"

Grady shifted cautiously, pushing the collapsed airbag off

her lap. There were several ominous twinges of newly born bruises, and her head hurt, but not with an unbearable ache. She was starting to feel more alert, at least enough to be keenly aware of Elena all but lying against her, both of them sprawled against the driver's door. Elena's fingers were beneath her hair, probing the base of her neck.

"I think I'm good." The odor of gasoline reached her. "Can we get out of here?"

It took several more questions and repeated probing, but Elena finally allowed Grady to move. She swung the side door open. "We'll have to go out this way."

They climbed out gingerly, bracing each other. Grady felt some post-crisis shakes, but she stood erect on the bank of the irrigation ditch without swaying. Elena looked pale but unscathed, and Grady was grateful for her supporting arm. The road before and behind them was empty, not even the dust of their pursuer in the air now.

Grady looked glumly at her canted truck and fished in her pocket for her cell phone.

"Are you calling your students?" Elena asked.

"I'm calling the cops." Grady frowned. "No, I'm calling my students." She clicked the keys quickly to find Sylvia's number.

"Grady, there's no use—"

Grady lifted her hand for silence, a new anxiety filling her. "Sylvia? Grady. Where are you?"

"Hey, hello." Sylvia's voice sounded tinny, but friendly and carefree. "We're all back at my place, Grady. We had a fantastic talk with—"

"Great. Stay there. Elena and I had some trouble a few minutes ago. Someone ran us off the road. We're all right, but I want the three of you to be careful tonight. I'll catch you up when we meet in the morning. Is that clear?"

Sylvia was silent for a moment, and Grady could hear her suppressing a flood of questions. Janice's voice asked something in the background. "Yes, Grady, we'll be careful. Are you sure you guys are okay? Do you need help?"

"No, you three stay away from here. Eight a.m. sharp tomorrow, please. Take care." Grady tapped off, then started to dial 911 when Elena touched her wrist. "What?"

"There's no use calling the police, Grady. I'd rather we didn't."

"Elena." Grady's thumb still hovered over the last key. "Someone just tried to kill us both. I think nice little Manny made a call himself while we were talking to his grandmother. To a man you apparently recognized, right? Someone named Barela?"

"It was Rudy Barela's truck. Hector Acuña was driving it. He's a Mesilla deputy marshal."

Grady lowered her phone. "Are you saying the cops will refuse to help us?"

"I'm saying Mesilla is a small town. My family has never been able to turn to the law for help. Grady, we can talk about this later. I don't like your color. Let me call my friend Rita for a ride."

"Elena, my family has always been able to turn to the law for help, and besides, I promised your mother I'd look after you."

"You *what*?"

"I promised your mother I'd look after you." Grady couldn't believe she'd said that, to say nothing of saying it twice, but suddenly nothing made much sense anymore and her knees hit the dirt road with a solid thud.

CHAPTER TWELVE

Grady didn't faint, and she explained that to Elena several times. She explained it to Elena's friend Rita, too, when Rita drove up in her battered Toyota to give them a ride to Elena's home. Grady recognized Rita as the customer she'd seen in Elena's store, which she offered as evidence of her mental acuity. In an odd cultural role reversal, Elena hammered at Grady to go to an ER for a head scan, and Grady stubbornly refused.

"You blacked out twice," Elena repeated as she unlocked the door to her shop.

"I did not black out the second time," Grady explained again. "I just sat down hard. Elena, I've had a concussion before, I know what one feels like. I don't have a concussion now. I have a bump on the head. I really don't need a nursemaid."

"Well, you don't have a choice about that." Elena waved her in impatiently. "Someone needs to watch you for a while, so unless you have a better nursemaid to suggest, you're stuck with me."

Elena escorted her to the back room she used for healing sessions. "Take off your boots and get comfortable, please. I'll just be a minute."

Grady sighed. She had to admit it was good to be out of the day's heat and glare. The bed in the cool, dim chamber looked freshly made and inviting. If that curvaceous young crab out there was going to order her around, at least she gave orders Grady could live with.

She sat cautiously on the edge of the bed, wincing at the ache in her side, and began the difficult business of removing her boots while simultaneously opening her phone to tap through stored numbers. By the time she was bootless and had finished her call, Elena was stepping through the bead curtain, carrying a small tin dish. She glanced at Grady's phone.

"The police?" Elena sounded resigned.

"No, Triple A. Arranging to have my truck towed." Grady tossed her cell into her boot. She hadn't made up her mind to keep the law out of this, but she was willing to mull it over for a while. "I might have to borrow your horse to get home, if you ever spring me."

"Don't worry. There's a very used Ford out there in the stall, along with my horse. I'll get you home." Elena set the dish on a side table and then sat beside Grady on the bed. "I am sorry about your truck, Grady."

"Well, the back end damage looked fixable."

"Good, but I'm sorry for the two boxes of sugar-free chocolate pecans that are melting all over the seat right now."

Grady chuckled, and Elena smiled up at her. They were sitting close enough that their shoulders touched.

"Are you going to let me look at you?" Elena leaned against her briefly. "You cushioned the landing for me a bit, but you hit your door pretty hard."

"Nah. I'm really all right. Appreciate the thought, though." Grady was largely telling the truth. Her body aches were minor and her raw nerves were beginning to settle. But if having Elena look at her meant the removal of any pertinent clothing, she didn't think she could take any more adventure today.

"Okay. Lie down, please."

"Lie down?" Grady frowned. "You're still worried about my head?"

"Not your head." Elena rose and pulled back the light bedspread and sheet. She went to the side table and struck a match to the dry shredded leaves in the tin dish. "Will you trust me?"

Grady hoped Elena realized what a crucial question that was. She asked for trust herself, every time she intruded upon the people of a new culture. She had asked Leigh for trust. The side of Elena's face flared a soft red-gold as the leaves caught, and her dark eyes held a grave serenity.

Grady lifted her feet and stretched out stiffly on the bed. Her side twinged, and the firm coolness of the pillow cushioned her aching head. Elena struck another match and lit a tapered candle on the table, then turned off the small lamp, throwing the room into near darkness. She breathed deeply of the thin smoke swirling from the dish. Then she came around to the side of the bed and clasped her hands.

"Would you please move over a bit? I need to touch you to do this." The corner of Elena's mouth lifted. "Don't worry. This isn't sexual. I would probably only crack us both up anyway if I tried to make a pass."

Grady shifted cautiously, feeling her shields rise as tangibly as the lifting of steel. Elena lay down next to her, close against her side. Grady lifted her arm automatically so Elena could rest her head on her shoulder. The bed was narrow enough that there was really nowhere else for her to go.

"What now?" Grady asked politely.

"Let's just rest for a while. We need to wait until you start feeling less like an ironing board."

Grady waited. It was late afternoon, but the fierce sunlight couldn't penetrate the shadows of the quiet room. The flickering light from the candle glinted against the healing icons on the wall above it. Elena's head was a pleasant weight on her shoulder, her arm draped lightly across Grady's waist.

Grady breathed in the mild scent of the smoldering leaves. "Is that salvia?"

"No. Not salvia, not cannabis." Elena's voice was a low murmur against her chest. "It's a blend my grandmother found when she traveled to Mexico. It isn't a euphoric and it doesn't inspire visions, it just clears the mind." She paused. "Grady, I would never try to trick you with a drug. You know that, right?"

Grady heard faint distress in her tone. "Yes, I do know that. Don't worry, Elena, I'm easy." And she found she was getting there; she was relaxing into the bed.

"I'm starting to think you were right about protecting your students. What if one of them had been with us today?" Elena fingered the sheet beneath them. "I never intended to pull you into all the hatred and fear around Llorona, Grady. I'm so sorry you were hurt."

"Not your fault." Grady stared at the dark ceiling. "This is my work, Elena, exploring legends like this. You've been honest with me about the risks."

She didn't know if it was the smoke or the girl, but her mind was definitely clearing. Grady was intensely aware of the soft swells of Elena's breasts against her side, her breath on her throat. What puzzled her was that her response was not immediate arousal. Intrigued her, actually, because this comely curandera had begun to appear in Grady's more private fantasies as mysteriously as Maria appeared by the river. But she lay quietly beside Elena, and it was enough.

"There are things I have to know now, Grady." Elena's tone was kind, but there was still a vulnerable note there. "Not for Llorona, not for the work we must do together. Just for me. Are you ready?"

"Yes. I hope so."

"Do you understand why you can hear Maria's cry?"

"I believe I do." Grady closed her eyes. "The only women who can hear Maria are women who have lost a child. Is that right?"

"Yes." Elena was quiet for a moment. "But there's more.

The only women who can hear Maria are mothers who have murdered their child."

Grady kept her eyes closed, savoring the darkness. She wondered how many people truly appreciated the beneficence of sleep. Deep sleep wiped the memory clean and silenced echoes. She had talked to Elena from the lost reaches of sleep once, calling Leigh's name. "I let him walk on the outside," she said. "And I let go of his hand."

Perhaps an hour passed. Grady didn't keep track of the time, but the candle on the table guttered down to an inch. She didn't doze, and neither did Elena, who hummed softly, stroking Grady's arm with the lightest brush of her fingers. Finally, Grady began.

"Max was two years old when I met him." She smiled in the darkness. "He had the biggest ears of any kid I'd ever seen, and he loved dancing to Creedence songs. Max got a kick out of jazz, too, which Leigh loved. He liked me right away, but then Max liked everybody. He was a very sunny kid. He was crazy about dogs. He tried to hug every dog he saw. Leigh wanted to get him a puppy for his fourth birthday, but I talked her out of it. It wasn't because of the mess or trouble, Elena. I would have loved to have a puppy in the house. I just thought Max should grow for another year before taking on a pet."

Elena murmured something, a listening sound.

"So instead of a puppy, Leigh and I took Max camping in the mountains for his fourth birthday. We went hiking that morning. The trail was pretty narrow, lots of gravel. Leigh was on my right. Max was on my left, on the outside of the trail. I was holding his hand. His nose was running, so I let go of his hand to reach for my bandana. A squirrel ran past us and Max ran after it. I grabbed for him but I missed. He slid in the gravel and fell over the side. It was only about ten feet. But he landed badly, and he died two days later."

Elena drew in a long, slow breath and released it.

"Leigh and I lasted almost a year after that, which was probably a miracle. Leigh didn't blame me for Max's death, she really didn't. Except for the days when she did. She couldn't help it, and neither could I. I don't blame myself, either."

"Except for the nights when you do," Elena whispered.

"Except for those nights." Grady shivered, and once she started, she couldn't stop. Elena pulled the spread over them both and tucked it against her side, then rested her head on Grady's shoulder again. By the time Grady's shaking eased, the candle had winked out.

"So that's what La Llorona and I have in common?" Grady was comforted by the darkness, and by Elena's warmth against her. "We both killed our—"

"You and Llorona both feel terrible guilt for deaths you could not prevent," Elena said. "You both blame yourselves for your lost children, when no just and humane person would ever blame either of you. Hush, Grady. This isn't about Maria right now."

"What is it about?"

"Me. You and me. I had to hear the truth about the woman I'm falling in love with. Just lie still. Let me hold you."

Grady's chin brushed Elena's hair. Her curls smelled like fresh rain on parched desert earth, and that's how Elena's tears felt as they fell on her chest. She began to whisper a low prayer in Spanish, a musical, chanting sound.

Grady's own tears scalded her at first, behind the red darkness of her closed eyes. Then they brimmed and coasted silently down her face. Her breathing didn't change and her body didn't tense; she lay perfectly still beneath Elena's stroking hand. It was how Grady had always wept, at least as an adult—reluctantly, and only when depleted by emotional exhaustion. She had never cried with anyone but Leigh over Max. She had never cried over Leigh at all, until now.

Sleep was starting to claim her by the time Elena finished her prayer. Elena's palm circled Grady's heart, a more intimate genuflection. *"Deseo que podría curar tu dolor, hermana,"* she whispered. "I wish I could heal your pain."

Grady nodded her thanks. A faint memory was trying to tug her away from the seductive pull that wanted to draw her under—something about Elena falling in love with her. Either the pull was suddenly too strong, or the thought was entirely too intense. Grady ran like the weary coward she was and spiraled down into dreamless sleep.

CHAPTER THIRTEEN

*M*y *lips move silently tonight, mi Diosa, so as not to disturb this grieving woman's hard-won rest. She lies still beside me, her body soft and relaxed at last, her strong shoulder cushioning my cheek. My heart breaks, knowing the full enormity of her pain.*

I pray now for the spirit of a little boy I never met, who resides with You in the stars. He has big ears and he loves to dance. Please bestow all Your blessings on young Max, and help him find a way to send his love to Grady, and his forgiveness.

I know it is true that an immortal spirit can carry rage and a thirst for vengeance far beyond the darkness of the grave. Maria's soul is still steeped in such hatred, centuries after her death. But it is also true, then, that love and compassion survive. If the fury of a bloodthirsty witch can still ravage lives today, then surely the love of a small boy can ease the ache in Grady's noble heart.

Our two River Walkers, Diosa. Both torture themselves for the deaths of their children. Their guilt is their only bond, the only commonality between two spirits who could not be more different, the light and the dark. A self-imposed and punishing guilt that neither of them deserve. Please, help them both find peace.

I know I should also pray to You to ease the pain in Hector Acuña's heart. As with Maria, his hatred is born of suffering. He loved the brother La Llorona stole from him, and that is what drove him to try to harm us today. But Hector Acuña injured my friend, this woman who already bears too much sorrow. I find it easier to plead for Your intervention in Manny Herrera's troubled life. I remember him as a little boy with ice cream smeared on his chin, asking about everything in our shop. Manny is still young, and can still turn back toward the light.

And lastly, Dear Mother, were You listening when Your Elenita finally, for the very first time in her life, told a woman she was falling in love with her? Did You catch the woman's reaction? She FELL ASLEEP. Ha ha ha, I now see why Your sense of humor is so useful.

I will not close my eyes tonight. This time with Grady is too precious to squander in sleep. Like You, I will keep watch over her until the sun rises. Even if there is never anything more between us, I thank You, mi Diosa, for these few hours holding her in my arms.

Please smile down on Your weary daughters, and direct our steps along Your path. With love from Your Elena.

Chapter Fourteen

Grady surfaced slowly, as if drifting up through warm, languid waters, and awoke alone in Elena's healing room. She blinked several times at the ceiling, a little awed by a sense of comfort and peace that rarely blessed her mornings. She sat up gingerly, and the twinge in her head reminded her of yesterday's more bruising highlights, but neither her body nor her heart felt nearly as battered as she might have expected. She swung her legs over the side of the bed and touched her chest. There was a light dampness on her shirt, and she remembered the tears Elena had shed the night before.

Inez's querulous voice sounded from upstairs, and Elena's soothing tone responded from the shop. Tantalizing aromas were wafting through the beaded curtain, and Grady groped for her boots, her mouth watering. She was not ordinarily a breakfast person. Her stomach was often half sour from a sleepless night of churning through old memories, and all she usually wanted was a bracing flood of strong coffee. But she hadn't eaten since yesterday's lunch, and whatever Elena was cooking woke her appetite with a vengeance.

She stepped through the strings of beads and down the two steps into the shop, tucking in her shirt and trying to claw her hair into some semblance of neatness. She saw Elena standing by the oak table in the corner, which was laden with steaming platters and plates. Elena was adjusting a vase filled with fresh flowers at the center of the table. Grady watched her move it two inches to the left, then back again. Elena stepped back, as if to judge her centerpiece, then moved it two inches to the right.

"Good mrng." Grady's voice was a little hoarse with sleep, and she smiled shyly and cleared her throat. "I mean, good morning."

Elena turned quickly and clasped her hands behind her, color touching her cheeks. "Ah, *buenos días*, Grady. Did you sleep well?"

"I did, as a matter of fact." Grady walked to the table, brushing her hands together greedily. "Are you feeding the neighborhood?"

"Uh, no, just the house. I hope you're hungry."

"Well, it would be bad manners to turn down a breakfast my hostess must have been slaving over since dawn, right?" Grady held Elena's chair for her, then circled the table and sat in the other. "Like Mrs. Herrera says, I'm very polite."

Elena giggled, and Grady realized she was nervous. "I hope you like *chorizo*."

"I'll force myself, somehow, given my good manners." Grady lifted the platter of fragrant sausage and helped herself. "Any chance your mother might join us?"

"Not a chance in the world." Elena spooned an abundant helping of steaming scrambled eggs with green chile onto Grady's plate, then filled her own. "Don't worry. Mamá got first choice of every dish. She's happy up there."

Grady would have engaged in some kind of pleasant small talk, but she felt no real need for it. They loaded their plates, and Elena poured them huge glasses of chilled orange juice. Grady remembered to thank her soundly before she dug in, because she didn't think she'd be able to talk once all the chewing started.

But once Elena relaxed, they managed to inhale vast quantities of food and converse at the same time, and the ease of their talk surprised Grady. She had told this maddening curandera about the most painful year of her life last night, but she felt no solemn veil between them now. They didn't talk about any of the secrets revealed, or dead witches or blue trucks, because they found many other interesting topics to explore. Grady didn't know if it was the protein or the solid night's sleep—or the shedding of overdue tears, or Elena's healing prayer—but she felt ten years younger this morning.

"…and I thought I'd bring us a real desert Christmas tree." Elena swallowed mightily and continued, waving her fork. "So I found this great little yucca tree out on the mesa, and I hauled it back here and stuck it in a big pot and decorated it. And it was great! And then that night, when the heater was on and the shop was warm and so was the yucca tree, we heard this low, awful buzzing start up."

"Uh-oh." Grady grinned, anticipating what was coming, and bit into her toast.

"Right. The hornets were awake! The hornets that were passing this nice peaceful winter tucked into yucca pods, until this stupid girl came along and dragged them inside and woke them up. I ran down here and they were flying all over the place. I was jumping around and flailing my shawl—" Elena did a great demonstration, and Grady sputtered laughter into her orange juice. "I got most of them out, but we kept hearing little isolated buzzing sounds in here for weeks afterward. Mamá threatened to burn down the shop to chase them off for good."

"Hey, that would have worked." Grady sat back in her chair, sated and happy. "Elena, I will never eat again. This was wonderful. Thank you."

"You are most welcome." Elena stretched, running her fingers through her tumbling hair. "Every bite of this breakfast is going immediately to my hips, and I do not care. I will be proud to carry an extra pound as a tribute to our time together this morning."

"I wish it didn't have to end." Grady checked her watch. "But my seminar is meeting pretty soon, and I need to head up there." She had a thought. "Any chance you might want to come along?"

"To the campus?" Elena brightened.

"Yeah. You might be able to help me convince my three intrepid students that writing this paper is getting too dangerous."

"And I could see your classroom?"

"Well, I don't really have one room, but I could show you where I work. My office. You've showed me yours, I can show you mine. I mean…"

Elena laughed. "Grady, you don't do sexual humor any better than I do. But yes, thank you. I would love to see where you work."

They gathered the plates and glasses and stacked them in the deep sink at the back of the side room. Grady was touched with a pleasing sense of domesticity as she helped Elena wash them. Their wet hands touched occasionally, sending a warm tingle through her arm. They were heading toward the shop's door when Inez called from upstairs.

"Go ahead, leave me all alone up here! I'll try to have my heart attack nice and quiet so my death throes won't disturb you when you come back, if you ever do."

"Have a wonderful heart attack, Mamá." Elena turned off the lights, and the shop was filled with the striated morning light coming through the slatted windows. "It's my day off, and I'm going to school. Say good-bye to Grady, please."

"Good-bye to the gringa who ate up all our food."

"Take care, Inez," Grady called, fishing her keys out of her pocket.

Elena shook her head and twirled her own set of keys. "Your truck is nose-down in a ditch, remember? Elena drives."

"Ah, that's right," Grady sighed. "Can we take your horse?"

"We might get there faster if we did. Wait till you see my little car."

❖

Elena's ancient Ford rattled all the way to the campus, but it got them to Breland Hall. Grady unlocked the door to her office and waved Elena through.

"Whoa." Elena lifted her hands and stopped abruptly, bringing Grady up short. She turned in a slow circle, taking in the artifacts on the walls and the tall shelves full of books. "Grady, this is a wonderful office. I want to spend all day in here."

"I like it too, but it's a little cramped for a meeting of five." Grady went to her desk and scrawled a few lines on a legal pad.

"Will you tell me where all of these things came from someday?" Elena's hand hovered respectfully over a small twig of petrified wood on Grady's desk. "Like this stick?"

Grady smiled as she tore the sheet off the pad. In the richness of the art in her office, no one else had ever noticed the simplest of her souvenirs, and her longtime favorite. "That was a gift from my first field assignment. It's a prayer stick. An old holy man from a Cayuse tribe whispered a prayer for me into it, some kind of wish. I still don't know what he asked for, but he was a funny, kind man. It was something good. He told me to keep it close, and I always have."

"You always should." Elena's eyes were shining. "There's a story like that behind everything in here, isn't there?"

"Pretty much." Grady couldn't imagine a better morning than sharing those stories with Elena, but she was already eager to leave. She wanted to be outside, breathing in the desert's crisp air, while the sun was still mild. And that urge had nothing to do with restlessness, for once—Grady simply felt good.

She taped the note telling her students where to find them to her office door and ushered Elena out.

The awakening campus was alive with birdsong as they walked among the handful of students dedicated enough to sign up for early-morning summer classes. Grady had developed a real fondness for this college and its widely diverse citizenry in her six months in Las Cruces. NMSU wasn't small, but it felt almost cozy after the political in-fighting of other universities.

Elena strolled with her hands clasped behind her, close beside Grady—perhaps closer than usual, as she was a guest on Grady's turf. She wore one of her many light skirts and an old-fashioned white blouse, a unique style among the proliferation of jeans and shorts on campus. But Elena smiled openly into every face they passed and received more amiable nods in reply than Grady would have expected from sleepy students.

The graveled rooftop of the Pan American Center would be hell on earth in four hours, but this early in the day, it still provided a cool refuge. The high stadium offered an unobstructed view of the Organ Mountains that Grady found hard to resist, and she wanted to share it with Elena. Her boots crunched over the gravel as she led the way to a raised cement slab near the east side of the roof. Grady sat on it cross-legged, a little appalled when she couldn't quite suppress an uncouth belch as she settled. "Excuse me."

"I can't crack an egg," Elena said suddenly.

"I'm sorry?"

"I can't cook. My mother made our breakfast this morning. Not me." Elena sighed and sat on the cool cement beside her. "I couldn't tell you because you kept thanking me for cooking it, about a hundred times. I got locked into my terrible lie. Now I've confessed, and I'm once again free of sin."

"I'm glad my burp led to the unburdening of your heart." Grady grinned at her.

"I made the orange juice."

"And exquisite orange juice it was." She let her gaze sweep the majestic vista, the distant mountains tinged red by the sun. "The first time I came up here, I thought you guys were kidding, with this light."

"Us guys?"

"You New Mexico people, and your desert light. Look at

those mountains. The Organs are a small range, and they must be what, ten miles from Las Cruces? But those jagged peaks are crystalline, like someone punched up the contrast key on Photoshop."

"You're such a romantic, with your Photoshop praise." Elena slid her arm through hers, so easily Grady didn't even tense. "The mountains are beautiful from here. The Spanish who settled in this valley thought those peaks looked like the rising bars of a pipe organ, but they've always reminded me of my grandmother's hands. Battered and stately and lovely."

"I can almost picture her now. Your grandmother." Grady touched Elena's shoulder. "You're bringing her alive for me."

"I'm glad to hear it." Elena smiled and nodded toward the mountains. "Do you see that patch of reddish rock, at the base of the center peaks?"

Grady pulled her gaze back east. Elena was pointing out a landmark she had noticed before, a tight grouping of small red cliffs near the bottom of the range. "Yeah, I see that patch. Does it have a name?"

"It's a special place. I'd like to show—" Elena broke off as a door opened behind them, and she and Grady unwound their arms and scooted an inch farther apart. They blinked at each other and laughed softly at their sudden transformation into guilty teenagers caught out of class.

"Grady?" Janice's voice.

Grady shifted and shaded her eyes. "We're over here."

Janice turned toward them and smiled shyly. "Hello, Elena."

"Hey, Grady, you brought Elena?" Sylvia emerged behind Janice, carrying the essential box of doughnuts under one arm. "Great! You wouldn't make Elena take one of those death marches, right? We're not walking anywhere?" She came to the cement slab and plunked down happily beside Elena, then gave her a quick kiss on the cheek. "I'm glad to see you, *amiga.* I have something for you."

"Chocolate sprinkles?"

To Grady's amazement, Elena was peering longingly at the doughnuts. Maybe her secret *curandera* super powers made it possible to accommodate chocolate sprinkles after a huge breakfast of *chorizo* and eggs.

"Good morning, Elena." Cesar sounded pleased as he joined them, water still shining in his black hair. "Hello, Grady. Are you going to tell us what happened yesterday?"

"Yeah, please start there." Janice sat on the far corner of the slab. "Hey, will Elena be helping us with this paper?"

"I asked Elena to join us today for a few reasons." Grady shook her head at the glazed doughnut Elena offered her. "First, she's going to help me impress upon you that this project has passed into bedrock dangerous territory. And I think her input will be helpful in terms of where we go now."

"My being here this morning was kind of a spontaneous thing." Elena licked chocolate from her thumb delicately. "We don't know yet how much I can help you."

"First order of business." Grady forced her gaze away from Elena's lips. "No more interviews on this project, and no more field work."

"Man." Sylvia's eyes widened. "How come? What happened to you guys yesterday? On the phone you said something about being run off the road?"

Grady nodded. "By a man Elena recognized. A brother of one of the suicides."

"Sheesh. Which one?" Janice fumbled her Droid out of her backpack and clicked keys. "A brother of Jaime Barela? We interviewed his widow yesterday. I brought our notes."

"Just a minute, Janice." Sylvia looked troubled. Cesar, sitting at her feet, encircled Sylvia's ankle in his fingers. "I still don't understand what happened yesterday, Grady. Why would these men want to hurt you?"

"Because she was with me." Elena lifted her face and caught a brief, light breeze that puffed her hair off her forehead. "I've been trying to bulldoze my way through all this trouble these last few months. I thought if I stood up to these men, they'd leave us alone. I didn't want to let them scare me into silence, to make me stop talking about Maria. But their fear is too great. They honestly believe I'm a witch, and that every witch is under Llorona's thrall. They think I'm a threat, that I'm casting spells to help Maria kill them. And it's not just me and my mother in danger anymore. I've drawn all of you into this, and these people are serious." Elena was answering Sylvia, but she was looking at Grady.

Grady may have enjoyed a sound and deep sleep the night before, but she realized with a pang that Elena had not. She looked suddenly tired, even in this beneficent morning light.

"Grady's right," Elena added. "No class paper is worth risking your lives for."

"But we can contribute some really valuable stuff." Janice sounded plaintive. "Can't we just sign a release or something?"

"If you had signed an employment contract for a field project, yes, you could decide how much personal risk to take on," Grady said. "But undergrads, taking a summer seminar? No. After yesterday, I'd deserve to lose my job if I didn't pull you three to a quick halt."

"But this isn't just about the paper, Grady." A crease formed between Cesar's thick brows. "Elena told us we can help stop the suicides in Mesilla. It still seems to me that's important enough that maybe we should take some risks."

"No one said you had to stop working with Elena, Cesar." To her consternation, Grady was swept by an unexpected sensory memory of the sweet weight of Elena's head resting on her shoulder. The light hairs on her forearms tingled, and she made herself focus on Cesar. "The best way to help her is starting the solid practical research we need to ground this project. Put in some library time. Don't just rely on the Internet. We've got our two local interviews as contemporary sources, but we need a detailed history of Llorona's appearances."

"Hey, if anyone's an expert on the River Walker, it's Elena." Sylvia smiled and brushed powdered sugar off her chin. "You'd be a great interview, *amiga*."

"Yes, we can consider Elena a credible local source." Grady glanced at Elena apologetically. "But she's just one source. We can give her account due weight, but we have to provide historical perspective, too." She felt Elena's gaze on her face.

"But will the two of you still be sticking your necks out talking to people?" Janice was watching Grady with a worried frown. "You and Elena. You guys have already been run off a road. What's going to happen the next time a body washes up at the river? Will they come after you, Elena?"

"Yes, that might happen," Elena said. "I promise I'll be as mindful of my safety as Grady is asking you all to be."

Janice still looked concerned, so Grady shifted focus. "All right, folks. Let's hear about your interview, please."

"We got some great quotes, Grady." Sylvia brightened. "We listened for the cues you taught us. Mrs. Barela liked Cesar and his good manners. She really opened up to him."

"She's a sad lady." Cesar nodded at Janice. "Janice, read what she said about punishment. Jaime Barela was a real assho—a real jerk, Elena, just like you told us the others were."

Janice consulted the small screen in her hands. "Here it is. Cesar asked Mrs. Barela if other people in her family ever helped her, when her husband beat her up. Here's her answer. 'There was never any help for me. No one lifted a finger. Now there's no help for him.'" Janice looked up. "She never spoke her husband's name, the entire time we talked. 'Now he is the one who is punished. Now he cries out, and no one helps. Now he roasts. I spit on his grave, and on my knees every night I thank the dead *bruja* who put him there.'"

"There was no expression at all on her face when she said that." Sylvia stroked Cesar's shoulder, as if for comfort. "It was like she's already dead inside."

"It sounds like you all handled this with compassion and

respect." Grady was proud of her bairns. In the shiny light of the morning sun, they all looked older somehow, more mature. "Good job. I'd like a transcript of your notes by—"

"Grady, I know of one other interview your students can help us with." Elena was watching Janice thoughtfully. "One that won't put any of us in danger. Janice, can you come with Grady and me tomorrow morning?"

"Sure!" Janice cut Grady off before she could speak. "I can reschedule my biology test. I'll take it today." She bounced lightly on the slab. "Where are we going?"

"And why aren't we all going?" Sylvia said.

"Where are we going, and why are any of us going there?" Grady frowned at Elena.

"We're going to talk to another man who has heard Llorona." Elena spoke as calmly as if this weren't news to Grady. "But he isn't a well man, and all five of us can't crowd into his bedroom. So only three of us will go. All right?"

Elena looked up at her, and Grady realized she was asking for trust. She struggled for a moment, but the hopefulness in Janice's expression wore her down. "All right. Tomorrow morning. But after that, it's the library, for all of you. Are we clear?"

"Yes, oh mother of us all, the library, we're clear. Okay!" Sylvia grinned and riffled through her purse. "Before we disappear into boring research." She drew out three small creamy envelopes and handed them to Elena, Grady, and Janice. "It's in two weeks, so I know it's kind of last minute, but we hope you guys will come."

Grady smiled, knowing what she'd find before she slit the envelope with a thumbnail and pulled out the folded card. She was right. The front of the wedding invitation bore a distinguished brown-ink rendering of San Albino Church.

"Wow." Janice looked a little surprised. "Thanks for asking me."

"Hey, you decided on San Albino?" Elena sounded pleased.

"We did." Sylvia's cheek dimpled. "We had to fight our

families a little, but we fell in love with that church. We went there after our sessions with you, Elena. We had to pay a mint to print up new invitations, but it was worth it. We want to marry there. Cesar and I have history with San Albino now, you know?"

"I do know. What about your dress?"

"*Oh* my God. Elena, you have to see it! I look like a big, sexy, lacy white burrito in this dress. It's a thing of beauty."

Grady leaned back on her elbows and listened to them chatter, enjoying the sound, light as carefree gossip between high school girls. Sylvia and Elena had formed a quick friendship in the brief time they'd known each other. Sylvia was closer to Elena in age than Grady was, a somewhat disconcerting thought. Cesar had rested his head against the concrete block, apparently dozing in the sun. She noticed that even asleep, the big kid's fingers still gently encircled Sylvia's ankle. Janice sat quietly among them, a little apart, watching the mountains.

Finally Sylvia patted Cesar's head. "Come on, *hijo*. All the doughnuts are gone, since you ate four of them on the way here. We have to go to work." Cesar shifted and stretched.

"Do you have time for a short hike today?" Elena asked Grady.

"Elena, no, save yourself." Sylvia got up quickly and pulled Cesar up with her. "Do not walk anywhere with this person. She never stops!" Her eyes twinkled with affection, and Grady spared herself one wistful hope that she'd ever feel as happy and safe again as Sylvia Lucero felt today. "Come on, Janice. We'll be in the nice, cool, air-conditioned library if you need us, Grady."

Grady waited until her students gathered their things and crunched across the graveled rooftop to the double doors. Then she turned to Elena. "Do I get to hear about whoever we're interviewing tomorrow morning?"

"Yes, you do. I'll fill you in."

"And do I get to know why we're taking Janice?"

"Because Janice is lost in the world and she needs you.

Helping us will be good for her, as well as for our work with Maria." Elena shielded her eyes from the sun. "Now. Your head is better this morning, right?"

Grady felt the bump on the side of her head, and it gave off only a small twinge. "Yep, it's fine."

"As I was saying. Do you have time for a short hike?"

Time. Grady was behind on the fall syllabus due to Dr. Lassiter in less than two weeks. She had to take care of her half-squished truck. She had a stack of unpaid bills on her desk, in her dust-laden condo. "I've got all day. Where are we going?"

Elena smiled mysteriously and nodded toward the Organ Mountains.

There was some doubt that Elena's decrepit car could successfully deliver them over ten miles of increasingly rough road to the base of the mountains. At least there was doubt on Grady's part. She kept one hand firmly clamped on the brace in her door, and her right boot frequently shifted to an invisible brake pedal. It wasn't that Elena was a bad driver, or a particularly fast one, but even at a sedate pace, her small Ford rattled like a tin pail full of rocks.

But the jagged purple peaks ahead kept looming steadily closer until they filled Grady's sky, and she grew so fascinated by their contours she even let go of the door brace.

"You see that?" Elena asked, pointing through her dusty windshield. "That vaguely heart-shaped spot, halfway up the left side?"

"Yeah. That shape's even noticeable from Cruces."

"It's a field of red rocks, really striking up close, surrounded by this beautiful meadow. We call it the Heart of the Mountain. It's where I wanted to scatter my grandmother's ashes, but a plot in the San Albino churchyard won out." Elena cranked the wheel and her struggling little sedan chugged onto a wide turn-off from the dirt road. She keyed off the engine, then quirked an eyebrow at Grady. "So. You want to meet a different kind of ghost?"

"No," Grady said at once.

Elena laughed. "You'll like him, I promise. Everyone does."

Grumbling, Grady opened her door and ducked out of the car. She winced a little at the clatter she made closing the door, as if she'd let out a disruptive bellow in a quiet church. The desert wasn't always silent, but the bugs and birds of the morning had quieted down, and the evening critters wouldn't begin their songs for hours. The crystal air around them was utterly still. Grady drank in the peace of it like cool water.

Then she realized Elena was several yards ahead, striding toward the opening of a narrow trail in the sagebrush. Grady followed, reaching automatically into her back pocket for the strips of twine she carried there for desert field work. She used them to tie the cuffs of her pants legs to her boots, lest anything crawly wish to venture up there. Those strips, of course, were in the glove compartment of her half-squished truck. Grady eyed Elena's shapely bare calves flashing under the hem of her skirt and cursed herself for a weenie. She trotted to catch up.

They were walking into the pale red rocks Elena had pointed out to Grady from town. The cliffs stood high and thick enough here to block the view of the mountain range behind them. The trail narrowed and steepened, and Grady found herself mesmerized by the slow shifting of Elena's hips as she climbed. The sun beat down on their heads, strong enough now to remind her the temperature often crested a hundred before noon this time of year. She took out her bottle of water and swigged from it, then saw Elena stop abruptly a few yards up the trail. She seemed to be staring at the base of a large prickly pear cactus.

"Ish," Elena said faintly.

"Ish?" Grady called.

Elena nodded. "I'm sorry, but ish." She pointed to the stones around the cactus. "I know how girlie this is. I'm okay with snakes, with centipedes, with scorpions, but these? Ish."

"Ah." Grady smiled and sauntered over. She wasn't much daunted by desert fauna, even the creepier varieties, and Elena's uncharacteristic timidity was charming. Then she stopped short. The tarantula sunning itself on the flat stone was easily the size of a soup bowl.

"Ish," Grady said.

"I know."

Grady pointed her water bottle warningly at the magnificent bug. She took Elena's hand, and together they sidestepped a stiff, wide arc around it. The spider glared at them.

"Did you know they can jump?" Elena whispered. "And *hiss*?"

"Elena, I'm going to have to call in a helicopter to airlift me out of here, if you insist on discussing this."

"Creeped you out too, eh?"

"You could see that thing from space."

They finally put enough distance between their ankles and the sullen spider, but Grady kept her hold on Elena's hand. Elena seemed to notice this, too, and she turned back questioningly. Grady opened her mouth, but nothing came out, so she just smiled.

Elena pressed her fingers gently. "We're almost there."

Clasping hands like two trusting children, they climbed higher into the silent wedge of red rock. The yucca and barrel cactus that studded the desert floor grew more sparsely here, but the honey mesquite brush was thick on either side of their trail. A wet drop rolled between Grady's shoulder blades, and she wasn't sure if she was sweating because of the exercise, the blazing sun, or the cool hand resting in hers.

They topped a small stone rise and Grady spied the large, nearly rectangular opening in the rock's face. She grinned in delight.

"La Cueva, the cave." Elena, slightly breathless from the

climb, obviously enjoyed Grady's reaction. "We think Indian tribes—the Jornada Mogollon, some nomad Apache—found shelter in this cave as early as the sixteen hundreds."

Grady's mouth actually watered, and she tugged Elena on. She knew there would be no real artifacts left at such an accessible site, but the rich history of the place called to her like enchiladas to a starving woman. She had to duck slightly when they reached the cave's opening but found she could stand almost fully erect once inside.

La Cueva was about as long and deep as a railroad boxcar. Stepping inside it was like entering another ecosystem. The shadowy interior was blessedly cool. No tarantulas were readily apparent.

Grady walked the cave's length, brushing one hand lightly and respectfully over the craggy wall's surface, the soot-stained ceiling, listening for the echoes of a hundred lost voices. Elena seemed to understand that quiet would be appreciated, and she sat cross-legged on the stone floor just inside the entrance.

Images of her office kept appearing in Grady's head as she explored, and for some reason, flashes of the small healing chamber in Elena's house. This ancient space held the same aura of friendly reverence, and Grady was puzzled by how personally benevolent that energy felt.

"His name was Agostini Justiniani. Most of Mesilla just calls him *abuelo*, grandfather." Elena was looking out the cave's entrance, at the achingly beautiful view of the wide vista of the Mesilla Valley below. "He was born in eighteen hundred to a noble Italian family. He studied to become a priest but refused to take his vows."

Grady deduced this guy had to be dead by now and steeled herself for the ghost story. She sat on a flat raised rock beside Elena, relieved to feel her lower back crackle loose. Elena still looked tired, but now her features held that familiar dreamy cast, and a small smile played about her lips.

"He renounced his wealth when he was twenty years old,

Grady. He spent the next forty years traveling all over the world, mostly on foot. Everywhere he went, he learned about healing, and about God. They called him *El Ermitaño*, The Hermit. And he walked into Mesilla in 1867."

Grady rested her elbows on her knees, enjoying Elena's hushed voice. This was so vividly different from listening to Elena tell stories about homicidal witches. Her face was shining, as if she was sharing a much-loved tale from her childhood.

"Some families in Mesilla are honored, even today, because their ancestors befriended the Hermit. They still tell stories of his kindness and healing powers. But my *abuelo* was a truly solitary soul, and he chose to live the last years of his life alone here, in La Cueva."

"This was in 1867?" Grady whistled softly. "This must have been pretty rough territory back then."

Elena nodded. "Yes, it was dangerous. Lots of bandits and renegades passed through this valley." She smoothed her hand over the stone beneath her. "The Hermit promised his friends in Mesilla that he would light a fire here at the entrance every Friday night to assure them he was safe."

"And one Friday night," Grady guessed, "the cave remained dark."

"That's right."

"And the Hermit was found lying in here, a smile on his face, having died peacefully in his sleep?"

"Well, no." Elena sighed. "He was found with a knife in his back. It's one of New Mexico's great unsolved murders. *But*," she added quickly, "tell me how you feel right now, Grady."

"How I feel?" Grady leaned back against the rock wall and considered it. She felt great. The long muscles in her back were relaxed, she was cool, her mind was clear and content. Elena watched her face, and then nodded as if satisfied.

"That's my *abuelo*. We can't see him, but he's here." Elena rested her elbow on Grady's knee. "There's so much goodness in the realm of the spirit, Grady, as well as meanness. Just like here.

I brought you to La Cueva because I wanted you to feel that. In death, Maria chooses to kill and spread terror. But the Hermit continues to heal and give comfort, just as he did in life."

A pair of dark smiling eyes filled Grady's mind, their edges crinkled with age. They looked like the eyes of the old Cayuse holy man who had breathed a prayer for Grady into a stick of petrified wood. She felt Elena's fingers brush the side of her face.

"It's just that you keep surprising me," Elena said softly. "You don't act like a brainy gringa with no belief in any god. You don't look down on me, or the beliefs I cherish. You try to protect everyone you care about. You're a kind woman, Grady, and you have a brave heart. I'm proud that you're my friend."

Elena sat close against her, her face tilted up. Grady knew it was only a matter of lowering her head a few inches and letting their lips meet. She began to do just that. Then the aged eyes in her mind changed into wide, laughing blue ones, fringed by lavish lashes. Max's eyes. As if it were happening that moment, Grady felt his small, pudgy hand slip out of her own, and he was gone.

She sat up.

Elena was still, but if she sensed Grady's withdrawal, she chose not to mention it. They sat together quietly for a while, watching the valley.

"I'm hoping they buried the Hermit at your Heart of the Mountain," Grady said at last. "I bet that's a beautiful spot."

"It is, and that would have been the perfect choice." Elena looked pleased. "But of course everyone in Mesilla wanted to visit his grave, so he was buried in the cemetery. The oldest section. His headstone reads, 'Agostini Justiniani, Hermit of the Old and New World. He died the seventeenth of April, 1869, at sixty-nine years, and forty-nine years a hermit.'" Elena yawned, and rested her head in Grady's lap. "You still see fresh flowers on his grave all the time."

Grady let her hand hover over Elena's shoulder, then settle on it gently. Her feelings for this woman were a bewildering morass of tenderness, irritation, protectiveness, and outright lust. One moment she was on the verge of a stroke at Elena's stubbornness, the next she wanted to take on anything in the world that might dare harm her. Right now, Elena's touch felt light and sisterly. She spoke so quietly Grady almost missed her words.

"Do you think you're ready to face her with me?" Elena asked.

Grady blinked, playing quick mental catch-up. "You mean face Maria?"

"That's who I mean."

"And what would that entail, exactly?"

Elena's shoulder shook as she laughed. "*Now* you sound like a brainy gringa, Grady. It would entail going with me to the river at night. As many nights as it takes. Waiting until she comes to you again."

"To me? You think she comes to me?"

"Well, some people in Mesilla live their entire lives without ever hearing or seeing Llorona. You just moved to this valley, and you've heard her twice in one month."

Grady shivered, uncomfortable with the role of spook bait. But Elena thought she had a brave heart. "All right, and if Maria does show up? What then?"

"When Llorona comes, I'll speak to her through you. I think she'll hear you, Grady. You'll give her my message."

The part of Grady's heart that clearly remembered the shriek of the River Walker was not very brave, and she settled on the first of many possible objections. "Elena, my Spanish vocabulary consists of about thirteen words."

"I know, and you mispronounce ten of them." Elena smiled; Grady felt it against her thigh. "That's why the professor needs to take lessons. To learn phrases like *Usted no tiene que protegerme.*"

Grady squinted and attempted to translate. "I don't have to program you?"

"You don't have to protect me," Elena said, so softly Grady wondered who she was speaking to. "I have about twenty messages like that for Maria, and you'll have to learn them all."

Grady was glad Elena couldn't see her face. Sensitive as she was, Elena couldn't know what she was asking; she had never heard Llorona's wail. Grady wasn't sure she could bear to expose herself to it again. She was equally sure she didn't want Elena going to the river alone, not with thugs in blue trucks after her. Therefore, she would find the *cojones* somewhere.

Grady drifted her fingers gently through Elena's curling hair.

"Also…" Elena's voice was drifting off. "*La matanza debe parar*…the slaughter must stop."

"Yes, it must," Grady murmured. If she helped stop the River Walker, would Elena's goddess reward her with letting her see Max again? The thought revealed such craven longing she shrank from it. This aspect of the afterlife, reunion with those lost, was too tantalizing to consider rationally. And, paranormal experiences aside, she was still essentially a rational woman.

Elena had fallen asleep. Grady was a connoisseur of sleep, and she recognized deep and peaceful slumber when she saw it. She leaned closer to her.

"You are *sayen*," Grady whispered. "That's a Mapuche word meaning 'lovely.' I might have messages to teach you, too, curandera."

Because Grady was still essentially a rational woman, the swish of robes behind her, and the hand that rested gently on the crown of her head, had to be her imagination. The long fingers patted her hair and then withdrew.

Elena slept for a solid two hours, and Grady didn't stir once.

CHAPTER FIFTEEN

The next morning dawned bright and hot. Grady slammed the door of her battered truck with her hip, balancing two big paper tumblers of coffee in her hands. The truck had been deemed dented but serviceable by her trusty mechanic, but the door creaked loudly in the dawn stillness and didn't close quite true.

Grady still didn't understand why Elena insisted they hold this interview so early or exactly why they were talking to this man at all. But the sight of Elena's pleased smile when she opened the door to her shop convinced Grady that this outing was a terrific idea.

"*Buenos* morning." Grady handed Elena one of the tumblers.

"*Ay, caramba.*" Elena laughed as she tucked a small satchel under her arm and accepted the steaming cup. "It's enough coffee to keep half of Mesilla awake for a week."

"This is not coffee. This is clover-brewed blend, filled with flavorful nuances, with a piquant aftertaste." Grady waited while Elena locked the door to her shop. "You'll have to trust me on this. The desert Southwest knows salsa, the Pacific Northwest knows coffee."

"Thank you for this exotic drink from your strange culture, Professor Gringa." Elena stepped down off the boardwalk and nodded down the street. "We're going this way."

Grady strolled beside Elena, taking in the awakening village. Mesilla was never a buzzing hive of activity, but on this early weekday morning, the street was starting to fill. Slow cars trundled down the road past them. Kids were out of school for the summer, and she and Elena dodged around two of them running into a store.

"I guess Janice isn't joining us." Grady had mixed feelings about this development. Janice was supposed to have met them at Elena's shop, and Grady was surprised she hadn't shown. She had seemed excited about being in on the interview. Grady had to admit she wasn't overly sorry Janice had slept in, though; she was enjoying this time alone with Elena.

"Oh no, Janice will join us." Elena sipped tentatively from her cup. "She's just running a little late. She called me this morning to ask how to get to the house."

"Ah," Grady sighed.

"Are you unhappy that I invited her?" A line of worry appeared between Elena's brows. "I know I should have asked you first."

"Well, you've said this interview won't be risky, so I'm okay with Janice tagging along. I guess I still don't understand why you singled her out for it, though."

"Janice isn't coming so she can 'tag along.' I feel she needs you, Grady." Elena touched Grady's arm to turn her down a dirt road dotted with small adobe homes. "She seems very much alone to me, and she's looking for a guide, a mentor."

"You feel these things about Janice?" Grady was developing a healthy respect for Elena's curandera super powers. "Dr. Lassiter tells me the same thing about her."

"Your hero, Dr. Lassiter?" Elena smiled. "I like what you've told me about her."

"You would like her. Both of you are ganging up on me to be Janice's hero." Grady kicked a pebble with the side of her boot. "I guess I'm not sure I'm up to that yet."

"Then heal as fast as you can, Grady. Nurturing our young is a sacred thing." Elena smiled. "I don't mean to sound like a nun, but it is. I'll never bear children, but I will always look for ways to help young people."

"This sounds like some more good teaching from your grandmother."

"From my grandmother, from *mi Diosa*. But it's the teaching of Mesilla, too." Elena nodded at the opposite sidewalk, where an elderly woman walked clutching the hands of two small children. "So much of Mesilla is good-hearted and wise. I never forget that."

In another life, where Grady's heart wasn't tattered and she and Elena were not walking down a residential street in Old Mesilla, she would have lifted her arm and settled it around Elena's shoulders. The prospect of doing so was a light and natural urge, which Grady quelled with some difficulty. "So tell me what I need to know about our mystery man, please."

"Yes, okay. This is excellent, by the way." Elena waggled her tumbler of coffee at Grady. "To understand our mystery man, you're going to have to think back. To the night we met, as a matter of fact. The night you first heard the River Walker."

Grady frowned. "Will I like where this is going?"

"It's doubtful." Elena sounded sympathetic. "Think back and tell me when the body of Enrique Acuña was found. The fourth man to drown himself in the river."

Grady calculated. "About three weeks ago. My seminar had just started. Oh, it was the day after you and I..." Her voice faded.

"That's right. The first time you heard Maria on the riverbank, Enrique Acuña heard her, too. He drowned that night."

Grady had never made this simple connection, and it creeped the crap out of her now. It was all too easy to picture this man flailing in the dark waters of the Grande, gasping for his last agonized breath under that horrible wail.

"Hold it." Grady stopped walking, and Elena turned to her. "What about the night Cesar heard Llorona's screams? That was over a week ago. There was no suicide that night. Was there?"

"No, there wasn't." Elena nodded toward a neat two-story house on the corner of the next street. Grady saw Janice leaning against her car, parked in front of the house. "Maria does not always bring down her prey, Grady. The night you brought Cesar to me, Maria attacked the man who lives in that house. He escaped with his life. Or most of it."

Elena crossed the street, leaving Grady behind her with her mouth hanging open. She trotted to catch up.

"Good morning, Grady." Janice smiled at them both. "Sorry I was running a little late."

"That's okay. He what?" Grady said to Elena. "This man did what?"

"Janice, I was just telling Grady that the man we are about to meet encountered Llorona at the river and lived to tell about it." Elena shaded her eyes and checked the position of the sun. "We should go in. He won't be awake much longer."

"My God. He didn't drown himself?" Janice caught up to Elena quickly and followed her up the stone steps to the house. "But is he abusive, like the others? How did he—"

"Janice." Grady tapped her gently on the shoulder. "All good questions, but this is a time to listen." She felt some empathy with her student. Her mind teemed with the same thoughts, but working with Phyllis Lassiter had taught her the discipline of patience.

"Oh, of course." Janice looked crestfallen. "I'll hang back and watch, I promise."

Elena pulled open a screen door and knocked on the inner one. "We should remember to speak softly, and not make any sudden movements or loud noises. Mr. Perez's hearing is very sensitive right now, and he startles easily."

"Hey. I know that car." Grady looked at the battered Toyota

parked at the curb. "That's Rita's car." Elena's friend had picked them up in it, after they were run off the road.

"Yes. Rita is Mr. Perez's daughter." Elena turned as the door shot open and two small boys tumbled out of the house, each with a big towel slung over his shoulder. Their happy shrieks rattled Grady's nerves, but then she was often rattled when she saw boys Max's age.

"*Vámanos*, go, get gone!" Rita appeared in the doorway, flapping one hand at the scrambling kids. A hulking man came up beside her, yawning as he pulled on a T-shirt. Rita reached up to grip his chin in her fingers and pulled his head down for a smacking kiss. "I owe you for this," she told him. "I promise I'll take them swimming three times next week."

"Yes, you will," the man muttered, but he was smiling and his smile broadened when he saw Elena. "Hey, Elena. Glad you're here. Glad I'm gone."

"Good morning, Tomás." Elena held the screen door open so the big man could inch past the three women on the front porch. "It's good to see you."

"Come on, hurry. The flies will get in." Rita flapped them into the house much the same way she had waved her sons out of it, and Grady and Janice followed Elena into the narrow entry.

A much humbler abode than that of Manuel Herrera, the home Santos Perez shared with his daughter and her family was cramped and dark, but messy with the kind of happy chaos that characterized a home with children. Toys and clothes lay scattered over the furniture and floor, and Grady heard the theme from *Thomas the Tank Engine* whistling from the television. Rita snapped it off, then straightened and pushed her hair out of her bloodshot eyes.

"You've been up all night?" Elena frowned at her.

"Tomás spelled me for an hour or two. I'll catch a nap later." She smiled at Grady. "And how is our *loca* professor this morning? The one who absolutely never faints?"

"I'm good." Grady liked Rita, a large woman with a generous laugh. She noted her slumped shoulders, the lines beneath her eyes. A sister in sleeplessness. "Thanks for letting us come today."

"Rita, this is Janice Hamilton." Elena touched Janice's shoulder. "She's one of Grady's students. I've told them we need to be quiet and calm around your father. He had a difficult night?"

"No more difficult than the last nine nights." Rita shrugged. "And in some ways, he's better. Those herbs you gave me to put in his soup are helping a little, Elena."

"I'm glad."

"His dreams aren't as bad." Rita stifled a yawn. "He still won't close his eyes at night and he can't be alone when it's dark outside, but at least he's sleeping better in the day."

"Are you sure your father's all right with this interview, Rita?" Grady asked. "Sounds like he's in rocky shape."

"Yeah, he's fine with it. I asked him again, just now. He trusts Elena." Rita sighed and gestured for the stairs leading to an upper floor. "Let's go chat with my daddy."

The four of them caused considerable creaking on the worn steps, and Rita gestured to them to climb carefully. Bright light issued from the hallway at the top of the stairs. Rita began talking in a low, soothing voice several yards before she reached the closed bedroom door.

"Dad, it's just Rita, bringing friends to visit you. Elena is here. She's brought the ladies she told you about, from the university." Rita paused at the door. "Is it all right to open the door?"

"Yes." The voice inside was guttural and faint.

"Okay." She turned and whispered to them. "Walk slow, don't move your arms around a lot. You can ask him about what happened, but don't say her name." Rita didn't have to identify "her." She opened the door and ushered them inside.

The large bedroom was bathed in light—electric light, as the curtains to the two windows were drawn tightly shut. In addition to the overhead fixture, Grady counted three standing lamps set around the room, blazing brightly, and a table lamp on a stand beside the bed.

The brightness hit Grady only a second before the smell. The humble haven of Santos Perez stank with the funk of unwashed man and long nights of fear sweat. The two fans set close to the bed did little to dispel the stench. She felt Janice recoil slightly behind her, but she made no sound.

Grady thought the man sitting up in the double bed had to be Rita's grandfather. His whiskered face was weathered and creased, his mustache and sparse hair an oily, dirty white. The sheets on his bed had been tucked in recently, the many pillows piled neatly behind his back. He was watching them with glazed eyes.

"Hello, Señor Perez." Elena spoke as gently as Rita had. "May I come and sit beside you?"

"Yes, you can come." His gaze drifted without interest over Grady and Janice.

Elena stepped quietly across the large room and sat in the comfortable armchair near the bed. She spoke to Perez in a whisper of Spanish, too softly for those near the door to hear. It went without saying that the communication between the curandera and her patient would be private, not part of the project interview.

Perez answered most of Elena's questions with a slow nod. Grady gathered she asked if she could touch him, and he allowed it. She checked his vision, listened to his heart, and smelled his breath without passing out.

"There lies the meanest man I've ever known." Rita's low voice drew Grady out of her rapt focus on Elena. Her tone held little rancor. She was watching her father with a mixture of pity and indifference. "He was worse when he was wasted, which was a lot of the time when I was a kid. He's mellowed out some since my mom died. Which is a good thing, because he has to live with us now." Rita's expression grew fierce. "I wouldn't let him around my boys if he was still throwing kids into walls."

Grady felt cold fingers brush her wrist. Janice was looking at her pleadingly, and Grady nodded permission. They were far enough away from Santos Perez for privacy, and Rita seemed to want to talk.

"Can you tell us what happened to your dad at the river?" Janice asked softly.

Rita let out a long breath and leaned back against the door. "Tomás had to work that night. So I took my father and the kids to a barbecue at my friend's house in Picacho. We stayed late. We were driving home, with the boys asleep in the backseat. I took the shortcut, the frontage road by the river."

Rita scratched her scalp, scowling. "I didn't even think. Most people around here have the sense to avoid the river at night right now, but I just turned onto that frontage road like an idiot. And about a mile later, my father just went crazy. Yelling, clawing at the windshield. He kicked open the car door, and I could barely slow down before he jumped out."

Rita paused. Grady glanced at Janice to keep her from interrupting with a question, but Janice didn't need the warning. She waited quietly while Rita gathered her thoughts.

"He scared the kids to death. They were screaming and crying. But when he took off toward the river, I knew I had to leave them and go after him." Rita looked back at the shrunken man in the bed. "It was a damn close call. I had to knock him down and lay on top of him to keep him from jumping in. I'm a big girl, but he was bigger then. I almost couldn't hold him."

Grady saw Elena place her hand on Perez's sunken chest and close her eyes. They began a prayer together, the man's voice halting and reedy. Grady remembered Elena telling her that certain conditions must be met for Llorona to bring down her prey. Santos Perez had not been alone at the river when he heard the witch-ghost roar. The daughter who had endured his cruelty as a child had saved his life and nursed him with obvious care now.

"I got him home, and he's been like this ever since." Rita rubbed her nose. "I'm sorry about the stink in here. He won't let me wash him. He's afraid of water now. He'll drink juice and the tea Elena brings him, but nothing else."

The prayer Elena shared with her patient was lengthy. When it was over, Elena opened the small satchel she carried and drew out several packets of herbs. She still spoke quietly but turned in the armchair to include the women by the door. "You can stir these into any hot beverage, Señor Perez. I want you to try to get out of bed for a while after you wake up. Just let Rita or Tomás walk you around this room a few times. You must get strength back into your legs."

"I will." His gaze drifted toward the curtained windows, and Grady didn't believe him. She couldn't imagine this frail old man leaving the safety of his bed.

"Grady?" Elena rose slowly from the chair. "Would you like a few minutes?"

Grady hesitated, and looked at Janice. Everyone had a first test. "Go ahead," she whispered.

"Me?" Janice squeaked.

"You, yes. Just focus on what he needs to tell us. Let him guide the story."

"Grady—"

"You can do this, Janice. I'll be right beside you if you need help."

Janice closed her mouth. She looked uncertainly at Elena but followed Grady closer to the bed. Grady held the armchair and Janice slid into it. Even their gentle approach made Santos Perez tense, his fingers clenching the sheets. Grady stood next to Elena, close enough to hear Janice, but not crowding the bed.

"Hello, Mr. Perez." Janice cleared her throat quietly. "Um, my name is Janice Hamilton. And this is Dr. Wrenn, my instructor. Is it okay if we talk for a while?"

"Yes. It's okay." His fingers relaxed in the sheets. "You're Elena's friends."

"That's right." Janice glanced at Grady. "We're trying to learn more about…what happened to you, the other night."

Perez's breathing changed; not dramatically, but it quickened in his hollow chest. He blinked hard. "She got me away." He jerked his chin in Rita's direction. "That one."

Janice nodded. "Rita got you away?"

"Yes, that one." Perez gazed over Janice's shoulder at his daughter, who stood silently across the room. "I kicked her mother in the belly, when she was in her womb. I slapped her when she was still in a crib. And still, she got me away. Before the water."

Grady studied him dispassionately. There were clumps of thin white strands on the pillows; his hair was falling out. Standing quietly beside her, Elena was watching Perez with more compassion than Grady could conjure at the moment.

"Rita saved your life, then." Janice's body was relaxing into the chair, instinctively taking on the unthreatening posture this fragile man required. Grady sensed his need to talk, to confess, and apparently Janice was attuned to it, too. "She stopped you before you could jump into the river?"

"That one, Rita, she has four brothers." His raspy voice lowered. "Only one of them speaks to me now, and only when he wants money. I'm a man without sons." His red eyes welled with tears that Grady attributed to self-pity. "My sons hate me. They should cut my throat. I drove their mother, my Lucy, to an early grave. She was an angel on this earth, and I made her life a hell."

Not selfish tears, then, Grady realized. Remorse. Shame emanated from Santos Perez in waves, like the smell of his unwashed body.

"What was it like for you, Mr. Perez?" Janice was doing well, using a light hand in keeping her subject focused. "The night you ran for the river?"

"Like the Virgin Mother herself turned her face from me forever. God save my evil fucking soul." Perez's eyes had taken on a dead sheen, the kind of flat stare Grady heard was common in soldiers fresh out of combat. "The witch is the Angel of Death. She came for me. She showed me what I am. I wanted to tear off my skin. Only the river could end my shitty waste of a life. Even now." Perez punched his chest weakly. "Even now, a bathtub would be my coffin, or just a sink. I'd drown myself just to kill her screams, and my memories."

Janice started to speak, but Grady's light touch on her shoulder quieted her as Perez began to weep. At first his sobs were the weak sputtering of the aged, but then they deepened, seemingly wrenched from subterranean caverns of regret.

"This'll go on, for a while." Rita didn't sound callous, just pragmatic. "He'll drop off pretty soon."

"It's best if we keep this talk brief anyway." Elena rested her hand on the sheets over his leg, and he didn't flinch from her touch. "Señor Perez looks tired."

Grady doubted they could learn much more from this wretch, and it would be a relief to be out of his presence. She nodded at Janice.

"Mr. Perez, thanks very much for talking to us today." Janice paused, and her voice was kind. "I'm sorry you're suffering like this. I hope you're better soon."

Perez didn't acknowledge her. His bony hands were clenched over his face, and his sobs were becoming reedy and whistling again as he tired.

Grady left Rita and Elena to help him lie down and adjust his bedding. She ushered Janice out of the room, down the stairs, and out of the house. They didn't speak until they stood together on the front porch.

"Grady, I wasn't expecting to hear that." Janice looked

pensive. "I thought Llorona's wail chased men into the river, and they died trying to get away from her. He sounded more like he wanted to kill himself, that he thought he deserved to drown. He sounded sorry."

"Yeah, he sounded sorry. But in all his sorrow, I never heard him apologize to his daughter." Grady was tempted to ask Janice for a cigarette. She had never smoked, but she could make an exception. Santos Perez depressed the hell out of her.

She heard Elena and Rita coming, and she focused on Janice again. "Hey, you did well in there. We'll break down the interview in class, but I don't have many notes for you. You're showing a real nice touch for field work, Janice."

"Well. That's good. Thanks." Sunlight flooded Janice's face, but she quickly assumed an aloof and professional expression. "I'm going to go write out my notes, while they're clear in my head. Thanks, Grady." She waved at Elena and Rita and hurried down the stone steps to her car.

"And you simply must get more rest yourself, Rita." Elena sounded stern as they stepped through the screen door and joined Grady on the porch. "Tomás should help more. You know this may not get any easier."

"He's going to die, isn't he?" Rita sounded resigned.

"*Mi amiga*, that's possible. I can make him more comfortable, but the witch's hold on him is still very strong."

Rita caught Grady's look, and she chuckled without humor. "That old man up there is forty-eight years old, Grady. That's what Llorona did to him. He's been shrinking, getting smaller and weaker, ever since." She shook her head. "Maybe hearing the River Walker is something you can't come back from. Something you shouldn't come back from. Not if you're a certain kind of man."

Rita's eyes filled with tears, and Elena lifted her hand and held it. They stood together, listening to the sad piping of birdsong from the tree outside.

"My mom would want me to forgive him." Rita's tone held

bitterness for the first time. "She made her life's work forgiving that man. I think the cancer in her stomach was made up of all the excuses she made for him. She would tell me he's sorry now and our church tells me I should accept his repentance." She scrubbed her hand across her eyes. "But I can't get there yet."

"Forgiveness can be very hard." Elena pressed her hand. "I think your mamá understands better now what growing up was like for you, Rita. The two of you will talk all of this over someday."

Rita found a weary smile, and she pulled Elena into a hug. "I don't know how I'd get through this without you, *chica*. I hope you're being careful out there. I don't want you getting run off any more roads."

"I'm careful, I promise." Elena's voice was muffled against Rita's plump shoulder.

Rita released Elena and turned to Grady. "You be careful, too. And look out for my ballsy little friend here."

Grady accepted Rita's unexpected embrace willingly. "I'll do my best."

Rita straightened and brushed her fingers through her messy hair. "I need to go check on him. He can't call for me. He's even scared by his own voice if it's loud."

"Thanks, Rita." Grady went to the steps, the morning sun a welcome benediction on her head. "You get some sleep."

Elena cupped Rita's face in her hand. "I'll call you tonight." Rita nodded and went back into the house, closing the door with a quiet click.

Grady and Elena walked together silently, Elena with a faraway look, her hands clasped behind her, Grady grinding her teeth. Elena's shop was in sight before Grady finally spoke.

"It's justice," Grady said. "What's happening in that house."

Elena didn't respond.

"The man kicked his pregnant wife in the stomach, Elena."

"Yes, he did. But Llorona doesn't have the right to impose

this kind of mortal justice. Santos Perez should be punished by the laws of Mesilla, and by his God. Maria doesn't set things right. She murders these men in cold blood. Their widows might see some benevolence in that, but you and I can't afford to. Do you understand?"

"Yes. I do." Grady sighed. "Anyway. Thank you for letting us see Perez."

Elena's smile returned. "Thank you for letting Janice take the lead back there. You've taught her well."

"Yeah, I was impressed. Janice did fine."

"I saw her face when you were talking on the porch. Janice's eyes as she looked at you were exactly like yours when you talk about your Dr. Lassiter." Elena glanced both ways, then went up on her toes and kissed Grady's cheek. "Now *vámanos*, gringa. I'll see you tomorrow for your Spanish lesson."

Grady slid her hands into the pockets of her jeans and jangled her keys until Elena disappeared behind the door of her shop. She walked to her truck, pondering vengeful witches and mortal justice and the lovely softness of Elena Montalvo's lips.

CHAPTER SIXTEEN

Your fall syllabus, Dr. Wrenn. When may I expect it?"
Grady hadn't seen Dr. Lassiter appear in her office doorway, and her cold voice startled her from a rather pleasant reverie. She quickly lowered her feet from her desk and sat up.

"My syllabus? Isn't it due to you next wee—"

"We'd best discuss your plans for the fall term. The Lava Room, one o'clock." With an arched eyebrow, Dr. Lassiter turned and clicked down the hallway.

Grady's shoulders relaxed. Her dean had a rather peremptory way of inviting her to lunch, but that had indeed been her intent. She checked her watch, looking forward to this outwardly mandatory meeting. Between Elena and Dr. Lassiter, Grady figured she must be developing an inordinate fondness for the company of crabby, bossy women.

If Grady felt no real urge to kneel upon entering a Catholic church, she had to resist that reverent gesture every time she walked into La Posta. The light aromas issuing from the historic restaurant's kitchens would inspire instant piety in the most adamant atheist.

Grady followed the red brick hallway past the gift shops and the glittering tank of piranhas—yes, piranhas—in the lobby. The friendly space was alive with screeching music from the large aviary in its center, where macaws, African grays, and cockatiels offered a usually raucous welcome to La Posta's diners.

She found Dr. Lassiter seated in the Lava Room, so called for the porous black rock lining the adobe walls, visible through the greenery festooned from the eaves overhead. In keeping with Grady's religious theme, her scowling mentor looked almost angelic, bathed in the natural silver glow of a skylight, peering at her menu through her glasses. The menu peering was a ruse, as they both always ordered the same thing.

"Tostadas compuestas and coffee." Ignoring Grady, Dr. Lassiter handed her menu to their smiling server.

"Combination plate number two, please, no egg on the enchilada." Grady lifted a tortilla chip and slid it through a small bowl of savory salsa. "Can we have sopaipillas?"

Dr. Lassiter sighed. "It's like dining with a five-year-old," she said to the server, and waved him off.

"I can't help it. Sopaipillas are crack." Grady crunched her chip contentedly, the spicy salsa making her eyes stream. La Posta was fairly affordable; maybe she and Elena could bring Sylvia and Cesar and Janice here to celebrate the upcoming wedding, and ply them with sopaipillas. If they liked glazed donuts, sopaipillas had to be on their hit parade.

What gave Grady pause was she could picture this happening. Having lunch with her students and with Elena, who was proud that she was her friend. Sitting with them at one of these red-clothed tables, just like any woman who had friends, who talked and laughed with them over lunch. She hadn't been that woman for well over a year; she hadn't considered even wanting friends again. Interesting. She thoughtfully munched another chip.

"And who resided in the room behind the balcony above our heads?" Dr. Lassiter polished her glasses with her cloth napkin. "Back when this building was a luxurious hotel?"

"That creep Kit Carson." Grady was happy to play the apt

pupil, knowing the dean relished the rich history of this square block in Mesilla. "And the man who built this place died up in that room. Of the *plague*," she added, not above enjoying a few morbid details herself.

A glint of humor softened Dr. Lassiter's austere features. "Before our victuals arrive, I have something for you." She lifted her omnipresent briefcase onto her lap and opened it, then drew out a small package wrapped in plastic and handed it to Grady.

Grady recognized a new gleam of greed in her teacher's eyes. She felt an answering chime of excitement go off in her belly. "What's this?"

"I found it in the archives at the Brannigan Cultural Center. We absolutely cannot keep it, but Vera Schrader was kind enough to lend it to me for a day. If you spill salsa on this, Dr. Wrenn, I'll see to it that you never work in this field again."

"I believe you. I'll be careful." Grady unwrapped the plastic delicately, eager as a kid with a Christmas present. Inside the protective wrap, a transparent binder further shielded a single sheet of paper. It was the color of yellow smoke, thicker and more like parchment than modern paper, perfectly square, about six inches to a side. Grady handled it lightly, noting two small circles in one corner of the page that might have been drops of lamp oil or candle wax.

She turned the page in her hands, skimming the many lines of spidery black writing on the other side, faint but legible. The letter was written in Spanish, but the date at the top of the page was clear: *el 23 de abril 1903*. Grady wished she could handle the page itself, breathe in whatever faded scent might linger in the candle wax. "Do we have a translation?"

"We do." Dr. Lassiter shook out another sheet and adjusted her eyeglasses. "This letter was written in 1903 by one Señora Elodia Martinez of Mesilla, New Mexico Territory. It was addressed to her sister in Santa Fe, but apparently never mailed. It was found among the family's papers when their estate was settled several years ago." Dr. Lassiter offered Grady the translation.

Grady shook her head, her gaze still on the letter. "Would you read it, please?"

"Surely, if you wish." Dr. Lassiter was in her sixties, and her voice matched the age of the woman beginning to form in Grady's mind, the writer of this century-old message. The penmanship was cramped but neat, the lines more orderly than those drawn by a younger woman. Dr. Lassiter began to read, and the hum of conversation and clinking glasses around them faded for Grady as she stepped into the past.

"'My dearest Fatima.'" Dr. Lassiter's tone was measured and formal. "'I pray this finds you in good health, and safe in the merciful grace of Our Lord. I am sorry but you must not visit here. Mesilla is no longer safe for God-fearing Christian families. The Weeping Woman has taken three lives, and her servant, the Hidalgo witch, is always searching for more mortal souls to feed her. We should burn the wretched woman at the stake! God will turn His eyes from us forever if we suffer a witch to live. But until the cowardly men in this village destroy Hidalgo, the she-demon who commands her will continue to kill. You and the children stay safely in Santa Fe until this cursed season has passed. Please pray for us! Yours in the promise of Life Eternal, Your Loving Sister Elodia.'"

Neither of them spoke as their server came to the table bearing a tray of fragrantly steaming dishes. Grady stared at her plate: a folded taco, a chile relleno, and a green chile enchilada with refritos and rice. No egg on the enchilada. Elodia Martinez probably prepared meals very like this for her family a hundred years ago, when she wasn't wishing a fiery death on Juana Hidalgo.

"Thoughts?" Dr. Lassiter asked at last.

"This is amazing." Grady returned the letter carefully to its plastic wrapping, still immersed in the age in which it was written. "Thank you for finding it."

"I knew you would be pleased." Dr. Lassiter dug into her tostadas compuestas with relish. In her more inelegant moments, she referred to this dish—toasted corn tortilla cups filled with frijoles and red chile con carne—as an orgasm on a plate. "Señora Martinez comes across as a bit bloodthirsty, but doubtless this letter is an accurate expression of the paranoia of the day."

"That paranoia drove Juana Hidalgo to slit her wrists on the banks of the Rio Grande." Grady fingered her taco, remembering the small, sad stone in the weeds, forty paces from consecrated ground. "Some remember her as a good woman, kind to her neighbors."

Dr. Lassiter laid down her fork. "Do you know more about this alleged witch? Wonderful. Tell me everything."

Grady shifted in her seat. Elena's history felt like a private thing, a story shared in trust. She heard Elena's voice in her mind: *If we're going to talk about such things, I need to see your eyes.* In Dr. Lassiter's eyes, Grady saw intelligence and curiosity and a reverent respect for the past. "Do you remember the night Cesar Padilla went into that strange trance at the river? The curandera I brought him to is descended from Juana Hidalgo."

She traced Elena's story to present day, omitting such details as La Llorona's perch on her family tree. Grady would let Dr. Lassiter absorb this tale over time, if further discussions were necessary.

"So now Elena Montalvo is persecuted by the people of Mesilla, just as Juana Hidalgo was a hundred years ago." Dr. Lassiter stirred her coffee thoughtfully. She frowned at Grady. "You reported your mishap on the road the other day as an accident, Dr. Wrenn. You might have told me it was the result of mob hysteria and a modern-day witch hunt."

"I guess that's a more colorful way of putting it."

"A more dangerous way." Dr. Lassiter pointed her coffee spoon at Grady. "You were entirely right to pull your students out of field work after this 'accident.' I'm thinking of pulling you out, as well."

"Well, you can pull." Grady's voice was polite, and she meant no disrespect. But she was going to the river with Elena tonight, and no sixty-year-old department head was butch enough to stop her.

"You will take all precautions, at the very least." Dr. Lassiter sighed and regarded the skylight overhead. "What must life be like, I wonder, for this young curandera. Despised by the people of her town, harassed on the street. Her very life threatened."

"But Elena's loved in Mesilla, too." Grady remembered the expression of gratitude on the face of the old woman in Elena's shop, and Rita's heartfelt thanks. "People go to her for help, and she's known as an excellent healer. It's a source of great sadness for her, I think. Elena wants friends, she cares about her community. It's killing her to be hated and feared."

Dr. Lassiter patted the corners of her mouth with her napkin, studying Grady. "Has Ms. Montalvo come to mean something to you?"

Grady assumed a relaxed slouch. "What makes you ask that?"

Dr. Lassiter's rare smile flickered. "You've never been much good at dissembling, Grady. Your candor is one of the first qualities I admired in you. Your body language changed entirely the moment this curandera's name came up."

Grady gave up on the slouch. She started to answer, then stuffed an entire chile relleno in her mouth instead.

"I have all afternoon." Dr. Lassiter lightly drummed her neatly trimmed nails on the tabletop.

Grady swallowed hard, twice. "She might be," she said finally. "Coming to mean something to me."

"I thought as much." Dr. Lassiter's smile held warmth this time. "Look at you. Your eyes are clear for the first time in months. That haunted look is starting to leave you. Perhaps we have Ms. Montalvo to thank for this."

"She's also responsible for these." Grady raked her fingers through the gray streak in her hair.

"I like her already." Dr. Lassiter lifted a small sopaipilla from a basket and broke off a corner. She tipped a small jar over it, watching Grady as the light bread filled with warmed honey. "You've been spending considerable time with Elena?"

"We got together a few times this week for Spanish lessons. And we're supposed to go river-sitting tonight."

"You lesbians have such odd courting rituals." Dr. Lassiter passed Grady the dripping sopaipilla. "All right, Dr. Wrenn. Just see to it that you're as protective of your own safety as you are of your students', moving forward. I'm certainly not paying you enough to risk bodily injury for an undergraduate seminar."

Grady bit into the warm pastry and entered into holy ecstasy. Bullies and witches were far from her mind. All was well in her world, for now. Her belly was full, her boss was her ally, and she was seeing Elena again in ten hours.

Grady pulled up to Elena's shop, turned off the engine, and checked her hair in the rearview mirror. Her collar was slightly crooked, so she straightened it. She touched her fingers to her tongue and patted down a stubborn cowlick. She started to open the door to her truck, then checked her hair in the rearview mirror again.

"This is ridiculous," she said to her reflection. "We're going to the river to wait for a ghost, not to the senior prom." She stared sternly at herself, but saw the corners of her mouth curve irresistibly. She was going to the river with Elena.

She ducked out of the truck and brushed her butt off, just in case. Twirling her keys in her hand, Grady grinned again as Elena stepped onto the boardwalk in front of her shop. She was dressed in denim shorts and a light cotton blouse, an alluring sight in the moonlight.

"I got your present," Elena called. She waved a small box at Grady, then began to open it. "Thank you, for whatever it is."

"I got you a present?"

"Well, someone did. It was sitting right here, in front of the do—*ay, mierda!*"

"Elena?" Grady bolted around the truck. Elena had dropped the box, and she was clutching her wrist. "What is it?"

"I don't think this was from you." Elena nudged the box with her foot and peered closely at her index finger.

Grady took Elena's hand gingerly. There was a red indentation in the tip of her finger, a single drop of blood welling from it. "What the hell stung you?"

"It didn't sting me, it bit me. It's a *niño de la tierra*. Don't worry. They're not venomous."

"A who?" Grady spotted the small creature scuttling out of the light cast by the bulb over the shop door, and she crouched beside it. "Ah, man. A Jerusalem cricket. I haven't seen one of these in years."

"You don't find them in town much. Just give me a second, Grady, I'm going to go put something on this."

"Is it hurting a lot?"

"Less and less now. But it'll itch like crazy if it's not treated. I'll be right back."

Grady nodded, fascinated by the little nightmare crawling slowly along the base of the wall. Jerusalem crickets looked like they were assembled by a psychotic and vindictive child. Well over two inches long, the bizarre bug had the striped body of a bee and a spider's thick, jointed legs, albeit only six of them. The clumsy monstrosity was topped by a round bald head, bearing its most distinctive feature—markings that looked eerily like a human face. Grady wiped her palms on her knees, glad to see the sinister insect creep off into the shadows. She knew Elena was right—in spite of their alarming appearance, they weren't poisonous. But the bugs had powerful mandibles and could inflict a painful bite, and Grady wanted to know what the hell one was doing gift-wrapped on Elena's doorstep.

She got up and retrieved the box, shaking it out carefully to be sure it was empty. It was an ordinary cardboard box, about an inch deep and a few inches long. A sour odor clung to it, another unattractive feature of this species. It might not be able to poison anyone, but it could stink up the place.

Elena emerged from the shop, smoothing a Band-Aid over the tip of her finger.

"What a lousy place to be bitten." Grady took her hand again, tilting it toward the light over the shop door. "Must have hurt like crazy."

"It did, for a few seconds. It's better now."

Grady was tempted to plant a healing kiss on her finger, but contented herself with a lame pat on the wrist before releasing her hand.

Elena was watching her with a slight smile. "What did you call it, by the way?"

"Oh. A Jerusalem cricket, but I know it's not a cricket. Some creatures are just so peculiar we can't come up with a fitting name."

"We come closer. We call it a *niño de la tierra*, child of the earth. It's because they have faces, I think." Elena looked around the worn planks of the boardwalk. "You didn't kill it, did you?"

"No, but maybe I should have. I wouldn't want it to get in and scare your mother."

Elena laughed. "If it gets in and my mother sees it, that's going to be one terrified little *niño* in the two seconds before Mamá blasts it to bug heaven with her shotgun."

"Who put it here, Elena?" Grady stepped down off the boardwalk and scanned the dirt lining the edge of the street, hoping for distinctive footprints. "Best guess. Hector Acuña? Antonia Herrera's grandson, Manny?"

"Possibly." Elena went to the truck. "Or Rudy Barela. The cousin of the second man to kill himself last spring."

"You sound pretty casual about all this."

"*Ay.* Bullies, Grady. How much power can we give them? It's not like they put a scorpion on my porch."

"Well, they could have. It might have been." Frowning, Grady opened the passenger door to her truck, and Elena slid inside. "You think it was a warning?"

Elena nodded. "Lots of people are more afraid of *niños de la tierra* than they should be. They think they're the souls of unbaptized children, as if our Mother would allow such a cruel thing. Supposedly, if you put a *niño* on a witch's doorstep, you could trap her. She wouldn't be able to leave her house."

"Sheesh. I remember reading something like that in a book on Mexican folklore."

"Stop fretting, Grady." Elena reached through the open window of the truck and patted Grady's face. "I'm out of my house. Either that was a really incompetent little *niño*, or I really am the pious and devout curandera I claim to be. Come on, it's a beautiful night. Don't let this cowardly act spoil it."

Muttering, Grady went around the truck and slid behind the wheel. She opened her glove compartment and tossed the box inside. "Heaven forfend I should *spoil* a night where we hope to see a bloodthirsty, murderous ghost-witch."

Elena laughed again, a light and carefree sound, and Grady turned the truck toward the river.

❖

"Try this one," Elena said. "'This woman is the last of your line. She speaks to you through me.'"

"*Esta mujer es la última de tu línea.*" Grady closed one eye to better engage her mental translator. "*Ella habla a través de mí.*"

"Not bad." Elena sidestepped a snarl of high grass, her features illuminated by the bright moonlight. They had parked Grady's truck close to the river, near the Picacho Bridge, so it wasn't a long walk. Elena had chosen to return to the section of the river where they first met for this night's witch-waiting. "How about, 'You must promise the killing will stop.'"

"Usted debe prometer que la matanza parará." The words rolled off Grady's tongue like Spanish silk.

"You've been practicing." Elena patted Grady's arm approvingly.

"You're a good teacher."

They reached the riverbank and fell silent for a moment, taking in the glittering ribbon wending through the valley. The blasting sun had dipped beneath the west mesa hours ago, leaving the night air cool and fragrant. The moon washed their surroundings in silver light, and Grady caught the flash of Elena's smile.

"Can you say, 'It feels kind of weird to get naked in front of a college professor'?"

"Oh. You mean we're…" Grady turned quickly and studied the river as Elena slipped off her light cotton blouse. "Ah. For some reason, I thought river-sitting had something to do with actually sitting beside a river."

"You may sit wherever you like, of course." Elena kicked off her sandals and slid her shorts down. "But as you know, I prefer my rivers up close and personal."

"Ah," Grady repeated inanely. Elena, who was naked as the day she was born, more even, stepped down the steep, shallow bank. Grady lifted a hand toward her when she started to slip. Elena steadied herself gracefully and waded into the water, lifting her hands slightly for balance.

Watching her, Grady again felt the odd, pleasant slippage of time this ancient desert valley seemed to inspire. The strange light from the moon outlined Elena's lush and sensuous curves in a way that rendered her image somehow mythic.

"You're Lethe," Grady murmured.

Elena turned back. "Please what?"

Grady thought fast and covered her eyes with her hand. "Would you please sit for pity's sake down, before I go blind?"

Elena's laugh was genuine, if a bit high-pitched. She moved slowly toward the middle of the river, the water rising to cover her hips.

"Lethe," Grady whispered again, unable to take her eyes off Elena. One of the Greek Naiads, Lethe was a river nymph, one of the few to take an interest in the fate of humanity. She appeared to men and women who had died, and offered them a goblet of water from her stream. If the mortal souls drank from Lethe's cup, they would forget all the sorrows of their earthly life, and move on into the afterworld in blissful peace. Elena brought Lethe alive in that moment, two ethereal spirits who sought only to ease the grief of the troubled dead.

Elena settled herself carefully in the center of the stream, the slow current swirling just beneath her chin when she was seated. Grady heard the light lapping of water when she patted the space beside her. "Will you join me?"

Grady tapped her thighs uneasily to buy time, remembering her nightmare. She frowned at the river, searching for snakes. "Uh, *yo no quiero mi muerte.*"

Elena's soft laugh was easier. "You don't want your death? Grady, I don't think even a brainy gringa can drown in three feet of water. And there aren't any sharks in here."

"Where did the piranhas at La Posta come from?"

"Not from the Rio Grande," Elena called patiently.

When did you become such a joyless prude, Wrenn? Grady blinked at the vehemence of her thought. It was the stern inner voice she used on herself when she had to gather her courage. She plucked the shoulders of her T-shirt and slid it over her head. She shoved down her shorts and stepped out of them. That was the best she could do. Her undershirt and her briefs stayed on. She would just drive home wet.

Grady's modesty might be misplaced, but it felt practical and wise. She was here, to some extent, to serve as Elena's bodyguard, and she didn't want the sense of vulnerability that came with being naked. She stepped cautiously into the water, which was pleasantly cool. Walking into a river was nothing like entering a pool. The Grande's current was gentle but primal, sluicing slowly around her ankles with supreme indifference, following the course the gods set for it centuries ago. Grady waded out to Elena, trying to minimize her splashing because it sounded loud in the still night. She lowered herself beside Elena, squeaking softly as the water touched her more sensitive areas.

She could have guessed, to a tenth of a centimeter, the distance between her and Elena. Grady sat on a mild rise in the riverbed so her head rode higher, the water lapping against her shoulders. She was acutely conscious of the lumpy, rocky sand beneath her.

"See? No sharks in here. No tarantulas, no *niños de la tierra*." Elena sat back, resting on her hands, and the swells of her full breasts lifted briefly into the moonlight. She was watching Grady with a mysterious half-smile that at first seemed flirtatious, but then she nodded at the water moving past them. "What do you think?"

Grady pulled her gaze from Elena and tried to focus on the river. Five seconds of that and she couldn't focus anywhere else. "Wow," she said quietly.

"I know."

Elena was right; this was very different from lounging on a distant riverbank. Sitting cross-legged in the middle of the most storied river in the American Southwest, beneath a star-spangled, luminous sky, brought out a certain humility in the human heart. Grady had discovered long ago that the richest moments of her professional life were these brief glimpses of awe, kindled by her love of the past. A small Spanish cemetery, a cave in the foothills of the Organs, this grand and silent river. The sense of wonder that filled Grady now was all she knew of worship, as close as she could come to reverence.

Elena was still watching her. "Have you ever been to Carlsbad Caverns, Grady?"

"I haven't. I'd like to go."

"You should." Elena let her head fall back into the water to wet her long hair. "At the bottom of the deepest cave there's a pillar of stone they call the Rock of Ages. They figure it's over five hundred thousand years old. It was old when our gentle brother Jesus walked on this planet. And now the stone is covered with a kind of lichen that absorbs light. You know what they used to do when the Caverns first opened, on the walking tours?"

"Digame," Grady said. "Tell me."

"At the end of this long walk through the caves, everyone would gather near the Rock of Ages. And then the lights were turned off."

Grady smiled, imagining it.

"My grandmother described what it was like, how dark it is a thousand feet underground," Elena continued. "That kind of blackness is alive, she said. It touches your face. But then, out of that stark, deep midnight, in all that silence, this ancient stone pillar began to glow. It's a muted, shadowy green, a subtle light. And then there was quiet music—a recording of a beautiful tenor voice singing the hymn. Do you know what the people who were watching did then, many of them? At least the adults."

"They cried," Grady said.

"That's right." Elena looked at her in surprise. "How did you know?"

"It's what I'd do, I think."

"Yes, me, too." Elena leaned back and let her feet play with the current. "It's just being in the presence of something so profoundly ancient. Such powerful feelings must come up."

"You said they used to turn off the lights at the Rock of Ages." Grady rocked with an eddy in the current. "They don't anymore?"

"No. My grandmother said they stopped doing it after World War Two broke out. Because people would just sob."

"I don't doubt it." If Grady gave up every vice she ever had and lived a pure life, maybe some god somewhere would let her sit with Elena Montalvo in the Rio Grande for eternity and listen to her stories.

Grady's body had adjusted to the mild chill of the water. Like Elena, she rested back on her hands to accommodate the easy push of the current. She allowed herself the fancy of feeling the cool flow trickling through her ribs and bathing her heart, washing years of dredge from its sore and weary walls.

She watched Elena's profile, silvered in the moonlight. Just as the ageless waters of the Grande were cleansing Grady, just as Lethe soothed the suffering of the dead, this curandera was bringing her back to life. It was a grandiose and shamelessly romantic thought, but Grady let it stand. Then she remembered she wasn't here for romance; she was supposed to be looking out for Elena.

Grady tuned her ears tightly to the quiet night air, which suddenly seemed too quiet. She braced herself to hear the opening snarls of Llorona's fearsome wail, but a more prosaic warning signal reached her—the far-off sound of a passing car.

This section of the river was not so remote that traffic was unheard of, even at this time of night. But cars were rare—and they didn't usually come to a stop in the middle of the bridge spanning the water. Grady twisted and looked back at the bridge, frowning.

"What is it?" Elena asked.

"Do you recognize that car?"

"Grady, I can hardly see that car." Elena squinted. "Are you sure it's not a van?"

"Too far to tell." Grady's frown deepened when a weak light ignited from the vehicle's interior and played out over the surface of the river. She and Elena were much too distant to be detected by a flashlight, but the driver's effort made her nervous. She considered and rejected the possibility that it was a police patrol car. A cop would have used his cruiser's powerful searchlight.

After a few seconds, the faint beam switched off and the vehicle continued over the bridge and down the road. Grady still couldn't get a sense of its size. It could have been a van, it could have been a blue truck. Her pulse didn't return to normal until the headlights faded in the distance.

"The hang-up calls have stopped," Elena said.

"What?"

"The hang-up calls have stopped."

Grady summoned her patience and tried to be more specific. "What hang-up calls, Elena?"

"They'd gotten worse in the last few weeks." Elena rested the back of her head in the water and her dark hair drifted with the current. "Someone calls my shop, and they don't speak after I say hello. They're just quiet for a few seconds, and then they hang up."

"Haven't you traced the number?"

"Mamá refuses to have any phone in the house but the one she bought in the stupid eighties, so we can't trace anything." Elena shrugged. "What can I say? My mother surrounds herself with the familiar and the safe."

"But why haven't you mentioned these calls before?"

Elena scowled up at her. "Hey, don't take that hectoring tone with me, Grady. I'm only saying something now because they've stopped calling. Maybe we've seen the worst of the hassles these men have the *cojones* to think up. Maybe they're backing off."

"Elena, one of them ran us off the road less than a week ago."

"Well, maybe that shook them up as much as it did us. They know I know their names. Maybe they're scared we'll call the cops."

"The cops you don't want to call." Grady tried not to sound skeptical. "One of those men put that damn box on your porch tonight. You really think they're backing off?"

Elena was silent. Then she sighed and sat up, pushing the river past slowly with her hands. "No. I know better. These men wouldn't care if we called the whole state patrol. They've got nothing to fear from the police."

"You worried me there, for a moment." Grady shifted in the water, trying to see her face. "I have to know you're taking all this real seriously, Elena. If you're starting to blow this off as no big deal—"

"I'm not, I promise you." Elena sounded despondent. "It's just that you seem to worry about me, a lot." She reached up, water cascading down her bare arm, and swept cool, wet fingers across Grady's brow. "Look, your forehead was smooth two minutes ago, and now it's all lined and tense again."

Grady took Elena's hand before it could disappear into the water. The gesture felt so automatic as to be preordained.

"It's just that I would like to be more to you than a source of worry." Elena swallowed visibly. She spoke so softly Grady had to lean closer to hear her. "It's hard to want to be closer to a friend when you're responsible for someone driving her into an irrigation ditch. But it's what I want, Grady. To be closer to you."

There it was, as artless and natural an invitation as Grady had ever received. She turned toward Elena and slipped her free hand beneath the cool curtain of her hair to cup the back of her neck. The first meeting of their lips was warm, sensual and sweet—for the few seconds it lasted. Grady opened her eyes to discover Elena had not closed hers yet, and they stared at each other in bug-eyed puzzlement. Grady laughed into Elena's mouth and Elena laughed into hers, and then the kiss was on again, in earnest this time.

It probably wasn't the most sophisticated kiss the river had ever witnessed, because Grady was out of practice and Elena seemed to be too, but it was a really good kiss. Friendly and warm and a little tentative at first. Then rich and happy. Grady felt the first small flash of open desire go off in her sex.

What are you doing? Grady's inner voice was incredulous this time, and her lips stilled against Elena's.

Suddenly Grady was kissing Leigh again, that last, formal, heartbreaking peck as they parted for good at the airport. She was kissing Max's pudgy, sticky cheek the morning of their last hike. *And you're suddenly willing to risk caring that much again? Two years of loneliness is adequate payment for that moment of tragic distraction? What are you doing?*

Grady resisted that voice, hard, but it wouldn't shut up, and she lifted her head. She let go of Elena's fingers and slid her hand out from beneath her hair.

"What?" Elena asked softly, searching her face. "What are you doing?" And that finished Grady for the night.

"I'm sorry, Elena. I don't think we should do this."

"Oh." Elena sat up. "I see." She sounded calm, even accepting. She had no further questions. They sat together quietly for a full minute, the river pushing gently against their bodies.

Then Elena stood. She lifted herself out of the water slowly, as if not wanting to splash too much. It was the only time Grady had ever seen Elena move in a way that wasn't graceful. The careless ease with her body was gone. She waded clumsily toward the shore and stepped out of the river before Grady could find her voice again.

"Elena? It's not you. Honestly."

"Of course it isn't me." Elena stepped into her shorts. "Could you look away, please?"

Grady did, hating herself. "Do you understand? At all?"

"I do." Elena was silent as she pulled on her clothes. Then she stood still on the bank and folded her arms across her chest, her hands cupping her elbows. "I know you've had terrible sadness in your life, Grady. I know you need to take care of yourself, now. But…that wasn't easy for me. Do you think it's easy to lay your heart open at someone's feet like that?"

"I know it's not." Grady's throat ached.

"Good." Elena nodded once, then turned to walk back toward the road.

"Hey?" Grady clambered quickly to her feet, not caring about splashing. "Where are you going?"

"My home isn't too far to walk." Elena kept going.

"It's a good three miles," Grady called. "Elena, you shouldn't be walking around alone out here!"

"Go home to your nice bed, gringa," Elena said, just as she'd said on the first night they met. "I'll be fine."

"Elena!" Grady yelled. She waded the distance to the riverbank as fast as she could in sluggish current and bare feet. "Damn it, you wait for me!"

By the time Grady threw on her clothes, found her keys, and made it back to her truck, Elena was a distant white speck stepping onto the dirt road. Grady revved the engine higher than necessary and took off after her, gravel spraying beneath the wheels. Elena's figure got larger in the dusty glow of the headlights. Grady moved close behind her and stuck her head out the side window.

"I said I was sorry," she called. Elena said nothing and kept walking. "Elena! You're being childish! Let me give you a ride home."

"Go away, Grady." Elena turned her head, but she didn't look back and she didn't stop walking. Her damp hair looked tousled and wild against the white of her blouse. "I told you I'm fine."

Grady heard tears in Elena's voice, and she sagged in her seat. Elena trudged another fifty yards, outlined in the headlights, the truck inching slowly behind her, before Grady could think of anything else to say. She stuck her head out the window again. "I promise we don't have to talk!"

Elena didn't seem to consider that assurance worth comment. She kept walking.

So that's how Elena Montalvo got home that night—slowly, on foot, for three miles, outlined by the headlights of a small battered truck that followed close behind her. Grady actually considered the folly of stepping out of the truck, lifting Elena onto one shoulder, hauling her bodily back to the truck's bed, and dumping her in. She didn't attempt this for two reasons. First, Elena would fight like a crazed wildcat if her plea for privacy was ignored. And second, Grady had not earned the right to assert herself as Elena's protector. Of the two of them that night, Elena had displayed more courage.

She followed Elena into Mesilla. The village was silent and still in the lush moonlight, except for the stubborn curandera who crept through the twisting streets and the miserable anthropologist driving slowly behind her. Finally, Elena reached the boardwalk in front of her shop. She stepped up onto it, pulled her keys from her pocket, opened the door, and closed it behind her without looking back once.

Grady idled the truck in front of the shop. Through the window, she could see the light over the stairway go on. Then it went off, and a window on the second floor lit up. Only then could she pull away gradually, shaking a little in her wet clothes. As the truck rolled past the shop, she thought she saw a figure appear in the upstairs window, and she braked quickly. She craned her head out of the truck to look back, but the light upstairs went off, leaving the storefront quiet and dark.

Grady went home.

CHAPTER SEVENTEEN

*T*he *heart wants what it wants.*
It's one of the hardest lessons I've had to learn, Mother.
No matter how much it hurts, I must embrace that wisdom again tonight. I've never been able to make anyone love me simply by loving them first. Not those few girls in school, whose beauty made me ache inside. They weren't cruel girls, those secret crushes of mine, they were my friends. They might even have chosen to love me as I wished to be loved, if they'd had both the inclination and the power to choose. But their hearts did not choose me, and that wasn't their fault.

I can't be mad at Grady because her feelings for me are not strong enough to overcome her pain. I know she thought I was angry tonight, but mi Diosa, what I felt was great loss and bewilderment. How can I feel so drawn to this woman, and be so wrong about her attraction to me? I've touched some part of Grady Wrenn, I know I have. But when I finally found the courage to reach for her, she turned away. I had been so certain that our time was right, sure that tonight was meant to be our beginning. That it was my turn, at last, to experience the kind of love You seem to grant everyone but me.

I feel myself slipping into self-pity, my Goddess, and my spirit rises up to rebel against it. My mother gave in to feeling sorry for herself years ago, and that indulgence has crippled her more surely than any disease.

Do You remember when I was eighteen, the night I sat beside the river and pledged my life to Your service? I accepted, all those years ago, that such a life might have to be a solitary one. Tonight, I reach for that gentle acceptance again. Help me surrender futile dreams, Diosa, so I can focus on the good You want me to do in the world.

And please, comfort Grady in her loneliness. It's like she was in the river with me, and she started to float away. I grabbed her and tried to hold her close, but she left me, drifting away on her own sad current. I pray she someday finds someone, even far downstream, who can anchor her restless wandering and bring her peace.

Maria. Maria is the River Walker I must reach, somehow. Without Grady's help, if need be. Keep me strong, Sweet Mother. Send Your most errant daughter to me, and let her hear me. Give me the wisdom to do Your will. Lead us all home by Your path.

CHAPTER EIGHTEEN

G rady didn't go to the police to defy Elena's wishes. She went to the police because Elena wouldn't return her calls, and she was worried about her. She had no way of knowing if other little gift boxes had appeared on Elena's front walk, or if a blue truck was following her the nights she went to the river alone. If Grady couldn't be with her, she had to find another way to provide Elena protection.

Technically she didn't go to the police at all, because Mesilla was too small for a police force. She pulled up to a square, one-story cinderblock building bearing a sign reading MESILLA MARSHALS DEPARTMENT—"PROTECTING YOUR HISTORY, TODAY."

The air conditioner within was cranked to an arctic coolness. Should her own a/c conk out, Grady resolved that she would rob a convenience store in order to be taken here. It seemed to be a slow day for crime in Mesilla; most of the seats in the waiting area were empty. She took off her sunglasses and approached the young woman sitting behind the wire-meshed glass screen, who didn't look up immediately. Grady listened to the faint murmuring in the back offices, a blend of English and Spanish, until the receptionist finally offered a wan smile.

"Hello. What can we do for you today?"

"Hello," Grady said pleasantly. "I'd like to file a restraining order against Hector Acuña."

"Well, you wouldn't do that here. You'd go—" The girl's eyes widened. "Do you mean Deputy Marshal Acuña?"

"Yes, that's who I mean."

"Oh." She lifted the phone on her desk. "Would you mind sitting down for a minute?"

"Sure." Grady figured she wouldn't wait long, and she was right. A large man in a beige uniform bearing a five-pointed star badge on his chest emerged from an office less than a minute later. He pushed through the waist-high hinged wooden gate and extended a hand to Grady.

"Good afternoon, ma'am. I'm Sergeant Oscar Telles."

"Grady Wrenn, Sergeant."

He glanced at her left hand. "Please come back, Miss Wrenn."

"Dr. Wrenn." Grady followed the big man through the warren of cubicles behind the front desk. She glanced into each of them as they passed. Judging by the uniforms, the Mesilla Marshals Department boasted half a dozen deputies, all male. One younger officer sat on a desk, deep in conversation with a second man seated behind it. Both looked up and studied her keenly as she went by. Grady couldn't be positive, but the seated deputy bore a powerful resemblance to one of the men she had seen near Elena's shop. She hadn't caught much of a look at the driver who ran them off the road, but it was a safe bet this guy was Acuña.

"Please, sit down." The sergeant closed the door of his office and held a chair for Grady. She sat, a little amused. She hadn't been the recipient of such courtly courtesy in years. Telles didn't look old enough to be indoctrinated in old-school chivalry. Balding and too grand of girth to be on foot patrol, Telles lumbered around behind his desk and sat in a wheeled chair with a great creaking of springs. The wall behind him was dotted with framed photographs of the sergeant posed with local celebrities, few of whom Grady recognized. Then she blinked. There was one photo of Telles standing with the actor who played Mr. Rogers, his jowly face lit with obvious delight. Grady liked him a little better for it.

"Our girl tells me you have a complaint against Deputy Marshal Acuña." Telles opened a memo pad and clicked a ballpoint pen. "Is that right?"

"That's correct. He ran me off the road on July sixth."

"He ran you off the road." Telles wrote for a long time, then looked up. "Where was this?"

"On the back road that leads to Manuel Herrera's pecan orchard." Grady saw the flicker in Telles's eyes at the mention of Maria's first victim.

He kept writing. "Tell me what happened."

"My friend and I were coming back from meeting with Antonia Herrera. Her grandson, Manny, was also in the house. I believe he called Acuña, who smashed into my truck, twice, and ran us into an irrigation ditch."

"He was in his patrol car?"

"No. A large blue truck."

"Well." The sergeant looked up. "To my knowledge, Deputy Marshal Acuña doesn't own a blue truck."

"I believe it belongs to a friend of his." Grady summoned the name of the cousin of the second man to commit suicide last spring. "Rudy Barela."

Telles frowned and resumed scribbling. "And who was this friend who was with you?"

"Her name is Elena Montalvo." Grady saw that flicker go off in his eyes again.

Telles laid down his pen. He studied his notes for an inordinately long time. "You say this happened on July sixth, Dr. Wrenn. That was more than a week ago. How come you didn't report this right away?"

"I wanted to be sure about the identity of the driver." Grady figured that was close enough to the truth. "I believe Hector Acuña is one of a group of men in Mesilla who've been harassing Elena and her mother."

"But this blue truck." Telles ran a beefy finger over a line in his notes. "You didn't get the license number?"

Grady summoned patience. "No."

"No license number." Telles underlined the words in his notes. "Were you or Miss Montalvo injured?"

"We easily could have been. This wasn't an isolated event, Sergeant. Someone shot out the window of Elena's shop in June."

"Did anyone bother to report that back—"

"You're hearing a report now." Grady warned herself to slow down. She was too tired to mince words, but she needed this man's help.

"So can I ask how come Miss Montalvo isn't here with you today? You say she's the one being harassed."

"Elena doesn't have a great deal of faith in law enforcement. I'm hoping you'll prove her wrong." Grady glanced toward the door. "I thought I saw Mr. Acuña down the hall. We can ask him about this directly."

"Yes, Hector Acuña is here today." Telles wrote some more notes. "He came in even though I told him he didn't have to. He was out real late last night, looking for that little girl who went missing over off Guadalupe. We found her this morning. She's okay. You want some coffee, Dr. Wrenn?"

Damn. He'd found her weak spot. Well, coffee would ensure she'd be here a while, at least he wasn't dismissing her outright. "I would, thanks."

"Me too. I was out late myself." The sergeant lifted himself from his creaking chair. "Give me just a minute."

Grady closed her burning eyes as she waited. So Acuña searched all night for a lost child, and still came in to work the next day. She was willing to concede Telles's non-subtle point that the man wasn't a complete monster, but anyone who threatened Elena was far too monstrous for Grady.

She had driven through Mesilla's cemetery on her way

here, on the off chance of finding Elena scrubbing headstones. There had been no sign of her. She hadn't wanted to leave the graveyard. Its desolate loneliness had suited her mood. "Elena," she whispered. She sat up quickly as the door opened.

At first she thought Sergeant Telles had dropped twenty years and fifty pounds. The young officer carrying a steaming cup of coffee was the man Grady had seen sitting on a desk, talking to Hector Acuña.

"Uh, Sergeant Telles got called away. He asked me to bring you this and...finish things up."

Luckily, Grady took her coffee black and strong, as such niceties as cream weren't offered. She watched the deputy sit carefully behind the large desk and lift the memo pad to read Telles's notes. He was short and rather skinny; his uniform looked too big. He was trying hard to grow a full mustache and not having much success.

"So...I guess you didn't get the license plate of this truck that hit you?"

"My name is Dr. Wrenn, Deputy. And you are?" This guy was about the age of Grady's students, so the patient reproof in her tone came naturally.

"Oh, sorry. I'm Larry Ortiz. Uh, Deputy Marshal Larry Ortiz." He actually stood up behind the desk and extended his hand. Grady shook it courteously, and he sat again. "So...is there some reason you didn't come in and report this until now?"

Grady rubbed the back of her neck. "I've already been down this road with Sergeant Telles, Deputy. I haven't seen any indication that he intends to do anything about this, so I'm not sure why I should repeat myself. He didn't even stick around long enough to ask the same questions twice personally."

"Oh, no, that's not true. He's concerned." The deputy scooted his chair closer to the desk, looking earnest. "Sergeant Telles recused himself, just now. You know what that means? He knew he shouldn't finish this interview himself, because you said Rudy might be involved." He tapped the memo pad. "Rudy Barela? He's Oscar's—he's Sergeant Telles's cousin. So it's like he might have a conflict of interest."

Elena was right, Grady thought, *Mesilla is a small town.* Apparently, its chief law enforcement officer had also lost a relative to Llorona. Rudy's cousin Jaime would have been Telles's cousin, too.

"Did you get a look at the driver at all?" Ortiz was immersed in notes again.

"Just a glimpse. I believe the driver is the officer I saw you talking to earlier, Deputy. I definitely heard him. After he hit us, before he took off, he screamed 'death to the witches.'"

Ortiz looked uncomfortable. He touched a line on the pad. "Elena Montalvo. She was with you, huh?"

"That's right." Grady thought his tone had softened a little when he spoke the name.

"But she's okay?"

"The last I heard. What action is going to be taken in this matter, Deputy Ortiz? I believe Elena and her mother are in danger, and I need to know what will be done about this."

"Well, Sergeant Telles is talking to Hector now. He'll know better what to do after that. Um, let me get your contact information? In case he has questions later."

Grady supplied her numbers woodenly. She stood, giving the untouched coffee a look of regret. "Please tell the sergeant I expect to hear from him very soon."

"Dr. Wrenn?" Deputy Ortiz stood too and fumbled in his chest pocket. "I went to school with Elena. I was a couple of years behind her." He pulled out a business card and wrote on it, then passed it to Grady. "You or Elena could call me, any time. If for some reason you can't get through on our other lines."

Grady studied him. "Did you and Elena know each other well?"

"No, no. She was older than me. She really only spoke to me once. But Elena is kind of why I'm a deputy marshal today."

Ortiz folded his hands in front of him, his eyes on the desk. "I was really tempted to drop out of high school when I was a junior. Just didn't see any use for it. Elena talked me out of it. You know what she said?"

"No, but I imagine it took a very long time."

"Nuh-uh, she just said six words." He smiled. "'Quitting school would be stupid, Larry.' That's all she said, and that was it. I changed my mind, right there. And it's a good thing. You can't be a marshal unless you've got a high school diploma." Ortiz looked up at Grady, his face slightly red. "Tell Elena I said hello from Larry. Okay?"

"I will, Larry." Grady found a smile for him as she pocketed his card. "And I'll call, if anything comes up."

She made her way back through the warren of cubicles, keeping a sharp eye for the one she wanted. She heard Hector Acuña before she saw him. He and Sergeant Telles had their chairs pushed together near the far wall of his cubicle, and they were engaging in an intense, whispered conversation.

Grady waited in the doorway until Acuña looked up, his face flushed. The sergeant didn't look happy to see her, either. She reached into her breast pocket and pulled out the small box Elena had found on her porch. She tossed it onto Acuña's cluttered desk. "I think you dropped this, Hector."

She held his gaze for a moment, then walked out of the building and into the baleful sunlight, fumbling for her sunglasses. She knew she would drive by Elena's shop on her way home, like a lovelorn teenager hoping for the small comfort derived from glimpsing a face through a window.

Chapter Nineteen

G rady cleared her throat while she waited for the beep. She tried for an upbeat, casual tone. "Elena, hey. Just checking in with you again. You might have tried to return my calls today, but I was knee-deep in student conferences. Sylvia mentioned she hasn't heard from you for a while, either. She and Cesar and Janice say hello. They're still hoping you might be willing to help them out with their project."

Grady was shameless. If she could guilt Elena into picking up by implying she was neglecting her promise to her students, she was craven enough to try it.

"You know Cesar and Sylvia's wedding is coming up this weekend, right? I don't know if you still plan to go, but they sure want you to be there. We don't have to talk if we see each other. I promise I'll hide under a pew on the other side of the church, if you want. Heh." Grady's brow was dotted with flop-sweat. "I don't have to go to the reception, if you'd rather I stayed clear. Just say the word."

Grady sighed harshly and slid down the wall, to sit cross-legged on her generic carpet. "Elena, just say any word. Tell me to fuck off, if that's what you really want, but this silence is flat-out killing me. I don't know how to—"

An electronic shriek went off in her ear, and she nearly dropped her phone. She heard a great clattering, and a woman's voice muttering curses in Spanish. "Elena?"

"Do I sound like my daughter, you stupid gringa?"

The voice was older, the accent stronger. "Inez? Is something wrong?"

"Everything is wrong. How do I turn off this *pinche* answering machine?"

Grady waited until the echoing she heard on the line finally snapped off. "I think you found the right button."

"No thanks to you." Elena's mother had stopped shouting, but her voice was low and tense. "I got nothing to thank you for, Grady Wrenn. You said you would take care of Elena. What happened to your promise to me?"

"Inez, I've been trying to get Elena to talk to me for days. She won't return my—"

"What, do you think we have moved? Do you think we have packed up this house that has been in my family forever and moved into one of the big mansions on Alameda? You know where Elena lives! You know where she works! Why do you stay away?"

Inez was trying for pure righteous indignation, but even through her anger Grady heard the anxiety in her voice.

"I haven't come by her shop because…" Grady raked a hand through her hair. She had come by Elena's shop, at least a dozen times, but always driving. Sometimes she caught a glimpse of Elena through the wide window, just a flash of her behind the counter or reaching up to one of the wall shelves. She couldn't bear to face Elena until she could convince her to talk to her. If those beautiful eyes stared at her with flat rejection, if she ordered her out of the shop, Grady didn't think her bruised heart could take it.

"Because why?"

"Because I don't think she'd speak to me, Inez." Grady got to her feet and began to pace her small living room. "Tell me what's happening."

"What's happening is my daughter has turned into a little *bruja* who won't tell me anything. She goes out every night, even though I beg her to stay home. She won't tell me where she's going, or why she won't talk to you. Tell me why she won't talk to you!"

Grady paused, looking out the window at the lowering sun. *Your daughter won't talk to me because I kissed her, and that was the closest, most loving moment I've had in years, and still I turned her away.* Somehow, she doubted that this explanation would either placate or satisfy Inez. "It's a long story."

"That is what she says!" Inez sputtered incoherently, then managed to lower her voice. "Trouble is coming, Grady. And we are all alone."

"Inez, listen to me." Grady fumbled in her pocket and drew out a small card. "I went to the Mesilla marshal's office. I spoke to a deputy who knows Elena. His name is Larry Or—"

"Stop wasting my time! No stupid deputy is going to help us."

"This one might. Larry Ortiz knew Elena in high school, and he thinks highly of her. He gave me his number, and I want both of you to have—"

"I don't care what he gave you." Inez was crying now, angry, reluctant tears. "Those men are all in it together. They all hate us. I can't believe a big educated college teacher like you can be so dumb to think they would do anything."

"Inez." Grady closed her eyes. "Believe me, I want to help. Tell me what to do."

Inez didn't answer. The sobs rolled out of her now, and Grady could only listen to her harsh and helpless weeping. Finally, she heard Inez blow her nose, and the clatter of her lifting the phone again. "I'm the stupid one, for believing any outsider would help us. Maria trusts only her daughters. She will punish us for bringing in strangers like you."

Grady leaned her forehead against the cool glass of the window. "You still have my number, right? Will you promise to call me? If anything at all happens, I want you to call."

"Oh, sure I will." Inez sniffed. "I'll call you. The minute the mob pitches their burning torches into our shop, I'll run right to this phone and call you. We can have a nice little chat. Then you can come rushing over here just in time to toast marshmallows over our smoking bodies." She slammed down the phone.

Grady stood looking out her window. The view caught a corner of the Mesilla Valley, where the setting sun cast the desert in a warm red glow. It was a postcard image of a benign and beautiful land, surely blessed by heaven and watched over by all the saints. Grady watched until the sun sank over the western hills and the land went dark.

❖

Dr. Lassiter phoned two nights later, her voice clipped and formal. "Dr. Wrenn? May I ask what you could possibly be doing at your office at this hour? It's well after midnight."

Grady checked her watch. "Just finishing up that syllabus for you, ma'am. Sounds like you're working late tonight yourself."

"I am sensibly home and ensconced in my cushioned recliner, thank you, as any civilized woman should be in the middle of the night." There was a pause, and in that short space of time Grady heard Dr. Lassiter's considerable sensitivity and restraint. She had known Grady long enough to know when not to push into private territory. Her tone remained businesslike.

"I can't possibly make time to review your syllabus until the middle of next week, at the earliest. Go home, Grady. Try to rest."

"Yes, ma'am."

She hung up, and her eyes fell on the calendar over her desk, featuring fair reproductions of Georgia O'Keeffe's paintings. She noted the date. Sleep would prove even more elusive tonight than most nights, but she would try to abide by her mentor's command.

Grady's truck trundled across the sleeping campus and through the silent streets of Las Cruces. She turned up the driveway leading to the condominium complex that contained her supposed home. Her unit was sparsely furnished, but included the queen-sized bed that Grady loathed on sight. She pictured it waiting for her, that useless, mocking waste of a mattress. Then she braked, backed down the driveway, and turned west, toward the Rio Grande.

Most nights found Grady at the river eventually. It didn't matter which part of it she tried to search, she never saw Elena. She sometimes bargained with Elena's goddess, the one Grady didn't believe in, through these long, lonely drives. *You can keep me up all night, in exchange for Elena being safe. If I see her, I promise I won't try to talk to her. I'll just park where I can keep an eye out to make sure no one bothers her. You could at least intervene enough to make Elena return one of my goddamn calls.*

Either her blasphemy displeased the goddess or she didn't exist, because Elena never called and Grady never found her. She pulled up by a stretch of the river she hadn't visited before, at the far edge of the valley. The water that flowed past this spot was leaving Mesilla and New Mexico behind, and she doubted Elena would choose to go any farther in her quest for Maria.

She got out of her truck, flexing her shoulders to loosen the tightness in her neck, and began to walk. The quiver of anxiety went off in her stomach before she'd gone ten feet, another price Grady paid in her search for Elena. The fear that she might hear the wailing of Llorona begin at any moment was constant during these night walks. She wanted so badly to hold Elena's hand in her own that her palm itched.

It was a barren, featureless stretch of the river, with no trees and only patches of knee-high grass and brambles to break the monotony of the dirt bank. Grady walked carefully, keeping an eye out for a small pack horse or Elena's decrepit car. Either would be easier to spot than the curandera herself, if she was river-sitting.

A bomb of bells went off over Grady's heart and she

staggered, clutching her shirt. It was her phone, she knew that, but her pulse shot skyward anyway. She had set the volume as high as it would go so she wouldn't miss a call from Elena. Breathing hard, Grady yanked her phone out of her breast pocket and fumbled with it, trying to open it before it went off again. She stared at the display. It wasn't Elena's number. She didn't know this number, and she didn't know who else would call her at two o'clock in the morning. "Hello," she snapped.

"Grady?"

The voice was cultured and soft. Grady remembered the date, and the strength went out of her legs. She sat heavily on the riverbank, and watched the implacable dark ribbon of water flow by. "Hello, Leigh."

She heard the distant click of a lighter, and then a long, slow exhale of smoke. "Were you asleep?" Leigh asked.

Grady smiled sadly. "I think you know me better than that."

"Yes, I do." Leigh's voice was fond. "I can't sleep tonight either."

Grady closed her eyes. "Are you with your parents?"

"I'm visiting them for a week, yes."

Grady could picture Leigh in her childhood home in Portland, sitting curled in an armchair before the bay window, her fingers combing back her fine blond hair. She liked Leigh's folks and wanted to ask her to give them her regards, but the words died in her throat. She doubted the mention of her name would be pleasant for anyone in Leigh's family, especially today.

"I'm living in Seattle now." Leigh coughed, a short, harsh bark. Her voice was slightly rougher than Grady remembered it. "I took that opening at UW. It's working out pretty well. How about you?"

"He would have been six today."

Leigh was silent. Grady wondered if there was some small mercy in having a child die on his birthday. Most parents had two excruciating days to survive each year; she and Leigh had only one.

"We'll visit his grave in the morning. Mom says the butterfly bush we planted is beautiful."

Grady couldn't find any words.

Leigh exhaled smoke again, long and slow. "I called tonight because I wanted three things," she said at last. "Are you listening?"

"Always."

"I wanted to hear your voice again. You do have the most extraordinary voice, Grady. It can still make me feel calm, quiet inside. You remember all the times I told you that?"

"I remember."

"Second, I need to know that you're all right. We haven't spoken in several months, and we may never talk again. I can't say good-bye to you, I can't move on, unless I know you're okay."

"I am, honey." Grady cradled her phone against her cheek. "I will be, I promise."

"You always keep your promises. I'm counting on that."

Grady watched the river wend its way gently out of the valley until Leigh spoke again.

"And down to my bones, I want you to be happy, Grady. You deserve it. Of all the things I've ever said to you, before we lost…and after, that's the message I want you to take to heart. I said things that hurt you, and I want you to forget them all. When you remember me, I want you to remember only my wish for your happiness."

"I will. Thank you, Leigh." There was something in the sensation of smiling while tears ran down her face that captured Grady's feelings for this woman perfectly. She was still keenly attuned to every nuance in Leigh's voice, and she meant what she was saying. Grady also heard the farewell in her tone, and knew that this would be the last time they spoke.

"I'll never regret them," Grady said. "The years we spent together."

"Me either, babe. Please take good care. Good night."

There was a pause, then a small click, and she was gone.

Grady folded her phone carefully and slipped it back into her breast pocket. She rested her elbows on her knees and watched the small eddies at the river's edge, carrying twigs and grass away from the bank. Her tears continued to fall easily, and that was new for Grady. She remembered how her eyes burned the last time she had cried, the miserly tears she had shed lying next to Elena. She touched her breast, remembering the soft circling of Elena's hand at the base of her throat. She didn't understand how that night in Elena's arms loosened the vapor lock that usually gripped Grady's throat when she cried, but she was grateful for it now. Saying good-bye to Leigh and Max again rated a few tears.

"I don't think you're there," she said quietly to the night. "But Elena does. And Leigh does, or at least she used to. She told me she had Max baptized, and his memorial service was held in her parents' church. So thank you, for looking after Leigh. Thank you for looking after Max." Grady lowered her head, and her voice dropped to a whisper. "Please, take care of Elena. Please, man. Don't let anything happen to her."

After a few minutes, Grady climbed stiffly to her feet. She slid her wallet out of her back pocket and opened the flap that carried her family pictures. She had three of them—one of her parents, a posed photo of Leigh, and one of herself and Leigh together, tickling Max.

Grady replaced the other pictures and studied the one of Leigh for a long time. Her smile was polite and rather stiff, but her genuine kindness was clear in her eyes. Grady stepped to the edge of the bank and dropped the picture into the river, placing her first real love safely into the ancient care of the Grande. She watched the small square swirl away on the slow current, then looked up into the starry sky.

"Happy birthday, buddy," Grady whispered. She headed back toward her truck.

CHAPTER TWENTY

*M*aria will not come to me. Night after night, I search *for her. My prayers to You have become a new rosary, mi Diosa, repetitions of the same plea, over and over. Let me find Llorona before another man dies. Let her hear me. Let the killing stop.*

I'll keep going to the river every night. That's all I can do. I'll trust You to put me in Maria's path. And I admit I would probably leave my house every night, even if You hadn't charged me with the task of finding Maria. Forgive me, Diosa, but I need the time away from Mamá. She grows more afraid, and less reasonable, every day. She knows I will not discuss Grady with her. So she has taken to playing all the messages Grady leaves on our old answering machine, again and again, with the volume turned all the way up. It's partly my fault. I can't bear to erase those messages. They are all I have now of Grady's voice.

It was her three nights ago, at the river, I know it was. I recognized her truck. I ducked down below the surface of the water until she passed. It was only by Your grace that I found the will to do this. It was one of the hardest things I've ever done, and besides, Grady drove so slow I almost drowned.

I can't return her calls, Sweet Mother. Please do not think this is just my pride. All right, don't think this is only my pride. You have pointed out more than once that my stubbornness often leads to grief. But the hang-up calls have started again. The same long silence, before whoever is there slams down the phone. These cowardly calls terrify my mother, and they piss me right off.

I can't bring Grady back into this now. Maybe the River Walker was always supposed to be only our burden, the many generations of daughters of Maria. I don't care what my mother says, it isn't fair to ask Grady to share our danger again. She could have broken her skull when we were chased off the road. She could be shot if one of those pendejos—I'm sorry, Diosa, but You know they are—came around with a rifle. Grady has made sure her students don't take any more risks, but I know she would be willing to face them herself. I can't let that happen.

The tension in Mesilla is growing. I can feel it, like spiderwebs on my face, and so can Mamá. It's been more than a month since the last suicide. I wish I could believe that Maria is finished with Mesilla for another century, but that doesn't feel true to me. Grady needs to stay as far away from us as possible. She might think I need her macha self to protect me, but You know me better. You made me strong, and You made Mamá's shotgun even stronger, if we need it.

Let me find Maria before it comes to that. Please, mi Diosa. Grant Your stubborn, loving daughter that one boon.

Mamá is stirring, I must go to her. As always, I end by asking You to guard Grady's sleep, and please, go with me tonight.

Chapter Twenty-one

I f Grady was very lucky, she could catch a brief nap when she came home from her nightly wanderings, before the clock radio beside her bed blared its alarm. Those naps were deep and dreamless and desperate, as if her body was pulling hard for as much real rest as possible. Grady hoped no more nightmares would ever break through to disrupt that inadequate escape.

And no nightmares did, but a week after she spoke to Leigh for the last time, a dream of uncommon sweetness wended through her exhaustion and touched her sleeping heart. She rarely dreamed of Max at all anymore, and when she did, it was just quick, painful sightings of his hand letting go of her own. But tonight, Max was dancing.

Some vintage Creedence tune was rocking in the background, and Max was doing the delighted spinning-arms jumping thing that constituted quality choreography in his small world. He bounced in circles, his high-pitched yelps of laughter bringing a smile to Grady's lips. She felt it, even asleep. And nothing horrific happened. Max didn't suddenly disappear into a cavernous hole in the floor. He just jumped and spun and laughed.

But Grady recognized the song he danced to: "Bad Moon Rising."

A rattlesnake's deadly buzz cut through the music. Now in the dream herself, Grady blanched at the teeth-rattling hiss that filled her ears. She turned quickly toward Max, but he was gone.

Grady jerked awake and sat up. The clock's glowing green numbers showed it was still fully night, only two a.m. It was her damn phone again. She had left it on the metal filing cabinet beside her bed, set to vibrate, and the clatter could wake the dead. Her heart pounding, Grady snatched it up.

"Grady, another man is dead."

"Who is this? Janice?"

"Yes, it's Janice." She was speaking clearly and fast. "Another man is dead. I just heard it on the news, another drowning."

Grady scrubbed her hand across her eyes.

"They found the body this afternoon. I tried to call Elena just now, to be sure she knew. I think her mother answered. She screamed at me. I'm scared Elena's out there by the river tonight, and if those thugs are looking for her—"

"Thanks for calling me, Janice. You did the right thing." Grady whipped off her blanket. "Stay home. Don't leave the dorm. I'll fill you in when I can."

She snatched her boots and slammed out of her condo thirty seconds later.

By day, the streets of Old Mesilla were slightly shabby, but quaint. By night, at least this night, they seemed secretive and sinister, and Grady raced through the twisting neighborhoods much faster than caution allowed. Speeding and tapping keys was a precarious combination, but she tried twice to reach Deputy Marshal Larry Ortiz as she drove, and was sent straight to voicemail each time. She gave up and flung her phone to the floor of the truck in frustration.

Her stomach soured with the quick adrenaline of alarm, and she couldn't stop cursing herself for the nights she'd let Elena await Maria at the river alone. It took all of her intellectual muscle not to imagine what might be happening to Elena now.

The streets and cracked sidewalks were empty, which was not too unusual, even for a Friday night. But for the lateness of the hour, bright lights burned in the windows of entirely too many houses. Mesilla was awake, afraid and watchful.

Elena's shop and the home she shared with her mother was the only dark building on the block. Grady pulled up fast in front of it and jumped out of her truck before it came to a full halt. She leaped the two steps to the boardwalk and knocked hard on Elena's door. "Elena? Open up!"

The curtain above her twitched. Grady saw a flash and a blast rang out, shocking her stupid. A loud crack sounded at the base of the boardwalk, dust puffing inches from her boots. Grady's heart trip-hammered in her chest. *"Inez!"*

Inez Montalvo swept the curtain aside with the stock of her shotgun, her hair wild and streaming. She looked seriously crazy, and Grady instinctively held up a hand to calm her.

"I'll blast a hole through anyone who comes to my door tonight, *pendejos!*"

"Inez, it's me! Please just calm the fuck down! Where is Elena?"

"They were just here!" Inez clawed back her hair and spat the words down at Grady. "Hector Acuña, and two of his *pinche* friends! They came looking for my Elena!"

Grady's throat went dry. "She's at the river?"

"Just go, gringa!" Inez screamed.

Grady jumped into her truck and tore down the street.

❖

Second only to the ride from Max's memorial service to the cemetery, it was the longest drive Grady had ever endured. She would start with the Picacho Bridge, Elena's most frequent river-sitting site, and work her way south. The three miles to the bridge took an eternity to travel, no matter how hard she gunned it through the dark and sinuous streets.

"Okay," she kept saying, quietly but aloud. Meaning, *Okay, the Grande is a long river.* Acuña and his thugs could search a long time without finding Elena. *Okay, I'm sure she's fine.* The calm in Grady's tone soothed her, kept her focused, and gave her some hope of holding her raw terror at bay.

She veered onto the narrow frontage road running beside the river. Just as the bridge came into sight, Grady's headlights picked up a small horse trotting riderless off the road, reins trailing in the dust, shaking its head in agitation. Grady floored the gas.

The Rio Grande had witnessed more than one macabre death, and it took no particular interest in the violent events unfolding on its bank. Grady saw what was happening in surreal bursts, illuminated by the headlights of the large blue truck parked at a crazy angle near the water.

The rusty light washed over Elena, who was hissing with rage and fighting for her life. The three men must have found her just after she climbed out of the water and donned her clothes. Her blouse was unbuttoned, and her hair lay in wet ropes over her bare breasts. She held a long crooked stick over her shoulder like a bat, and when she swung it full-force at one of the two men closing in on her, he yelped and jumped back.

Grady caught a quick glimpse of the third man, who was younger—Manny Herrera, who had known Elena since he was a little boy, and who was now throwing a noose over a branch of a juniper tree at the edge of the wash of light.

Grady jammed one hand on her truck's horn, sounding its strident alarm in a prolonged blast. She jerked the wheel and sped off the road toward the river, dust boiling into her lights. She ground to a fast stop and jumped out.

The men turned at the horn's blare, but now they faced Elena again, feral dogs locked on cornered prey. Grady could hear Elena's terror in her shaking voice as she screamed curses at them, her hands clenched whitely around the stick she wielded as a club.

That's all Grady had time to see because she was running

full-out, and she kept running even as the larger, uniformed man turned toward her—Acuña. Grady saw him yank a service pistol from his gun belt. He bellowed something, then backed a step because Grady just kept coming. He was able to raise the gun, but Grady ducked and plowed bodily into him, her shoulder hitting him hard and dead-center.

Her momentum was enough to knock him off his feet, and they crashed to the ground with an impact that drove the air from Grady's lungs. She saw the pistol bounce off over the grass into the darkness, and that was a great relief, but she still had to deal with six feet of thrashing, intoxicated, pissed-off idiot. Grady was physically fit and sizzling with adrenaline, but she wasn't Xena, and she grappled desperately with Acuña's flailing arms. He was strong, but judging by the fumes, he was drunk enough to take the edge off his reflexes. He tried to buck Grady off, but she was able to ride him, until his hands closed around her throat.

Grady heard Elena scream her name. Elena ran toward her, but the other man jumped in her path and wrestled her to the ground, yelling for Manny to help him. Rudy Barela was smaller than the brute choking off Grady's breath, but he was wiry and furious, and Elena's desperate struggles couldn't shake him off. Before the spots appeared in her eyes, Grady saw Manny run to Elena with another rope. The blood pounded thickly in Grady's head and she knew, with sick despair, that she was starting to black out.

Incredulous, she realized the starlit sky overhead might be the last sky she would see, and Hector Acuña's hoarse cursing, and Elena's harsh sobs, the last she would hear—until a new sound drifted over the water. It began as a low, snarling cry.

Acuña's hands loosened from around Grady's neck. They stared into each other's eyes, and Grady felt hers widening slowly, just as his did, with growing horror. She was faintly aware that Elena was still screaming, but the other two men had fallen silent.

The rush of blood from Grady's head dizzied her even

through the swelling wave of audible rage sweeping the river, and she fell off Acuña. She lay on her side in the sparse grass, gasping for breath, her arms over her head to try to block Llorona's unendurable shriek. And then she felt Elena's arms around her, pulling her into her lap, Elena's hand pressing her face to her cool breasts.

"You c-can hear her, Grady? She's here?"

Grady could only nod and wrap her arms around Elena's waist and hold on. She thought she had heard Maria's cry before. She thought it was fearsome then. It was the hymn of a church choir in comparison to this night.

"Dios mío!"

She didn't know which of the three men cried those words, but he kept crying them over and over. She made herself lift her head to see their attackers, who seemed all but unaware of her and Elena now. Manny was crouched at the edge of the riverbank, looking around wildly, his hands pressed to his ears. Rudy Barela was inching toward the blue truck, his mouth gaping, his arms raised to defend himself. Acuña seemed frozen on his back like a crab, saliva dripping from his chin.

"Grady, we're safe." Elena had recovered her breath. She spoke to Grady quietly and she was shaking, but she held her with fierce strength. "Maria won't hurt us, *querida.* Just hang on to me."

Manny Herrera was sobbing now. He fell to his knees on the bank and clutched his head. Barela broke and ran for his truck, dropping his keys once, yelling incoherently.

The horrendous wailing went on and on. Llorona's rage was undiluted by grief tonight, and that made her cry immensely more frightening. Grady made a conscious resolve not to wet herself. That was the best she could do, and that was only possible because she was in Elena's arms. Now she could feel only the soul-shriveling terror this spirit inspired in men, but in spite of her fear, she preferred Maria's anger to her wrenching bereavement. Her fury terrified Grady, but her grief broke her heart.

Hector Acuña scrambled to his feet and ran for the blue truck, but Rudy Barela was waiting for no one. He cranked the engine to life and spun out, skidding in a reckless circle. Acuña managed to catch up and hurl himself into the truck's bed before it careened off for the frontage road.

"Elena!"

Grady sat up fast. Manny stood in front of them, shaking spasmodically, his hands still clenching his head. Elena kept her from rising, and Grady knew the kid presented no threat any longer. He stared at Elena, the whites showing clearly in his eyes.

"Save me, Elena!" Manny screamed, loudly enough to break through Llorona's cry. "Fuck, she's going to kill—" He ducked hard and staggered, then ran for the road, his gangly legs churning hard.

Grady watched him go, then let Elena pull her back into her arms, because the timbre of Maria's voice was changing now. Her wretchedness and remorse echoed all around them, and Elena cradled Grady until it finally began to fade.

"Is she gone?" Elena whispered.

"Hey." Sanity finally returned to Grady as blessed silence filled the night, and she pushed off Elena's arms so she could see her. "Hey. Are you all right?"

"I am." Elena touched Grady's face. "What about you? That *pendejo* was choking you!"

"It's okay. I'm good." Grady sat up stiffly, marveling at the merciful stillness around them.

"You are? You're sure?" Elena looked at her closely. "Because I need to do something."

"I'm sure."

Elena nodded, let go of her, and got carefully to her feet. Grady watched her walk over to the juniper tree on the riverbank. The rough hangman's noose still dangled over one high limb. Elena reached up and grabbed the noose, her blouse falling open to reveal one breast. Her face grew dark with distaste, and she pulled the rope from the branch. She coiled it in her hands, then turned and threw it hard over the water. Grady joined her, and they watched the rope unfurl and drift slowly away on the Grande's current.

Elena sighed and leaned against Grady, her full curves fitting so naturally against her side that they seemed sculpted together. Grady turned and took her in her arms, and Elena's head rested on the curve of her shoulder with the same light ease. Grady was grateful for her warmth; she was feeling a bit shell-shocked, and if Elena's trembling was any indication, she wasn't alone.

"They won't come after you again." Grady swallowed past the soreness in her throat, her lips in Elena's hair. "They wouldn't dare. You can tell your mother she's safe now, and so are you."

"Thank the Mother of us all for that." Elena squeezed her waist gently. "How did you know to come, Grady? How did you find me?" Grady didn't answer, and Elena lifted her head. "Grady?"

Grady closed her eyes, listening intently. The night wasn't silent anymore. But this new sound wasn't fearsome. It wasn't even ghostly. It came from the river behind them—the quiet, mournful sound of a woman weeping.

A chill went through Grady. "Elena?" She swallowed painfully. "What did you tell me about Llorona's cry? You said it's loudest, most powerful, when she's far away. And if her voice is very soft, then she…"

Grady opened her eyes, and Elena was looking past her, over her shoulder. Her eyes were enormous, and her voice was faint.

"G-Grady? I think you better turn around."

Chapter Twenty-two

It was La Llorona's banal normality that stunned Grady most, at least at first. That and the fact that she was a dead person floating above the Rio Grande, which made her normality discordant in itself. Grady hadn't expected Maria to appear even remotely human, but she had so obviously been alive, once. She was small, almost delicate, her thin shoulders hunched beneath gray, shapeless robes that fell to her ankles. She wore a tattered hood that concealed her face, for which Grady was grateful. From the angle of her head and the stillness of her posture, Maria seemed intent on Elena. Her chest hitched with another long, low sob.

Elena stood beside Grady, holding her hand tightly. Grady risked a quick look at her face. Elena was watching her ancestor with fascination, and her eyes were filling with tears.

Maria hovered inches above the river's mild ripples, about fifteen feet from the bank. Her body gave off a kind of murky luminescence, a dark, throbbing shimmer as different from the halo of an angel as it was possible to be. By that dim gray light, Grady could see Maria's feet were bare. They looked bruised and scratched, as if they had walked riverbanks for centuries.

"Grady." Elena grasped Grady's arm. "Speak to her."

Grady tried to clear her aching throat. Her voice emerged as a raw squeak. "Maria?"

"Dónde están mis niños?" La Llorona called softly, and Grady lost any fanciful notion that she was still human. It wasn't just the metallic rasping of her voice, it was the flesh-chilling, alien tone of it, as if the wretched spirit was chanting a mantra from an ancient nightmare. Stammering, Grady repeated the phrase to Elena.

"Where are my children," Elena translated. Her tears were falling freely now. "Go on, Grady. Give her my message."

Grady closed her eyes and found the words. *"Esta mujer es el último de tu línea. Ella le habla a través de mí."* This woman is the last of your line. She speaks to you through me.

And Grady would have remembered the rest of Elena's message, she would have spoken all of it, but then Maria lifted her pale hands and pushed back her hood, revealing her face. The blood drained from Grady's head and she fell to her knees.

Elena gasped too and knelt quickly beside her, but she wasn't looking at Maria. "What is it? Grady, what's wrong?" She seemed startled, but not terrified.

"Don't you *see* her?"

"Yes, I see." Elena stroked Grady's hair, and turned back to the hovering specter in the threadbare robes. "She's so young. Grady, she's no older than me."

Yes, Llorona was young, the age of all the women in the crude portraits lining the walls in Elena's house, probably the same age her descendant, Juana Hidalgo, had been when she cut her wrists and died beside this river. But Grady knew with certainty that while she and Elena might be looking at the same dead witch, they were not seeing the same face.

Maria was deeply and irretrievably insane. Grady had little experience with psychosis, but she needed no formal training to recognize a soul so hopelessly lost in madness. The dead woman's lunacy spilled through her sallow features. The corruption was in her eyes—the yellow, hollow abyss of her gaze, which seemed to stretch toward them as if to drag them into the river. Grady shook in Elena's embrace.

"Tell me what's happening," Elena whispered.

"I'm connected to her." Grady's mouth was dry. "I don't understand how. But I see what's true in her. I see *her*, Elena."

"All right." Elena's hand brushed soothing circles on Grady's back. "What is she telling you?"

Grady made herself get to her feet, and Elena rose with her. She pushed Elena's arms away gently and stepped closer to the river's edge. The white skin stretched over Maria's cheekbones looked parchment-thin. Small cords of muscle stood out in her throat, as if her teeth were grinding constantly. She turned her muddy, tortured gaze on Grady.

Grady summoned all of her courage. *"Dígame,"* she called. Tell me.

After a moment, Maria's bloodless lips parted and her rusty, abraded voice emerged again. She spoke in Spanish, a more antiquated dialect than Elena's, but Grady would have understood her words in Swahili because images came with them. Their shared grief, their shared remorse, allowed Llorona to show Grady flashes of the last night of her earthly life.

It was a night very much like this one, beside a stretch of the river much the same as the water streaming now below the ghost-woman's battered feet. The vegetation of this past riverbank was thicker, and the rain-smell of the creosote sharper and wilder. The Grande itself looked deeper and ran much faster. Unlike tonight, the moon was bloated and noxious overhead.

Grady reached blindly behind her and immediately felt Elena's warm hand slide into her cold one. She pulled her closer, her eyes never leaving the floating apparition.

"Él vino por nosotros!" Maria whispered the words, then cried them, a heartbroken, frightened keening. Grady repeated the sentence to Elena.

"He came for us," Elena said quietly.

Moonlight flashed on the weed-choked riverbank, on the water of the Grande as the terrified mother ran, panting harshly, struggling with her burden. Grady saw it happening through

Maria's eyes. Her lungs burned as Maria's had, her heart pounded as hard in her chest. She heard the screaming of the young boy Maria dragged along by the hand, the fretful wailing of the infant she carried in her other arm. Grady felt Llorona's head turn, and she caught a glimpse of a small girl stumbling far behind them, trying to catch up to her mother and brothers.

"*Él vino por nosotros!*"

"Elena." Grady felt Elena's arm slip around her waist. "She's showing me the murders."

"She's trying to tell you the truth of what happened." Elena held her close. "Easy, *querida*. Breathe slow and deep."

Grady steeled herself. She would see him next, the man chasing them, the father of these three children. The man who planted the seeds of five hundred years of fear and death in this valley. She would have to watch him take the lives of his wife and sons.

What she saw next was unspeakable.

When it was over, Grady couldn't move. She stared at Llorona's terrible, mad eyes, at her mouth yawning open in grief, at her bony hands clutching each other endlessly. Then she forced herself to look away, to turn to Elena and take her in her arms.

Elena rested her hand on Grady's breast, and she looked alarmed. Grady knew her heart was still pounding like a hot piston. "Grady, what did you see?"

Grady's lips were numb, and it took her a moment to form the words. "I saw them die. All three of them, Maria and her two sons."

"Are you all right? You look terrible."

"I saw her little daughter climb the juniper tree. She watched what happened." Grady swallowed. "Did you know that girl's name was Elena?"

"Yes. I know the names of all my grandmothers." Elena touched Grady's face. "Grady, are you sure you're okay? We... we need to get on with this. I don't know how much longer she'll be here."

"Of course." Grady stared down at Elena, savoring the warm reality of her in her arms, knowing she must tell her that her life's mission was based on a lie. She nodded toward the river.

Elena stepped to the edge of the bank. The two young women, one of them centuries older, regarded each other silently. The slump slowly left Elena's shoulders and she stood taller, her hands relaxed at her sides. Maria's features seemed incapable of portraying much besides a kind of poignant madness, but if Grady had to guess at a human emotion, she would have said Maria looked afraid.

"Do you know me, Grandmother?" Elena said. She glanced back at Grady and said the words in Spanish.

"Usted me conoce, abuela?" Grady repeated.

Maria's slight form seemed to flicker in its murky nimbus of light. To Grady's mingled dismay and fascination, that strange thread of understanding that connected her to the long-dead witch was still intact. "She knows you, Elena."

Elena nodded. "I am the last of your daughters. Your line stops with me. You don't have to protect us any longer. So the killings must stop, *abuela.* You must never kill again."

Grady got most of the words out in Spanish, Elena only having to correct her once. She honestly didn't know if Maria heard her message. The floating ghost kept repeating the same mournful word, over and over.

"She keeps saying *perdóneme*, Elena."

"Ay. She asks my forgiveness?" A sigh moved through Elena's body, and she looked back at Grady with real regret. "We must tell Llorona that her forgiveness is not mine to bestow, Grady. I cannot pardon her for taking the lives of so many men. Her redemption is a matter she must take up with her God."

"Perdóneme, hija!" Maria's cracked voice sounded again. Forgive me, daughter.

"She's not talking about the men she's killed, Elena." Grady went to Elena and took her face in her hands. "Listen to me. So much of your story is true. What you've been told about Maria and her husband's abuse is true. The stories all your grandmothers have passed down about the man's violence, his brutal beatings, really happened. I could feel her fear of him, her panic as she ran with her children to the river." She brushed a fresh tear from Elena's cheek with her thumb. "But her husband didn't kill them, sweetheart."

"What?" Elena whispered.

Grady closed her eyes, the scene replaying again in her mind in spite of herself. She couldn't tell Elena about the little boy's frantic struggles as his mother peeled his hands off her arms and cast him into the river—a river deep and fast enough in those days to swallow a child whole. She couldn't bear to relate the details of the infant, wound in its blanket, hurled into the swift current.

"She was convinced she was saving them, Elena. She believed her husband was coming to kill them all. But her mind was gone. He wasn't there. He wasn't anywhere near them. Maria drowned her two sons. Then she had a horrific moment of sanity and realized what she'd done." Grady had to clench her teeth to get past the visceral anguish of that memory. "She followed her children into the river."

"That can't be." Elena looked as dazed and vulnerable as if Grady had struck her physically. "That's impossible. You didn't understand her, Grady."

"I'm sorry, honey. I did understand her." Grady turned Elena toward the river. She stepped behind her and wrapped her arms around Elena's waist, supporting her until she could stand on her own again. "Maria has never appeared to you, or to any of her daughters, because of her shame. She's guilty of killing her children, and she couldn't face you."

Maria's doomed eyes brimmed with tears as she gazed at Elena. *"Perdóneme. Perdóneme, hija!"* Grady realized these were the last words the woman had uttered in life, a despairing plea to the little girl watching her from the spindly branches of a juniper tree.

"Can you do this?" Grady's lips moved in Elena's hair. "Can you forgive her?"

"I d-don't know." Elena's hands on Grady's forearm were cold.

"She was so crazy, Elena. So very sick."

"She murdered her sons."

"Yes."

La Llorona wept quietly, scrubbing her face with the backs of her hands, her thin shoulders quaking. The night was otherwise silent around them, the river so still it seemed nature itself had paused to await Elena's decision.

"Your heart is strong enough for this," Grady whispered into Elena's hair. "I know it is. You think with your amazing heart, so follow it now. I believe in you."

She heard Elena begin to pray. The words left her in a choked whisper. She sounded very much like the first Elena, who had sobbed in the same broken voice as the person she loved most in the world drowned her brothers. That small girl prayed for the soul of her mother. This Elena prayed for the grace to escape generations of conditioning in a single night. Finally, she quieted and rested the back of her head on Grady's shoulder. "Tell her this, please." Elena spoke the words in English, then Spanish, and Grady delivered her message.

"Grandmother. All my life, I have believed in the decency and goodness of your living spirit. Tonight, through the grace of my Goddess, I still do. I believe your madness blinded you. It tricked you. You never would have harmed your children, in your right mind."

Maria lifted her head from her shaking hands, her face still anguished, but a pathetic hope began to dawn in her features.

"I will forgive you, Grandmother, and in my name, you will have the forgiveness of all your descendents. But my mercy comes with a price." Elena lifted her head from Grady's shoulder, and her voice was firm and clear. *"You must never shed mortal blood again. The vengeance of La Llorona must end here, tonight."*

Maria stared at Elena, and with a disquieting twinge, Grady realized the undead murderess was finding the choice difficult. Maria was struggling with whether she could give up the dark pleasures of revenge, the joy of taking human life, in exchange for Elena's forgiveness. Just as Grady was content to consign this diseased spirit to any eternal hell out there, Maria gave Elena a look of such heartbroken, loving maternity that Grady felt tears rise in her eyes.

"Sí, mi Elena." The words were a rusty sigh lost on the light breeze coming off the river. *"Buscaré hombres no más."*

Grady repeated the words.

"I will hunt men no more." Elena pulled Grady's arms tighter around her waist.

The River Walker smiled shyly at Elena. And then she continued her search, without ceremony or farewell. Grady watched the weak dregs of humanity left to the ghost fade from her pale features, until she looked only damned and insane again. The grim gray light around her pulsed with her sorrow.

"Dónde están mis niños?" Maria rasped. Her haunted gaze drifted up the riverbank, and her battered feet carried her slowly upstream. Grady held Elena tightly while her shrouded form dwindled and then was swallowed by the night.

Then Grady held Elena tightly for a long while after that. They were both trembling at first, and a few minutes passed before Elena released a deep sigh and turned in Grady's arms.

"All those generations, Grady. My mother, my grandmother, every daughter in Maria's line. We all believed our destiny was to prove her innocence."

"And all Llorona ever wanted from you was your forgiveness." Grady traced Elena's brow with one finger. "Now you're the daughter who granted her that blessing."

"Yes. She carries such pain." The moonlight revealed the tracks of tears on Elena's face. "At least I was able to offer her that small comfort tonight."

Grady held Elena's face gently in her hands again. "Tonight, I'm hoping you can give me what you gave to Llorona."

"Forgiveness?"

"Comfort." Grady searched Elena's features, needing to be sure this was right for them both. She waited until the lines of Elena's body softened into welcome, and she knew to her core that she wasn't alone in wanting this. She lowered her head and brushed her lips across Elena's, then kissed her head-on, long and slow and deep. They managed to sink in tandem to the ground still in full liplock.

Making love on a historic riverbank was not as aesthetically erotic as Grady might have guessed, what with scratchy grass and tree roots and stony earth and so forth. But the kind of open eroticism that finally flowed between her and Elena didn't require a luxurious bed, and it didn't involve great carnal bombast. They touched each other with a gentle, sometimes clumsy fervor, and the sweetness of her hand cupping Elena's full breast at last flooded Grady's heart.

She couldn't stop looking at Elena, as mesmerized by her eyes as by the sensual contours of her body. They explored each other with languid curiosity at first, then moved together with an increasing heat. The long warm night seemed endless, and their passion was sated and became sweetness again, slow and searching. They were learning a new dance, one that bridged two cultures, and each in turn was patient teacher and eager student. The sun was beginning to rise when they lay still.

It occurred to Grady that five hundred years ago, a little girl named Elena witnessed three horrific deaths from the branches of a juniper tree. This morning, dawn was breaking over a young woman of the same name, lying under the same kind of tree, asleep and safe in the arms of her lover. Grady did find a measure of comfort in that, a small hope that the universe would finally offer healing, if they were only patient enough.

Chapter Twenty-three

When the sun had finished showering gold light over the peaks of the Organs to the east, Elena stirred in Grady's embrace, then gasped and sat up quickly.

"What?" Grady looked around, instantly on guard for bullying thugs or supernatural mayhem.

"I think something bit me." Elena pulled open the collar of her torn blouse and bared the cap of her left shoulder. Then she looked up at Grady.

"I know," Grady whispered. "I don't see it either."

The small, red birthmark on the top of Elena's shoulder was gone. Grady had brushed her lips against it more than once only hours ago, yet now the smooth, coffee-colored skin was clear.

Elena brushed two fingers over her shoulder. "My mother has a mark like mine, in the same place. So did her mother."

"I'm thinking every woman in the pictures on your walls had a mark like that. Maybe all the way back to Maria herself." Grady pulled the white cloth closed around Elena's throat again; the morning air was chilly. "And I'll bet Inez woke up a few seconds ago, just like you did, and hers is gone, too."

"I bet you're right." Elena reached up and patted Grady's cheek gently. "You surprise me, Grady. Tell me why you think so."

"Well, dawn means last night is over. It's the end of an era, isn't it? Llorona told you she would 'hunt men no more.'" Grady didn't know where her certainty came from, but she was sure. "I think that birthmark was her promise to each of her daughters that she would protect them from violent men. The mark has disappeared because Llorona made a new promise last night. She'll never kill again. You're free of that violent legacy now."

Elena gazed up at her, a mixture of wonder, fondness and amusement passing over her features. "Grady, you're talking like me. Do you hear yourself?"

"I know." Grady frowned. "Jesus, I hope I'm not still connected to that ghost—psychically, or whatever. I hope I'm not still…channeling her. Ish. Do you think?"

"No." Elena's palm slipped from her cheek and rested on Grady's heart. "I believe you're just learning to think from here, Professor Gringa. Finally."

Grady smiled. Their kiss this time was smooth, even graceful, as if they'd been intimate for several lifetimes.

Elena sighed and sat up again. "Catholics drive me crazy."

Grady found it an odd time to discuss comparative religion. "They drive you crazy in general, or a given Catholic in particular?"

Elena snickered. "Catholics drive me crazy because of their general fondness for early Saturday morning weddings."

"Oh." Grady checked the angle of the sun. The fact that Cesar and Sylvia were getting married in a very few hours had escaped her notice entirely. The prospect of a sedate church service seemed more than a little bizarre after a night of such extended ghostery.

"And yes, we must go," Elena said sternly. "It's a very special day for them."

"I think we must, too." Grady climbed to her feet stiffly, then helped Elena rise. "We need to let Inez know you're all right. I should call Janice and let her know, too. I want to stop by my office, then find some clean clothes." She brushed dead grass from Elena's back solicitously. "Sheesh."

"I know." Elena wrapped her arm through Grady's, and they started for her truck up on the frontage road. "Everything seems so simple, so ordinary, eh? Compared to the world we visited last night. I have to remind myself all the time never to forget how very thin the veils between worlds can be."

"Last night was probably a one-shot deal for me." Grady and Elena were both walking like senior citizens, leaning heavily on each other. "I doubt I'll ever see a ghost again. I hope not. I don't see how you can do this work, Elena, all this messing with spirits. My heart couldn't take it."

The truck started on the first attempt, as trucks are supposed to do. The drive back to Elena's store was uneventful, unmemorable. Except for their clasped hands, resting on Grady's knee. They both kept glancing down at their entwined fingers. They didn't look at each other much, but Grady chanced a quick glimpse of Elena's face, and she was smiling broadly.

She cranked the wheel and turned onto Elena's short street, then she braked swiftly. A thin figure stood in the middle of the road, his shirt flapping open, his arms raised. Manny Herrera's dark hair was matted and wild and his eyes were filled with tears. Grady heard him bawl Elena's name again, and she reached for her door handle.

"No, let me, Grady." Elena was already stepping out of the truck.

"Hey, wait. What if he's not—"

"He looks alone to me." Elena closed her door and peered in the open side window. "I promise not to barge in on the classes you teach, Dr. Gringa, and you must promise to sit back and let the spooky curandera do her job." She grinned, patted the windowsill, then went to the shivering teen awaiting her in the street.

Grady kept her window down, unwilling to lower her guard.

This kid had almost taken a noose to Elena last night. She could hear their voices, but most of their talk was in rapid-fire Spanish, so she got lost quickly. Luckily, their body language spoke volumes.

Manny was apologizing to Elena again and again, his hands clasped before him. He kept looking around furtively, afraid of pursuing vengeful ghosts, Grady surmised. Shorter than the boy by nearly half a foot, Elena shook a finger in his face and gave him the rough side of her tongue for a good five minutes. Manny kept nodding and apologizing, shifting from one foot to the other. Finally, he dropped to his knees and clenched Elena's leg, but Elena sighed and hauled him to his feet again. She spoke more quietly to him then, straightening his shirt, brushing his tousled hair out of his eyes. She took Manny's bandana out of his pocket, spat on it neatly, and used it to rub the sheen of dirt off his face.

"*Gracias*, Elena! Thank you, Elena!" Manny made half-bows as he backed away from her, obviously relieved.

"And you take good care of your *abuela*, Manuel!" Elena shook her finger again. "Every day, for the rest of her life."

"I will. Thank you! I will, Elena." Manny turned and ran down the far side of the street, then disappeared around a corner.

Elena sauntered back to the truck, looking pleased with herself. She leaned her arms on Grady's open window. "There goes a boy who's going to mind his curfew every night for the rest of his life. I told him there will be no more suicides, so word will probably spread all over Mesilla by noon."

"You have a generous spirit, spooky curandera." Grady wanted badly to plant a kiss on those full lips, but she remembered where they were. "You forgave him, just like that?"

"Well." The dimple in Elena's cheek deepened. "I figured I'm on a roll with the whole forgiveness thing."

A distant, hoarse voice called, "Hey!"

Grady and Elena both craned toward the sound. Inez Montalvo was leaning out of her open window, scowling down at them.

"My birthmark is gone!" she yelled. "Get up here and tell me what you two crazy *pendejas* did last night!"

Three hours later, showered and properly attired, Grady walked beside Elena down the carpeted center aisle of San Albino Church. The nave was transformed with fresh flowers, and white satin ribbons bedecked the side of each pew. The seats were filled with murmuring guests, a nice turnout. She remembered Cesar and Sylvia were born in this valley, and it seemed their large families had many friends, both Hispanic and Anglo, apparently none of whom objected to rising this ungodly early on a Saturday morning.

But surely all of whom could not possibly have heard about the dramas, mundane and spiritual, that had played out by the Rio Grande the night before. Grady didn't think she was being paranoid when she noticed an unusual number of heads turning as she and Elena were seated. Her senses prickled, ready to pick up the hostility and wariness Elena's presence sometimes evoked in the people of Mesilla, but there was none of that energy here. She caught only timid smiles directed Elena's way, even a few nods of welcome.

"Does news travel that fast in this town?" Grady leaned closer to Elena and spoke quietly. "If I'm not mistaken, they're looking at you like you're Gandhi."

"You're mistaken," Elena whispered back. "They're all ogling the cute atheist gringa sitting beside me. Oh, look, there's Janice."

Grady turned and spotted Janice hovering near the back of the church. She smoothed her blue skirt nervously with her hands, her gaze moving over the full pews. Grady looked at Elena and raised an eyebrow.

Elena smiled. "Of course."

Grady rose, and when she caught Janice's eye, she lifted her hand slightly in welcome. Janice seemed to sigh in relief, and she stepped carefully down the carpeted aisle to their pew. Elena patted the cushioned seat, and Janice settled beside her.

"Good morning, *mi amiga*." Elena kissed Janice on the cheek. "You look beautiful today."

"Not as beautiful as you. I'm so glad you're all right." Janice kept her voice low in the murmuring church. "Hello, Grady."

"Hey, you. Thanks for your help last night."

Janice smiled at her with shy fondness.

"Now hush," Elena whispered. "Or we'll all go to hell. It's starting."

All traces of weariness gone, Elena looked eager, as if they were watching the curtain rise on a well-loved play. Grady got it. Other cultures might celebrate rites with a dramatic flair, and other religions offered pomp and ceremony, but a traditional Catholic wedding truly engaged the human yearning for ritual.

A large woman in an elaborately ruffled dress walked demurely to the head of the nave, then faced the congregation. She sang the processional a capella, a sweetly formal old hymn delivered in a pleasing and reverent voice.

All the players in the pageant assembled, the priest, the couple, their many attendants. Cesar looked freshly scrubbed and handsome in his crisp Mexican wedding shirt. Sylvia glowed beneath the white lace mantilla covering her head and shoulders. The nuptial began, and Grady watched the draping of the long rosary over the couple's wrists. Cesar gave his gift to his bride, thirteen coins in a silk scarf, a symbol of his trust and confidence in their bond.

It would have been effortless reflex to remember the oppressive patriarchy of the Catholic Church, to see its expression in the very ceremony playing out before her. Easy for Grady to remember she and Leigh would never have been granted a church wedding, even if they'd wanted one. That was all true and it all still mattered, but now she was watching this pageant through

Elena's eyes, and she was able to lay grievance down for the day.

It was their faces. Not just Sylvia's and Cesar's, but every face Grady could see from their centrally located pew. The couple's parents, their friends. The simple happiness in their expressions. This community took such pure pleasure in the joining of their two children. Elena had said most of Mesilla's residents were good-hearted and sensible, and Grady was finally seeing that side of them.

Elena sat quietly beside her, listening to the homily. Grady felt a faint thrill of hope that both Inez Montalvo and her stubborn daughter might be more welcome in this small town now. Elena cared a great deal for Mesilla and for the afflicted here who came to her for healing. Grady wanted that for her, a community, friends, trusting neighbors. No more shot-out windows or sullen street mobs for this lady.

For my lady. Grady's sore throat tightened.

Janice watched the ceremony with tears in her eyes, but Grady saw more happiness for her friends than longing in her features. Janice glanced at her and smiled, apparently embarrassed by her tears. Grady winked at her. Janice was finding her home in this community, too.

"We're very, very, very glad to see you." In the reception line, Sylvia went up on her toes and kissed Grady's cheek. Her face was flushed with excitement, but she pushed back her *mantilla* to look closely at Grady and Elena. "You guys must have the wildest field trip report ever. When do we get to hear it?"

"Well, after you've been married for a few days," Grady said.

Sylvia hugged Janice. "I'll drag you to the ladies' room, Janice, you have to fill me in."

"What they're saying is true, Elena?" Cesar folded Elena's small hand in both of his large ones. "La Llorona is gone?"

"Not gone," Elena said. "Maria might walk rivers for

centuries to come, until she finds divine grace. But yes, it's true that she'll never kill again. Now, put all these ghost stories to rest, and enjoy your wedding day."

"Come on, Janice, you have to come to our party." Sylvia was already being pulled aside by other well-wishers, and she grabbed Janice's hand. "We've got an entire plank of tres leches cake. And the sangria will flow like a mighty river. I can't wait."

"Me either," Cesar said.

"Our best to you both, Sylvia." Grady steered Elena covertly through the crowd toward the doors. The lack of sleep was catching up to her, that familiar dry-lidded malaise. Elena had to be just as tired, and emotionally wrung-out, given their night. She was hoping they could stay awake for just a few more hours, though. She wanted them to make one more stop before they rested. Grady touched the small shape in her breast pocket to make sure it was still there.

The sun bombarded them as they stepped out of the cool shadows of the vestibule.

"Sheesh."

"Ay."

They both pulled sunglasses out of their pockets. Grady was now enough of a New Mexican never to be caught without them. They walked past the marble statue of Mary, who still held patient vigil over the church. Elena stopped and made a tsking sound. She went to the statue, untied her white scarf, and scrubbed at a spot of ash on the stone base. She glanced at Grady coyly. "Look, darling. It's just like our first date."

Grady chuckled. "Can I talk you into going home and changing into some pants?"

Elena laughed and shook out her scarf. "Silly gringa. You're supposed to want me to take my clothes *off*, not put more on. I have to teach you everything. Why do I need pants all of a sudden?"

"Well, I would get to see a lot of thigh if you tried to climb mountains in that lovely dress. Okay, skip the pants."

"We're climbing mountains?" Elena brushed the back of Grady's hand with one finger. "Okay, mountains it is. I don't care where we go. It just has to be someplace I can touch you."

Grady nodded. "I think I know just the spot."

CHAPTER TWENTY-FOUR

The Heart of the Mountain might have resembled a heart from Las Cruces, but it looked nothing like one when you were sitting just above its left ventricle. It looked like a straggling, random field of red rock, dotted with small barrel cactus and clumps of wildflowers in every color imaginable. Anatomically correct or not, it was an extraordinarily pretty spot, and Grady hadn't even banked on its loveliness. She simply knew Elena liked the Heart, and that's why they made their way up there after the wedding. But Grady admitted she also liked the imagery involved. Stone hearts finally flowering, and so forth.

"Shade," Elena panted.

"Shade," Grady said. Her truck had gotten them higher into the Organs' foothills than Elena's decrepit Ford could have, but it still took the better part of an hour to hike up here. The sun overhead baked them with unrelenting glee. "Over thar."

She led Elena to a patch of sandy ground cast into comparatively cool shadow by the sloping wedge of red granite and shale that formed the top of the "heart." The view was spectacular from this perch, which looked out over the stone field to the distant rock formations dotting the high hills of the Organs to the south. *"Bueno?"*

"Perfect." Elena sighed and flopped down. She was wearing frayed denim shorts that revealed the sexy curves of her legs, and a sleeveless cotton shirt that revealed not nearly enough of other interesting curves. Grady grinned, marveling at how little power her exhaustion held over her lust. Every muscle she had was creaking and sore, but every hormone in her body yearned for Elena.

"Why are you smiling at me like that?" Elena eyed her, unscrewing the top of her canteen. "You look ready to pour salsa on my head and eat me alive."

"I love it when you talk dirty." Grady brushed a curl of dark hair off Elena's damp forehead. "I'm smiling at this curandera who knows so much about healthy natural remedies, swigging her warm root beer on a mountain hike."

"Ooh, keep your mouth off my root beer, gringa. My root beer is a gift from the Goddess." Elena extended her canteen to Grady as if inviting her to drink, then snatched it quickly back to her own lips. "You've got your tasty water, drink that."

Grady uncapped her water bottle and obliged. They drank in unison, then leaned against each other with such deep sighs, Grady laughed. "You're running on less sleep than me, honey. At least I got in a nap last night before all the excitement began." She remembered her dream of a dancing little Max with poignant fondness.

"I can catch up on my sleep now." Elena rested her head on Grady's shoulder. "I'm not going to have to spend most of my nights sitting in rivers anymore."

"Hey, just because we've seen Maria doesn't mean we have to stop sitting in rivers. I kind of like river-sitting." Grady hoped Elena might doze off right now. It was so sweet to hold someone while they slept.

"I like it, too. And now we can sit in rivers for fun, instead of keeping watch for a forlorn ghost." Elena played with the buttons on Grady's shirt. "I wonder if she will remember me, Grady. If she'll find any lasting comfort in my forgiveness. Maria has so much sorrow, such remorse."

Grady thought about it. "It seems to me, if a woman can feel remorse, then forgiveness can bring her comfort. She'll remember you, Elena. You eased some of her pain." She realized she believed that. "But you told Cesar that Maria will still haunt rivers for centuries?"

"Until she finds divine grace." Elena nodded against her shoulder. "Haunting rivers is the punishment Maria imposed upon herself, and no mortal forgiveness will release her from that fate. But I believe that when she's ready, her God will offer her a chance to atone."

"How can a spirit atone for so many deaths?"

"A good question. I'm not sure. But divine grace can be tremendously creative, and it speaks to us in many different ways. A path will be found for Maria, when she's ready for it." Elena lifted her head, and her smile faded. She touched a tender spot on Grady's throat. "You have some bruising here. That *pendejo* Acuña really hurt you."

"He really tried, anyway." Grady yawned, then felt her throat gingerly. "We probably both have bruises we can brag on for weeks. Do you know of any anti-bruising herbal teas?"

"There's a wonderful salve I can mix, and spread lavishly over your entire bruised body." She patted Grady's face. "Have I thanked you? For hurling yourself like a freight train into that big, *loco* bully last night? The bully waving a gun, might I add. You should have seen your eyes. I was half scared of you myself."

"As well you should have been. I am much woman." Grady happily took advantage of this butch moment by drawing Elena into a kiss, a playfully passionate kiss at first, and then simply a passionate one. Elena's lips were soft and yielding against her own, and Grady felt a still-alien happiness shiver through her. She made herself sit up, and slipped her fingers into her breast pocket. She drew out a small twig of petrified wood.

"Hey." Elena's eyes lit up. "Isn't that your prayer stick?"

"This is my prayer stick. I'd like you to have it now."

"You want to give it up?" Elena looked troubled. "But, Grady, it was a gift. When we were in your office, I could tell by the look on your face that this stick is very important to you."

"It is. Do you remember its story?"

Elena nodded. "An old holy man from one of the Indian tribes you studied gave it to you, many years ago. You said he breathed a prayer into it—some kind of wish for you? A good wish."

"Yes, I've always trusted it was a good wish. But I've never known what that Cayuse holy man wished for me, until today." She handed the prayer stick to Elena. "I believe he wished that I'd find love, an honest, lifetime kind of love. He wished that I'd find you."

Elena stared at Grady, then down at the small stick in her hand, and her eyes filled with tears. She swallowed visibly, looking as moved as if Grady had just handed her a diamond engagement ring. Which in effect, she had. "Thank you," she said. "Thank you, Grady. I'll always treasure this."

"You're welcome." Grady leaned in for another kiss, but to her consternation, she yawned enormously instead.

Elena laughed softly and cupped her hand around Grady's neck. "My poor professor, you're so tired. Here, rest for a few minutes." She tugged gently, and Grady stretched out on her side and laid her head in Elena's lap. "I'll be sure to warn you if any more big, *loco* bullies happen by."

"Or tarantulas."

"*Sí*, or tarantulas."

"Or one of those *niño* earth-things."

"Or one of those. Hush, *querida*. Rest."

Grady felt Elena's fingers drift through her short hair, and she loved the sensation so much she beat back the lead weights threatening to close her eyes. She felt her body relax against the ground, muscle by sore muscle. A sip of cool breeze reached them, bringing with it the light, fresh scent of the wildflowers.

She had been right to insist they hike all the way up here. She knew she was right about the prayer stick's wish, and she was right about Elena. But Grady's bleary eyes focused on a distant rock formation, and she realized she wasn't right about everything. She wasn't right about never seeing ghosts again.

It was a small, craggy plateau, brightly lit by the sun, but too far distant to reveal much detail about the three figures on it. Grady saw what appeared to be two elderly men sitting on the rocky ground, several yards apart, facing each other. One of them had a long shock of white hair, like a certain old Cayuse holy man Grady had once met. He was rocking back and forth, laughing, clapping his hands rhythmically.

The other man's face was hidden behind a worn hood, but Grady recognized him too. She wasn't sure how she knew Elena's beloved Hermit, as he had been dead for 150 years, but it was him. He held some kind of wooden flute to his lips, and though they were too far away to allow its sound to reach her, Grady heard its light piping notes clearly.

Between the two old men danced a small boy.

"Elena," Grady whispered. "Are you seeing this?"

After a moment, Elena spoke softly above her. "No, my love. Whatever you're seeing is here for you alone."

The child spun and danced between the two old men, twirling to the music of the flute and the clapping hands. Joy was written in every line of his sturdy little body.

"Remember divine grace." Elena's fingers drifted through Grady's hair again, and her eyes began to close. "It can find creative ways of giving comfort, and forgiveness. I love you, Grady."

"Good," Grady mumbled. "I love you back."

Nestled in Elena's lap, Grady slept and slept and slept.

About the Author

Cate Culpepper is a 2005 and 2007 Golden Crown Literary Award winner in the Sci-Fi/Fantasy category, and a 2008 recipient of the Alice B. Toklas Readers' Choice Award. She is the author of the Tristaine series, which includes *Tristaine: The Clinic*, *Battle for Tristaine*, *Tristaine Rises*, and *Queens of Tristaine*. *Fireside* and *River Walker* are her first two offerings beyond the world of Tristaine's Amazons. Cate lives in Seattle, where she supervises a transitional living program for homeless young gay adults.

Books Available From Bold Strokes Books

Head Trip by D.L. Line. Shelby Hutchinson, a young computer professional, can't wait to take a virtual trip. She soon learns that chasing spies through Cold War Europe might be a great adventure, but nothing is ever as easy as it seems—especially love. (978-1-60282-187-3)

Desire by Starlight by Radclyffe. The only thing that might possibly save romance author Jenna Hardy from dying of boredom during a summer of forced R&R is a dalliance with Gardiner Davis, the local vet—even if Gard is as unimpressed with Jenna's charms as she appears to be with Jenna's fame. (978-1-60282-188-0)

River Walker by Cate Culpepper. Grady Wrenn, a cultural anthropologist, and Elena Montalvo, a spiritual healer, must find a way to end the River Walker's murderous vendetta—and overcome a maze of cultural barriers to find each other. (978-1-60282-189-7)

Blood Sacraments, edited by Todd Gregory. In these tales of the gay vampire, some of today's top erotic writers explore the duality of blood lust coupled with passion and sensuality. (978-1-60282-190-3)

Mesmerized by David-Matthew Barnes. Through her close friendship with Brodie and Lance, Serena Albright learns about the many forms of love and finds comfort for the grief and guilt she feels over the brutal death of her older brother, the victim of a hate crime. (978-1-60282-191-0)

Whatever Gods May Be by Sophia Kell Hagin. Army sniper Jamie Gwynmorgan expects to fight hard for her country and her future. What she never expects is to find love. (978-1-60282-183-5)

nevermore by Nell Stark and Trinity Tam. In this sequel to *everafter*, Vampire Valentine Darrow and Were Alexa Newland confront a mysterious disease that ravages the shifter population of New York City. (978-1-60282-184-2)

Playing the Player by Lea Santos. Grace Obregon is beautiful, vulnerable, and exactly the kind of woman Madeira Pacias usually avoids, but when Madeira rescues Grace from a traffic accident, escape is impossible. (978-1-60282-185-9)

Midnight Whispers: The Blake Danzig Chronicles by Curtis Christopher Comer. Paranormal investigator Blake Danzig, star of the syndicated show *Haunted California* and owner of Danzig Paranormal Investigations, has been able to see and talk to the dead since he was a small boy, but when he gets too close to a psychotic spirit, all hell breaks loose. (978-1-60282-186-6)

The Long Way Home by Rachel Spangler. They say you can't go home again, but Raine St. James doesn't know why anyone would want to. When she is forced to accept a job in the town she's been publicly bashing for the last decade, she has to face down old hurts and the woman she left behind. (978-1-60282-178-1)

Water Mark by J.M. Redmann. PI Micky Knight's professional and personal lives are torn asunder by Katrina and its aftermath. She needs to solve a murder and recapture the woman she lost—while struggling to simply survive in a world gone mad. (978-1-60282-179-8)

Picture Imperfect by Lea Santos. Young love doesn't always stand the test of time, but Deanne is determined to get her marriage to childhood sweetheart Paloma back on the road to happily ever after, by way of Memory Lane—and Lover's Lane. (978-1-60282-180-4)

The Perfect Family by Kathryn Shay. A mother and her gay son stand hand in hand as the storms of change engulf their perfect family and the life they knew. (978-1-60282-181-1)

Raven Mask by Winter Pennington. Preternatural Private Investigator (and closeted werewolf) Kassandra Lyall needs to solve a murder and protect her Vampire lover Lenorre, Countess Vampire of Oklahoma— all while fending off the advances of the local werewolf alpha female. (978-1-60282-182-8)

The Devil be Damned by Ali Vali. The fourth book in the best-selling Cain Casey Devil series. (978-1-60282-159-0)

Descent by Julie Cannon. Shannon Roberts and Caroline Davis compete in the world of world-class bike racing and pretend that the fire between them is just professional rivalry, not desire. (978-1-60282-160-6)

Kiss of Noir by Clara Nipper. Nora Delany is a hard-living, sweet-talking woman who can't say no to a beautiful babe or a friend in danger—a darkly humorous homage to a bygone era of tough broads and murder in steamy New Orleans. (978-1-60282-161-3)

Under Her Skin by Lea Santos Supermodel Lilly Lujan hasn't a care in the world, except life is lonely in the spotlight—until Mexican gardener Torien Pacias sees through Lilly's facade and offers gentle understanding and friendship when Lilly most needs it. (978-1-60282-162-0)

Fierce Overture by Gun Brooke. Helena Forsythe is a hard-hitting CEO who gets what she wants by taking no prisoners when negotiating—until she meets a woman who convinces her that charm may be the way to win a battle, and a heart. (978-1-60282-156-9)

Trauma Alert by Radclyffe. Dr. Ali Torveau has no trouble saying no to romance until the day firefighter Beau Cross shows up in her ER and sets her carefully ordered world aflame. (978-1-60282-157-6)

Wolfsbane Winter by Jane Fletcher. Iron Wolf mercenary Deryn faces down demon magic and otherworldly foes with a smile, but she's defenseless when healer Alana wages war on her heart. (978-1-60282-158-3)

Little White Lie by Lea Santos. Emie Jaramillo knows relationships are for other people, and beautiful women like Gia Mendez don't belong anywhere near her boring world of academia—until Gia sets out to convince Emie she has not only brains, but beauty…and that she's the only woman Gia wants in her life. (978-1-60282-163-7)

Witch Wolf by Winter Pennington. In a world where vampires have charmed their way into modern society, where werewolves walk the streets with their beasts disguised by human skin, Investigator Kassandra Lyall has a secret of her own to protect. She's one of them. (978-1-60282-177-4)

Do Not Disturb by Carsen Taite. Ainsley Faraday, a high-powered executive, and rock music celebrity Greer Davis couldn't be less well suited for one another, and yet they soon discover passion has a way of designing its own future. (978-1-60282-153-8)

From This Moment On by PJ Trebelhorn. Devon Conway and Katherine Hunter both lost love and neither believes they will ever find it again—until the moment they meet and everything changes. (978-1-60282-154-5)

Vapor by Larkin Rose. When erotic romance writer Ashley Vaughn decides to take her research into the bedroom for a night of passion with Victoria Hadley, she discovers that fact is hotter than fiction. (978-1-60282-155-2)

Wind and Bones by Kristin Marra. Jill O'Hara, award-winning journalist, just wants to settle her deceased father's affairs and leave Prairie View, Montana, far, far behind—but an old girlfriend, a sexy sheriff, and a dangerous secret keep her down on the ranch. (978-1-60282-150-7)

Nightshade by Shea Godfrey. The story of a princess, betrothed as a political pawn, who falls for her intended husband's soldier sister, is a modern-day fairy tale to capture the heart. (978-1-60282-151-4)

Vieux Carré Voodoo by Greg Herren. Popular New Orleans detective Scotty Bradley just can't stay out of trouble—especially when an old flame turns up asking for help. (978-1-60282-152-1)